FATED Path

N. D. JONES

KUUMBA PUBLISHING
CREATIVE MINDS.
PASSIONATE HEARTS

Baltimore, Maryland

Copyright © 2020 by **N.D. JONES**

All rights reserved. No part of this publication may be reproduced, distributed or transmitted in any form or by any means, without prior written permission.

Kuumba Publishing
1325 Bedford Avenue
#32374
Pikesville, MD
kuumbapublishing.com

Publisher's Note: This is a work of fiction. Names, characters, places, and incidents are a product of the author's imagination. Locales and public names are sometimes used for atmospheric purposes. Any resemblance to actual people, living or dead, or to businesses, companies, events, institutions, or locales is completely coincidental.

Cover Design: Jesh Designs
Original Concept Art: Phu Thieu
Editor: Chris at Hidden Gems

Fated Path/N.D. Jones. -- 1st ed.
ISBN: 978-1-7352998-2-2

Dedication

Baba Kweku Kemraha

Father
Husband
Friend
Author

Power and Grace . . . A Love Supreme and the Majesty of Blackness

Rest in Power

Special Thanks

To the winners of my name a planet and race competition

Scott Schieber for naming the Grul planet of Tsondelar

Germaine Harrison for naming the Malcareon race

Glossary of Key Asiyan Terms

Ab'ba:	Father
A'bra:	Mother
Affiq Band:	**Knowledge**
Anull:	Year
Dekull:	Decade
Devdas Band:	**Faith**
Dole:	Day
Einar:	High Star full-body armor
Euridice Band:	**Law**
Hern:	Hour
Iceril:	Winter
Ibor:	A twenty-five-foot, six-legged ancient Asiyan beast with wings, gills, and lungs
Ibor Armor:	Paladin bird-face war armor modeled after the Ibor predator
Marnil:	Mile
Mern:	Minute
Mor'up:	A natural resource found only in the northern mountainous region of Asiya; it is used in creating weapons, such as strong knives, as well as shields for all types of transporters
Paladin Band:	**Guardian**
Tolur:	Migratory bird
Seal of Eternal Breath:	Signet ring of the Regent of Asiya; it is designed to represent the Realm of Thuraya—the birthplace of all living beings
Verity Band:	**Truth**
Welk:	Week

Zot: Electronic tablet that comes in many sizes. Its functions are similar to an iPad and cell phone

Glossary of Key Races

AMAKAN

ASIYAN

GRUL

HUMAN

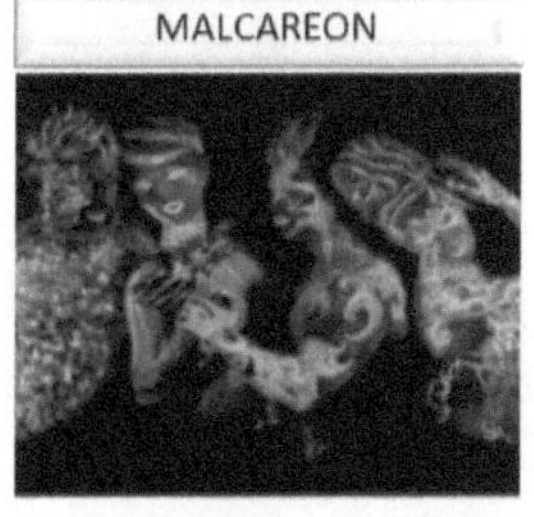

LUMERIAN

MALCAREON

UNBALK

YEGOTH

1. First Love

2252
Northeast Asiya
Regent Center of Khatra
Hall of Concord

"Lela is young and inexperienced," Yusef declared, a statement Ammon tired of hearing. "Certainly too much of both to be the next Chief Magistrate of the Verity Band."

"Yes, Lela is both young and inexperienced," Regent Etemaad agreed.

Ammon stood behind his seated father, Yusef, in the Council of Magistrates' Ruling Chamber. No one else was in the sun-heated room with them, including the regent's High Stars. Ammon shouldn't be in there either, listening to the two most powerful people on the planet discuss the political future of the woman he loved.

Regent Etemaad's dark gaze shifted from Yusef to Ammon, piercing him where he stood at attention, sweaty hands held behind his rigid back. The way the regent watched him, intense but with an unreadable expression, he desired nothing more than to disappear into the wall like the retracted solar panels.

"But Lela is no longer a girl," the regent continued. "She is an-ulls out of Sagacity. Only the finest of Verity scholars complete the rigorous training required to serve the people of this great planet. Need I remind you of her academic record?"

"Verity is the only band that comes close to rivaling Affiq as scholars. But even Verity does not share Affiq's thirst for knowledge. Verity seeks the truth in all things, be it knowledge for the sake of knowing or knowledge for a greater truth." Yusef leaned forward, his elbows going to the table. "No, I do not need a lesson on Lela's intelligence. No more than I need to explain why intellect is an insufficient antecedent of effective leadership."

As he spoke, Regent Etemaad divided his attention between father and son. "Insufficient, yes, but not unimportant. Lela has also served me well since I brought her here to live."

"Agreed. She's made an excellent disciple. I wouldn't dare deny what I've seen with my own eyes."

"You've seen only that which you've allowed your mind to accept as truth. You and members of the Council think of Lela as a child, perhaps even a pet I've spoiled and kept too close. She is neither."

Finally, Regent Etemaad released Ammon from what felt like an inescapable force field. A rush of breath slipped from him in a harsh sound that seemed to echo in the still room. The regent couldn't possibly know about Ammon and Lela. They'd been careful, hiding their growing feelings for each other in public while spending private time together when they could. Yet the way Regent Etemaad had stared at Ammon left him feeling cold and exposed.

"Lela is the leader Asiya will require in the future. I've seen it in my dreams."

At the five-letter word, Yusef leaned even closer to Etemaad. "In your dreams?"

Tone still serious but no longer with respectful challenge, Yusef's sudden shift didn't surprise Ammon. Most Asiyans did not dream. Of those who did, like Regent Etemaad, their dreams were often prophetic. Neither Ammon nor Yusef were among the rare Asiyan dreamers. In fact, the Paladin Band had the fewest dreamers of the five bands. Since dreams were connected to the Three Fates of Asiya—Purpose, Faith, and Truth—it was unsurprising that the Devdas Band, the spiritual foundation of Asiyan society, boasted the largest number of dreamers.

He wondered if Lela had dreams. If she did, what did she dream? Of him? Of them? Of ruling the largest planet of sentient beings in the Bazlorian Solar System?

"Yes," the regent confirmed.

"Are you saying the Fates have come to you in your dreams and have spoken to you of Lela?"

Ammon's fear of a future without Lela exceeded his bone-deep desire to hear the answer to Yusef's question. Regent Etemaad's spiritual connection to the Fates through his dreams had elevated him to a godlike status among their people no prior regent had known. Not even Devdas dreamers claimed the Fates entered their dreams, speaking to them and revealing their secrets.

For the briefest moment, Etemaad's eyes found Ammon's again. This time, they were soft, perhaps a little sad. For Ammon or for Etemaad, he couldn't discern. Ammon stepped backward, a soft retreat he hoped his father wouldn't notice until he'd exited.

Of course, being the leader of a band of warriors, Ammon was disappointed but not shaken when his father, back to him, said, "I did not grant you permission to leave. I requested your attendance in the chamber so you could listen and learn, not run away when you fail to comprehend the magnitude of the choices that lay before you."

Chief Magistrate Yusef didn't extend requests but issued orders, even to his family. Ammon wouldn't dare disagree with his father in front of the regent, so he swallowed his pride and moved back to the spot he'd vacated.

"The Fates do not speak to me in the way we are conversing now. I do not always understand the tri-voice they speak in or the images they show me."

"Then how do you know their messages?"

Etemaad turned his face away from Yusef and toward a beam of light that bisected the rectangular conference table. Lifting a hand, he stretched it toward the beam, as if, by mental will alone, he could compel it closer and into the palm of his hand. Nothing happened, of course, except Ammon sensed he'd witnessed something important in the regent's eyes when he shifted back to Yusef. Anulls later, he would reflect on the regent's expression with a worldly wisdom he didn't yet possess.

Instead of expounding on his dream, Etemaad squeezed Yusef's shoulder, a gesture of friendship and faith. "My dreams aside, the Verity Band has decided. The regent does not dictate the chosen leader of the bands."

True, but the regent had the right to refuse a band's nominee for chief magistrate. Thus, a band would do well to recommend a member who would pass favor with the regent. To do otherwise would humiliate the nominee's house if rejected.

"Is it not our role as mentors, Yusef, to teach and guide the youngest among us? Is it not our responsibility to lead by example? Were we not once disciples as innocent in the ways of Mother Cosmos as Lela?" Regent Etemaad nodded toward

Ammon. "The Fates have a plan for us all. The question we must ask ourselves is whether we are ready and willing to go down the path they've laid out for us, unaware where it will lead. Is our faith strong enough? Is our purpose clear? Do we lie to ourselves instead of facing the truth of our mortality and imperfections?"

Like a jacala burying nuts for a cold iceril season, Ammon stored the regent's questions away for later contemplation. Yusef, on the other hand, launched into a grand speech about "developing transformational leaders," "building cross-cultural relationships," and "honing communication skills." Except for using superior Asiyan technology and honorable warriors to maintain peace at home and abroad, this could've been the same speech Yusef gave Paladin High Star recruits their first day at Shielder, the Paladin Band's school for military training.

Regent Etemaad pushed to his feet, retrieved his hooded, lavender cloak from the chair, and slipped it on. "Understand this, Yusef, one doesn't acquire experience by being kept in a hall, even a hall as grand as this one. Birds have wings for a reason. We do not keep our winged friends in cages the way some races do. The entire sky is their home."

Yusef also stood, black boots silent on the polished floor.

Regent Etemaad nodded in Ammon's direction again but didn't seek to catch his gaze. No, his eyes were firmly on Yusef. "Birds come in all shapes and sizes. The worst crime we can commit against them is to clip their wings, thus denying them the ability to learn, grow, and experience life to its fullest. That also includes the freedom to fly in the wrong direction, at times. But as we know from the beautiful tolurs, they eventually turn themselves around and find their way home."

With a flick of his wrists, Etemaad pulled the hood of his cloak over his knee-length gray coils—purple liberally mixed throughout.

Despite decades of friendship, as well as the regent's approachable demeanor, Yusef understood a directive when he heard one, as did Ammon. The chief magistrates were to do a better job training their disciples—less lecturing and more modeling.

Ammon and Yusef bowed to Regent Etemaad, with Ammon's bow deeper than his high-ranking father's.

"There are many firsts in a male's life," the regent said to Ammon. "Some change us for the better. Some bring us heartache. Some stay forever in our hearts and minds." In the same way the regent had placed a hand on Yusef's shoulder, he touched Ammon's, firm yet comforting, and squeezed. "Then there are those firsts that improve and hurt us. Yet in the end, leave us feeling blessed for having had the experience. Be well, Ammon of the House of Eetu. I look forward to seeing you at the Luna of Analisia ceremony."

With that personal invitation, Regent Etemaad turned on his booted heels and left.

Ammon released another deep breath. For all that he'd seen the regent walk the halls of the planetary governance building, his lavender and black cloak heralding his entrances and exits, the male had never spoken so personally or cryptically to him before. He didn't like it, neither his forced attendance at the meeting nor the uncharacteristic attention the regent had paid him.

Angry and confused, Ammon turned to his father. "What are you not telling me? Why am I here? It isn't as if I'm your disciple. You've made it quite clear Gurion will be your successor."

Ammon didn't doubt, with Yusef's unyielding support, when the time came for his father to relinquish reins of the Paladin Band, the band would rally behind his older brother, propelling him into the position of chief magistrate. Ammon didn't covet the power and privilege that came with being a chief magistrate. But he took great offense when his father looked at and treated him as a second-class Paladin—devoid of a sharp edge and an unbendable spine. The greatest Paladins in history, according to his father, possessed both.

Yusef returned to his chair at the table. In brooding silence, Ammon joined him, claiming what would soon be Lela's chair.

Yusef's gaze held the too-familiar stare of disappointment, so Ammon braced himself for yet another lecture on what it meant to be a "Paladin of Valor."

"Your eyes conceal nothing. All of your emotions are harbored there, beacons of weakness for any enemy that would cross your path."

Out of spite, Ammon widened his eyes, allowing the full weight of his anger and hurt to flood into them. "Tell me, Ab'ba, what do you see now?"

Unperturbed by Ammon's passive aggressiveness, Yusef answered with a flat, "The same as always." He propped an ankle on a knee and considered him. "I see annoyance and anger. A tedious sight, I must admit, but your mother assures me your behavior and attitude are by-products of your age and gender. I'm certain there was an insult to males somewhere in her sweetly voiced statement, but I far more enjoy sleeping beside my mate in our bed than winning a pointless argument. Once you find your soulmate, you'll discover the truth of my words. Speaking of mates," Yusef said and pointed a finger at Ammon, "when you look at Lela, your eyes reveal your soul's deepest desires."

Despite Yusef's assertion of Ammon's inability to mask his emotions, he didn't flinch when he mentioned Lela. He may be unable to conceal his feelings for her from his father, but he was capable of not confessing to their unsupervised meetings.

Yusef smiled then nodded, his approval more grating than his words of, "Much better, but far too late. Did you hear what the regent said to you?"

"Of course."

"No, Ammon, did you listen with true understanding?" When Ammon remained silent, his father sighed, as if burdened with the worst Paladin son in Asiya's long history. "The regent and Lela's father only suspect what I know to be true. They may even believe the fondness you feel for Lela to be one sided. But they are not your father. Etemaad and Hasani do not know the boy I raised into the young man who sits before me now, protecting a female's honor with his stony silence."

That was the closest Yusef had ever come to likening Ammon's actions to that of a "true Paladin." Still, he would grant his father nothing. Ammon would always shield Lela from harm, even if that meant placing himself in front of her and taking the full force of whatever threatened his love. Not first love, as Regent Etemaad had implied. There would be no second love for Ammon, just as there would be none for Lela. Once she became chief magistrate, no one, not even the regent or her father, would dare stand in their way. They could, once and for all, announce their intention to begin the courting rituals.

"I know you think me unfair, harsh even. Believe it or not, there are times, Ammon, I wish I could be the gentle, patient father a young man of your sensitive bearing requires. But you've lived a sheltered existence, as has Lela. Even with your short travels to other planets, you have yet to see and experience the ruthlessness of life. We Asiyans know what it means to form ourselves from barbarians into civilized beings. Five bands formed from the endless wars we fought and the savages we once were. Five bands but no more blood and violence between us. Peace, Ammon, we grew to know and love peace. But that doesn't mean we've forgotten the beasts we once were."

Too much. Too. Much. Ammon needed to meditate. Needed time to reflect on everything he'd heard from the regent and his father. He stood. No, what Ammon needed was to see Lela. Being with her always had the miraculous effect of dulling the uncertainties that plagued him. When not in her presence, however, the sharp ache of them returned, especially when he spent extended time with his father.

Yusef neither rose nor tried to stop Ammon from leaving. But when he reached the doors, his foot a half step from sensors that would trigger the doors to open, he turned back to his father. "Speak your mind."

With a weariness only Ammon seemed capable of bringing out of Yusef, his father ran a hand over his forehead and up into the thick coils of hair piled atop his head. The effect was one of amateurish empathy. "Even if Lela loves you, you cannot clip her wings by asking her to stay here with you as your mate. And I cannot clip your wings by keeping you in the Hall of Concord, hoping to change a nature that is more Verity than Paladin. The regent will send her away from here. Not away from you, as you may think, but toward her destiny. For Lela to grow, she must spread her wings and fly away from home. Etemaad will send her on her first serious mission of peace and reconciliation soon after her induction into the Council of Magistrates."

"How long will she be gone?"

"One never knows with peace negotiations. Not that it matters. As chief magistrates, it is our duty to offer aid and comfort where we can." Yusef ran a hand over his forehead again, and then let his foot drop from his knee to the floor. "Lela is Verity. Ask her, when she envisions her future, if she sees you standing beside her, her mate and father of her children. She is too honorable to lie." With the palm of one hand on the table, Yusef pushed to his feet. "Are you brave enough to ask?"

Dark clouds had dimmed the impact of the sun's rays coming through the windows, cooling the chamber but not stilling his movements. Ammon made his leave, a belated retreat that left his head pounding forcefully and his legs moving hurriedly.

Running down corridors, one blurred into the next. He scaled stairs instead of taking a lift to the Northgard Residential Wing of the hall. When he reached his destination, sweat and desperation clung to him.

Ammon buzzed for entry.

The door slid open, revealing the person he'd run a quarter marnil to see.

"Ammon, what are you doing her—"

He stepped inside the suite, his arms going around her waist and pulling her to him. Then he was kissing her, and his secret fear of losing her slipped away with her return kiss.

"Lela," he whispered against her warm lips. "Lela," he repeated, unable to say more and afraid to let her go lest she and their love evaporate like water molecules from the heat of the sun.

Ammon kissed Lela again, and kept kissing her until the thought of him being her first but not her only love slinked away—forgotten but not gone.

2. Making Plans

Lela gazed up into eyes a swirl of cornelian maple. Ammon's gray and black coils hung down his shoulders and back, a glorious tide of hair he wore with pride.

"Thanks to you," he said, kissing the tip of her nose, "I must rewrap my coils before exiting your chamber."

Lela knew better than to untwine a Paladin's meticulous warrior's bun. She hadn't yet earned the right to see him thus. No more than Ammon had earned the right to recline beside Lela on the floor of her chamber, hands massaging sides and hips, and lips kissing cheeks and neck.

Yet there they were, a closed door all that hid their unsanctioned relationship from disapproving eyes. Still, from the first day Lela had met Ammon, a Paladin but not quite, she was drawn to him. Lela had never felt this way about any other male of her acquaintance. Love and desire, as she'd come to learn, encouraged the most reckless of actions.

"We weren't to meet again until after the Luna of Analisia ceremony." Her hand rose to his cheek, caressed with a gentle thumb before lifting to touch her lips to his. "What has you so upset?"

Just as Lela knew not to displace his hair, Ammon knew not to arrive at her chamber unannounced. Anyone could've been inside with her when he'd arrived. As it was, the door had barely closed behind him before he'd pulled her in for a delicious but ill-advised kiss. They could perhaps explain away his presence outside her chamber, but not inside, and definitely not their heated embrace.

Ammon peppered Lela's face with more sweet kisses before twisting onto his back, lacing their fingers and squeezing. "It's been an anull and a half since we began spending time together—talking and getting to know each other. If we were any other couple, we would've begun the courting rituals long ago."

"Quite true, but we can't ignore the expectations of others."

They'd had this discussion many times. Each one ended with Ammon reluctantly agreeing not to declare his intentions to Lela's parents. Her mother would welcome his declaration, while her father would encourage her to delay the union. If Hasani knew of their improper behavior, however, her father wouldn't be pleased. Worse, his disappointment in her would hurt them both.

"We are of age. Technically, we need not seek anyone's permission to court."

"Also true." Lela shifted onto her side to better see Ammon. Eyes that normally revealed much were hooded. Leaning over him, she pressed her lips to his—a languid kiss she hoped would remove the clouds from his eyes. "I made you a promise. After I'm sworn in as chief magistrate, we can sit down with our parents. They may disapprove, which is their right, just as we can proceed with the courting rituals without their support. I would like their approval, though."

"So would I. There are days, Lela, that I feel as if Mother Cosmos will conspire against our joining, that even the Fates do not wish us to become mates."

Lela wondered if Ammon would ask if she shared his foreboding. She waited, heart pounding with a truth she did not wish to utter beyond the boundaries of her conflicted mind. But when he only watched her, a hand going to her hip and rubbing in small, unsure circles, she knew he would not.

"I want us to be together."

"As do I."

"Are you a dreamer?" Ammon's fingers were strong yet sensual, and he kept them in constant caressing movement on her hip. "I've never before asked. Is it impolite for me to do so now?"

"The way I've permitted you to touch me—with your hands and mouth—such barriers no longer exist between us. I do not mind answering your question, although I am curious as to why you've chosen today to inquire."

"I asked if you were a dreamer. That was poor phrasing. I know you are a dreamer. It's one of the main reasons you were chosen by your band. You dream of a better and brighter future for all—not only Asiyans but all beings, no matter the planet or solar system. But you interpreted my question correctly. Are you like Regent Etemaad? Do you have dreams?"

Lela reclined on her back. She and Ammon spoke on a myriad of topics. The male was well learned, quick witted, and possessed a dry humor common in most Paladins. Yet there were days, like today, when Ammon would guide them to a river's edge, consider its depths from the safety of the bank but retreat before taking that fateful step forward. Simply put, Ammon did not want to know what existed below the surface of what he could see, feel, and control. In that regard, Ammon wasn't so different from most people, including Lela. All too soon, however, she would no longer have the luxury of walking away from the river. The plunge into the murky depths would be the biggest step of her young life.

She would answer his posed questions, but not the deeper query that hovered between them.

"Yes, I do dream."

Lela didn't turn her head to see his reaction. Beyond her family, no one knew she was a dreamer, not even her band. She suspected her father had shared her ability with Etemaad, although the regent had never inquired about her dreams or whether the Fates came to her in them. From the day Regent Etemaad had begun to treat his best friend's daughter as the daughter he and his mate never had, the trajectory of Lela's life had altered. With the Asheema family status in Asiyan society, Lela would've still traveled a path of leadership and service, but not on the scale as that of chief magistrate.

Little belonged exclusively to Lela. Her house, her band, the Council; she was an extension of each, part of and defined by them all. The truth of the constriction sometimes chafed, so she felt neither guilt nor shame for keeping small parts of herself for herself.

Ammon reached for her again, lacing their fingers once more. "My father suspects."

Of course the Paladin did. The only surprise was how long it had taken Yusef to discover their secret.

"Are you upset?"

"From the sound of your voice, it is you who is upset. I would rather him not know, but what is done cannot be altered. It must be faced with a matching truth."

"What is our matching truth?"

With a smile borne of belated purpose, Lela held on to Ammon's hand, tugging him to his feet as she drew upward. Shaking wrinkles from her white dress, the color worn by every disciple, her smile didn't waver despite the utter impropriety of what she was about to do.

The Fates did indeed come to Lela in her dreams. They never spoke to her, but they had been her companions since Lela was old enough to recognize them for who they were. To her knowledge, no Asiyans dreamed daily, much less were visited every time they did by the Fates. She had no explanation, not even an educated guess. But their presence brought equal parts warmth and hope—one bolstered while the other mystified.

"After I help you rewrap your hair, will you escort me to the Cetta Topiary Gardens?"

Ammon glanced down at their joined hands then back to Lela, his eyebrow arched at an adorable angle. "Holding hands like the humans you've researched . . . and in public for all to see?"

"Humans do seem to be rather fond of their public displays of affection. I must admit, I do find the courting custom of hand holding quite endearing. Shall we try?"

"You offer me a challenge?"

"Not at all. I simply wish to bring a smile to your face."

"And to spite my father. Perhaps even to spite those who seek to control the wind around your wings, pushing you in their preferred direction. You are an independent female, Lela, as I am an independent male."

Lela refrained from asking Ammon to clarify his wind-wing analogy, for she feared she grasped his meaning, as well as the implications for their future. What she chose to focus on was the smile that played about the edges of his mouth.

A lovely sight to be cherished.

Hand in hand, they walked toward the door, Ammon's warrior bun in place. With a long pause and two deep breaths, they exited her chamber. White floors and walls greeted them, nonjudgmental in their two-dimensional simplicity. Asiyans of all bands walked the corridors, absorbed in their own musings and unaware of the leap of faith Lela and Ammon had taken.

They hadn't jumped into a river of indeterminate depth, but they waded in neck-high waters—self-delusions all that kept them from slipping under.

Apion Solar System
Nikogeus Moonbase

"That won't be enough."

"You must not have the language translator programmed correctly. The down payment I wired to your account is half the price we agreed on."

"You change the job, the price changes with it. That's how it works. If you want my crew to add him to the count, that's going to cost you."

Quill slid his chair against the wall behind him. The bar in front of him was dark and the patrons oblivious to a lone Grul sitting by himself. This time of night there were more fists thrown and drinks poured than observations made. No one came to this bar and this part of Nikogeus without eyes in the back of their heads. Better, armed with the best weapons on the underground market.

Making sure he hadn't been followed and no one was listening, Quill surveyed the bulging crowd. Music played, but not loud enough to drown out the grunts of pleasure and the screams of pain coming from the upper level of the bar—from sex or fighting, or sex while fighting, the way Quill liked it best, he didn't know. What he did know, however, was that no one had made him the object of their unwanted attention.

Satisfied, he let his gaze fall to the audiovisual device in his hand, a top-of-the-line zot he'd won from a one-eyed Demite. Well, Demites had three eyes, but when he'd come after Quill with a knife, cursing him for rigging the card game, two of the Demite's eyes had been the price for calling Quill a "hairless three ball sucking cheater." He had cheated, but that wasn't the point. That reminded Quill; he reached into his jacket pocket, found the two eyeballs, tossed them into his mouth and chewed with greedy satisfaction.

"So, about the price. You have my new number."

"I don't have the authority to renegotiate."

The old woman must've thought Quill a space rock. No one without negotiation powers would've gone through the trouble of hunting Quill down for his services.

"You have two choices, Lumi," he said, enjoying the glint of affront at his deliberate use of the racial slur. "One, pay my fee. Two, get someone else for the job." Not that the Lumi could see the crowded bar, but Quill pointed in the direction of the raucous group. "There are plenty who would take the job. They'd take it but get themselves either caught or killed. Before they do, though, you know what they'll do?" Quill brought the zot closer to his face. "They'll talk . . . about you and your plan." Quill's smile wasn't pleasant or even boastful. He didn't have time for either. When a lie was pointless, he served up the truth like a baked ferine—the thick fish nasty going down but filling. "My crew is the best. We'll get the job done. Nice and clean." Quill laughed. "Bloody and quick, but it'll be nice and clean."

"No one can know we were behind it."

"No one will. That's part of what the extra payment is for. We'll disappear after it's done."

Showing his pointy teeth, Quill smiled again, confident in his skills. He didn't do complicated or messy. From his experience, the best jobs were the ones where the client kept it straightforward and easy. He left political machinations to people like the female Lumi frowning at him. If she were there with him, he would pour a drink down her throat and buy her a strapping Sinerus for the night. Between the alcohol and the unisexual Sinerus, the Lumi might just loosen up. Though, from the hard, imperial set of her chin, Quill retracted his previous thought. No wonder Lumis stayed embroiled in wars. They didn't know how to prop their feet up and relax.

For long breaths, the Lumi glared at Quill before doing something unexpected—she smiled. Lumis weren't the most attractive race of people, true, but that's not what had Quill moving the zot away from his face. Her ice-blue eyes matched the frigid lifting of lips at the corners, a silent, deadly gesture that explained, more than anything else, why her race couldn't maintain peace with their planetary neighbors.

"You're afraid."

A less experienced mercenary would've interpreted the Lumi's statement as a threat. While threats weren't above the still-smiling female, the Lumi hadn't given him one.

Her smile grew and her blue eyes all but glowed. "Your fear will ensure your success, as well as a speedy departure from my homeworld. Your fear is expensive. More expensive than I'd anticipated."

Finally, the Lumi had removed her mask. With the addition of the new target, the job's risk factor increased to a near-suicidal level. Quill salivated at the thought of a worthy challenge. The jobs, lately, were too easy, like removing that Demite's eyes. Even the sweet taste of them hadn't felt as good going down as in times past. But this job would test him and his crew. Even better, the payday would set them for the rest of their lives.

A drunk human bumped into his table, knocking over a half-empty mug of haze ale.

"Shit, where did that table come from?"

Bloodshot red eyes met Quill's then lowered to the amber liquid running from the table onto the sticky floor. The human shrugged then walked away, as if that was the end of it. Quill had no idea why the human was so far away from home. He hoped the man got a good look at the blue planet when he left because he wouldn't be seeing it or anything else ever again.

"Are you sure he's going to be there?" More than one mission had gone wrong because of faulty information.

"You have no idea how difficult it was to convince him to join the negotiations. But yes, he will be here. He will accompany their new chief magistrate."

"A Paladin?" Quill asked, rising to his feet. Zot clutched in his hand, he shoved the table out of his way. He may not have consumed all of the ale, but the liquid threatened to come out the other end. Deeming the bathroom too far away and his need urgent, Quill found the closest unoccupied corner and took a piss.

"No, Verity. A woman."

Inconsequential, the Lumi meant. The female wasn't as intelligent as he'd given her credit for being. No matter. As long as the new chief magistrate wasn't from the Paladin Band, Quill and his crew wouldn't have to worry about resistance from that quarter. Still . . . "Send me everything you have on the targets, including the female Asiyan."

Even if the Lumi didn't want the woman dead, Quill didn't believe in leaving witnesses or potential enemies behind. Unlike Lumis, Quill didn't live for war. He'd killed plenty, sure, but he didn't want to spend the rest of his life looking over his shoulder while trying to stay one step ahead of the so-called "honorable warriors."

Asiyans weren't what went bump in the universe. They were the dark universe. Lucky for Quill and Lumis, he'd never been afraid of the dark. Yet he was a cautious Grul, so he reclaimed his chair and sat. "From start to finish, tell me what you have planned."

3. Luna of Analisia

Lela opened her eyes, more centered than she'd been when she'd knelt on her prayer rug, lit five candles—one for each band—and started the breathing exercises that would usher her into a meditative state. The flames waned, her knees ached, and herns had passed since she'd cloistered herself inside her bedroom.

Leaning forward, Lela blew out the candles on the low table but didn't relieve her legs by standing and stretching them. Instead, she stared past the meditation table to the open closet. On the closet door hook hung a black and lavender hooded cloak. To most people, there was nothing noteworthy about the garment. Indeed, it was quite plain by Asiyan standards. No intricate embroidery. No artful pleats. No complementary textures.

Lela rose from the floor. No, there was nothing remarkable about the cloak except . . . Lela's fingers glided over the velvet-soft outer lining—the color as black as sight without vision. The inner lining—lavender silk—drew the eye's attention more so than it would've achieved alone. Two colors, yes, but only dynamic when combined under a purpose-driven guiding hand.

The significance of an object wasn't always evident, and so it was for the cloak she caressed—her touch reverent, the weight of responsibility the garment represented incalculable.

"Lela, do you require assistance?"

She turned away from her thoughts and toward her mother's voice on the other side of her closed bedroom door. "Come in, A'bra."

The door opened and Nenet entered. "Your father is worried about you. Do you plan on speaking with him before the ceremony?"

"I was unaware I wasn't speaking to Ab'ba. I was meditating, not avoiding him and our earlier conversation."

Her mother stepped further into her bedroom, footfalls as soft as her smile. Unlike members of the House of Asheema, who were known for their intricate ivory coils, Nenet of the House of Deeb had ankle-length hair the color of a sunset—pale orange with gold undertones. For Lela's induction into the Council of Magistrates, Nenet wore a lovely floor-length light blue gown with a square neck collar, bell sleeves, and black lace ruffles.

While Lela preferred warm, color-rich gowns, like the one her mother wore, her fondness for colors did not extend to her coils. For Asiyans, the primary house to which one belonged was determined by a child's coil color and pattern, both unique to each house. Thus, Lela's crisscross ivory coils made her an Asheema first and a Deeb second.

"Do you not understand Hasani's concerns?"

"What I understand is that I'm viewed as too young to decide when to take a mate but not too young to become leader of our band. How can both be true, A'bra?"

From Lela's perspective, they could not. Yet for the chief magistrates, both were. How could she be expected to rule by their side as an equal if they thought her incapable of successfully managing her professional and her personal lives?

Nenet's hand, warm and steady, took hold of Lela's. "Verity is the smallest of the bands. Philosophers, theorists, sages, logicians; we can be all of those titles, but we are not limited to those labels. Despite how others may seek to define us, as truth yes, but we are also wisdom made manifest. We do not lie, not because truths are easy to share, but because truths withheld is the greatest disservice we can do to ourselves and others."

Lela accepted Nenet's tight embrace. Her mother smelled of home—insight wrapped in sureness. The comfort she found in her mother's arms made her feel every bit the woman-child too many people thought of her as.

She burrowed closer, grateful for this private moment of vulnerability. The scared but knowing part of Lela interpreted the embrace for what it would prove to be. Once she joined the Council, woman or child, ready or unprepared, she would be a chief magistrate. In that role, Lela could never reveal this level of self-doubt again.

Lela hugged her mother even tighter while fighting back the tears that threatened. She'd already cried once. They had come unexpectedly, her father's voice regretful but firm when he'd said, "I cannot consent to your union with Paladin Ammon. Not now, Lela. In a few anulls, when you are truly prepared to be a mate and chief magistrate, Yusef and I will grant the two of you our blessing for a happy union. If you and Ammon are fated mates, waiting will only strengthen your feelings for one another."

Lela had miscalculated. She shouldn't have held Ammon's hand in public. News of her indiscretion had reached her parents' ears before their ship had landed in the capital city of Nazari. Her thoughtless, rebellious act had increased Hasani's resolve for her not to join with anyone until she acclimated herself to the role of chief magistrate. For the Council, her father's position was advantageous. Where then did that leave Lela and Ammon?

"Why must I sacrifice my heart for the Council, when they will have every other part of me?"

Lela didn't care that she also feared she and Ammon weren't destined to be together. She despised her traitorous thoughts, so she'd kept them to herself. Not a lie, by Verity standards, for she would disclose all if Ammon asked. Thankfully, he had not.

Still, Lela wanted to have Ammon for as long as the Fates granted her a sacred place in his heart and he in hers.

"Have faith, and trust the Fates have a higher plan for you."

"That's what most frightens me."

Nenet wiped away tears Lela hadn't realized she'd shed. "You weep on a day when smiles should be plentiful and contagious. Hasani and I are quite proud of you, daughter. Have we told you that lately?"

"Not since I left home to join Regent Etemaad here."

Her father knocked, but also peeked around the open door. "Then we have been most remiss in our duties as your parents." Hasani joined them in her bedroom, as tall and as broad shouldered as any Paladin male. "I wish only the best for my daughter. I did not mean to bring rain clouds to what should be your sunny day."

"I know, Ab'ba."

His eyes, her eyes, a swirl of black, brown, gray, and white watched her with a soft sadness she doubted had anything to do with their disagreement earlier and her uncharacteristic bout of crying.

Before she knew it, her parents had traded places. Her father stood in front of her, every inch the Sagacity Luminary, head of the Verity school for the next generation of regional and planetary leaders. Hasani rarely deviated from his typical attire. Today was no different. A black jacquard long coat with ruffles at the sleeves marked him as a band luminary. Only the Affiq Luminary wore formal clothing other than the standard black frock of her peers—a deep lavender long coat befitting her rank as Luminary of All. Lela supposed the other luminaries had also arrived for the ceremony, as would have regional leaders from across the planet.

"Breathe with me, daughter."

She did, following the smooth, slow cadence of Hasani's breaths. Nenet joined in, the way she always did when Hasani led Lela through this exercise. The sound of her father's measured breaths combined with the sight of his confident, serene eyes did for her what two herns of meditation could not.

In sync they breathed. Lela's mind, for the first time since accepting her band's nomination, was clear and focused.

No stress.

No self-doubt.

No fear.

The ceremony would begin in one hern. When it did, Lela's thoughts would be of her service to the people of Asiya. A woman's heart and tender feelings were secondary, so she followed her father's mental trail, finding tranquility in a turbulent sea of future regrets.

Mother Cosmos
Fate of Purpose

If the Fate of Purpose had used the energy from Mother Cosmos to conjure a body, she would've smiled down at her Lela, so proud was she of the young woman she'd grown into. Even without a form, Purpose's nonexistent stomach fluttered with cheer coated in a thin layer of anxiety. For now, though, she would focus on Lela, her long-awaited descendant, and hope for a much-needed slumber. But sleep was anulls into the future. Purpose and her soul-bonded mates—Faith and Truth—had much to do before they could rest in Mother Cosmos's lustrous bosom.

Her loves hadn't been as nervous about Lela's induction as she, so they had teleported to the planet in the guise of living Asiyans, an old truth. A small part of Purpose had wanted to join them. She had desired nothing more than to touch her feet upon the land of her birth, the air she would've breathed a visceral reminder of all that came before and all that could never again be.

High above the verdant grounds of the Hall of Concord, Purpose, like the crowd gathered in the Cetta Topiary Gardens, awaited the Council's arrival. A richly patterned mosaic walkway led from the Council of Magistrates' Ruling Chamber to the stone water fountain at the end of the garden. There were two pillars. Between the pillars were elevated statues of Faith, Purpose, and Truth. Under the center statue of Purpose was a stone-filled archway, its thick, wide base immersed in a reservoir. Chairs were placed in front of the fountain and on both sides of the walkway.

When the audience stood from their seats, she knew Truth and Faith were among them, their gazes, like everyone else's, on the seven figures who walked up the path and toward the fountain. Their hoods may have concealed their heads and faces, but Purpose didn't need conventional sight to identify the faithful servants of Asiya. Regent Etemaad led the procession, followed by Banou, Yusef, Chiku, Reth, and Mosi. Five feet behind the Council was Lela, the smallest and youngest in the procession. But her bearing was not dimmed by either. Indeed, she was as formidable and regal as the group she would soon join.

Lela is quite the sight, Truth spoke, their connection unaffected by distance or form. *She doesn't yet know her true value.*

She will come to understand much as chief magistrate, while grappling with even more. But she will prevail. I have faith in our Lela.

Of course the Fate of Faith did. But it wasn't their faith in Lela that most mattered but Lela's faith in herself.

Regent Etemaad, dressed in his lavender ceremonial cloak, removed his hood and addressed the dignitaries who had retaken their seats when the Council had stopped in front of the fountain. The Council faced their guests, with the regent in the center and his council to his left and right. A sole Asiyan remained on the walkway, her hood still on while the others had removed theirs. She hadn't yet earned the right to reveal her face to those who had traveled to Nazari, the capital of Asiya, or to the planet at large who watched the live broadcast.

The glow from the full moon seemed to shine upon Lela or perhaps it was Purpose's magic and happiness that radiated from her down to her descendant.

"We are gathered," Etemaad said, uttering the opening words of the ceremony, "on this day of Luna to welcome a new chief magistrate into our family of humble servants. I am because we are." Pausing, Etemaad nodded to the Council members to his left and then to his right. "I am because we are."

"I am because we are," the crowd spoke with the regent for the third, fourth, and fifth recitation.

"We are"—the regent pointed to the solitary figure on the walkway—"because she is. We are because she is."

Again, the dignitaries spoke in unison, reciting the line three times. They had turned toward Lela, speaking the proclamation directly to her.

"She is because we are. She is because we are."

Lela's parents and members of the Verity Band stood, turned to Lela, and repeated the regent's guiding words three times. "She is because we are."

Regent Etemaad stepped forward. "I am. We are."

"I am. We are," the chief magistrates echoed.

Etemaad gestured for those still standing to take their seats. He nodded, smiled, and then voiced the next words of the induction ritual. "Come forward Chief Magistrate of the Affiq Band, Mosi of the House of Faheel. Tell us who you are, what you wonder, what you hear, what you see, and what you want. On this day of Luna, your mind is unburdened, no ancient parchments to decipher. Share your understanding and welcome our truth."

Mosi, dark green eyes mixed with silver, her triangular patterned coils the same color combination, stepped away from the line of chief magistrates. With a confident gait, she walked toward Lela, stopping an arm's length in front of her. One hand went to Lela's lowered head. When Mosi spoke, it was with the meticulousness of the intellect of her band.

"I *am* knowledge and creativity. I *wonder* about life beyond my choosing. I *hear* the whispered secrets of the setting sun and rising moon. I *see* galaxies not yet birthed. I *want* to know why Mother Cosmos is so vast, yet we were given minds and life spans too limited to grasp it all. I *am* knowledge and creativity. I am because you are." Leaning in closer to Lela, her hand still on her head, Mosi repeated, "I am because you are."

With the same self-assured grace, Mosi returned to the fountain, claiming the space to Etemaad's immediate right.

"Come forward Chief Magistrate of the Paladin Band, Yusef of the House of Eetu. Tell us what you hope, what you feel, why you worry, what you touch, why you cry, and who you are. On this day of Luna, your warrior's spirit is unburdened, no innocents to defend. Share your honor and welcome our truth."

As Mosi had done, Yusef joined Lela on the walkway, his hand going to the top of her hooded head. Though Yusef's voice was stern, perhaps even tinged with irritation, his sentiments and heart were sincere.

"I *hope* there is as much honor in dying for a just cause as there is in fighting for one. I *feel* the indomitable shield of the first Paladin on my back. I *touch* prayers dripping from the trees of harmony. I *worry* apathy is a silent but deadly form of warfare. I *cry* for blood taken, hearts broken, and lives stolen." In a booming voice, Yusef proclaimed, "I *am* blade and armor." Reaching into a pocket of his cloak, Yusef pressed an item into Lela's hand.

Lela didn't react other than to store Yusef's present in her own cloak pocket. Strange; only Banou, as the outgoing chief magistrate for the Verity Band, was expected to grant Lela a gift.

Yusef rejoined the line, standing to Etemaad's left.

"Come forward Chief Magistrate of the Euridice Band, Reth of the House of Zadok. Tell us who you are, what you wonder, what you hear, what you see, and what you want. On this day of Luna, your mind is unburdened, no laws to interpret. Share your prescription and welcome our truth."

Reth was the youngest of the chief magistrates but still many anulls older than Lela. When he approached the inductee, vibrant blue-red eyes a stark contrast to his serious personality and snowy coils, Purpose could feel the genuineness of his smile.

Reth placed his hands on Lela's shoulders. As if reciting a code of conduct, he spoke clearly and loudly, enunciating every word. "I *am* justice and law. I *wonder* about covenants of the heart and decrees of the mind. I *hear* eruption fissures of disavowed commandments. I *see* the ghostly trails of mental mandates. I *want* safety and equity as canon." Before Reth retreated to stand beside Mosi, he told Lela, "I am because you are. You are because we are. Justice is not revenge. It is truth in action."

Lela nodded.

Purpose could feel her slow, calm breaths, as if they shared the same form. More, Purpose could sense Lela's resolve, her patience, her humility. For all that she could discern about Lela's physical and emotional states, she could not read her mind. There were limitations, even for an immortal fate.

"Come forward Chief Magistrate of the Devdas Band, Chiku of the House of Bagath. Tell us what you understand, what you say, what you try, what you hope, and who you are. On this day of Luna, your spirit is unburdened, your soul complete. Share your gospel and welcome our truth."

A tide of tightly coiled onyx hair trailed behind Chiku, nearly as dark as her skin, eyes, and cloak. The House of Bagath was rare in that one color dominated their bloodline—black—regardless with whom they reproduced.

Chiku didn't touch Lela on her shoulders or head. Instead, her wizened hands reached for Lela's, holding them between her own. A blessing meant only for Lela slipped past her lips. It was yet another unexpected gift from a chief magistrate.

The display of kindness pleased Purpose.

Dark eyes cast to Lela, Chiku bared the heart of a Devdas. "I *understand* Mother Cosmos is the origin of ALL. I *say* our belief exceeds our vision. I *try* to grasp the metaphysical purges of the universe. I *hope* conviction soothes self-doubt. I *am* fealty and faith."

Regent Etemaad stepped forward as Chiku walked to the fountain to take her place next to Yusef. "Lela of the House of Asheema, remove your hood and share your heart with those you will serve with honor. You have our ears."

Without a tremor, Lela pulled back her hood, revealing the sober face of a young woman poised to accept the challenges of the unknown.

Disinclined to watch this portion of the ritual from such a great distance, Purpose materialized behind the last row of dignitaries. Purpose joined Faith and Truth, who, to her surprise and delight, had left a seat for her between them.

She loved them dearly.

Faith kissed her cheek, his Asiyan form magnificent, the feel of his lips on her skin more so. "Are you prepared for what Lela's heart will express, for the commitment she will make? Once spoken aloud and given air, they cannot be withdrawn."

"I am aware. We have waited lifetimes for this moment."

"And we must wait one more lifetime," Truth reminded them. "We've been patient. Yet as the time of our eternal rest draws nearer, I find my patience waning." Truth nodded in the direction of Ammon, who sat on the opposite side of the walkway with his mother and brother. The Paladin's gaze was fixed on Lela. "I will watch over our young warrior. He will stumble and fall, as they all will. We cannot alter their fates."

"No," Purpose agreed, "but we can, if only for a meager moment of time, celebrate with them. Let us listen to Lela's truth, purpose and faith."

No one moved or spoke, except for Lela, who looked first in the direction of her parents then second to Ammon. Her gaze didn't linger on any of them. She didn't have to, for her eyes exposed her heart, as well as her choice.

Lela strode several feet forward, her head held high. "I *am* truth and wisdom. I *wonder* if rightness is cold comfort or warm relief. I *hear* principles rising from the ash of forgotten civility. I *see* starbursts in the eyes of children. I *want* hope disguised as certainty. I *am* truth and wisdom."

She moved three more steps forward.

Lela's parents and members of her band rose.

"I *hope* truth is a gift instead of a burden. I *feel* tendrils of stained realism gliding over my skin. I *touch* courage with fingers wet from my tears. I *worry* noble gestures are blind cultural insults. I *cry* for opportunities lost. I *am* truth and wisdom."

Lela advanced even more. Each step put her closer to the Council of Magistrates and her future. When Lela stopped, Ammon added his form to those already standing.

"I *understand* enlightenment is a winding journey. I *say* virtue devoid of balance is no virtue at all. I *dream* of empowerment and joy, freedom and kindness, happiness and compassion. I *try* to learn from every overcast day and sun-kissed morning. I *hope* love is forgiving and mercy is embraced. I *am* truth and wisdom."

When Lela finished, all in attendance had risen.

Without being directed by the regent, Chief Magistrate Banou, a hundred anulls, gestured with her chin for Lela to kneel.

Without haste, Lela complied.

"You are indeed truth and wisdom. Yes, truth is often a burden. That is why you have a council to help you hold it aloft."

In Banou's hand she held the very same gift bestowed on her when Banou had gone through the Luna of Analisia. Purpose recalled the indigo crystal well, for it was originally hers.

Banou placed a necklace around Lela's neck. "The Verity Band proudly grants Lela of the House of Asheema our most sacred artifact—the ver'ty. It has no beginning or end, like Mother Cosmos and our faith. I say unto you, let empathy balance knowledge, let love balance justice, and let you rise, Chief Magistrate of the Verity Band."

Ver'ty dangling from the center of Lela's necklace, she rose to her full height of five feet.

Regent Etemaad clapped his hands once, twice and his council followed. In unison, the Council offered their final message to the people of Asiya. "We are Affiq—knowledge and creativity. We are Paladin—blade and armor. We are Euridice—justice and law. We are Devdas—fealty and faith."

Banou escorted Lela to the Council and gave her the position next to Reth. With a shallow bow to the regent, Banou claimed the reserved chair in the first row to Etemaad's left—the sadika. Once the Luna of Analisia concluded, the Starlight of Shamoon would begin, an appreciation of faithful service ceremony in honor of Banou.

When Lela's presence completed the Council of Magistrates, she led the group in uttering the next line of their pledge. "We are Verity—truth and wisdom."

"We are *one*," Regent Etemaad exclaimed. "We are *Asiya*."

"We are *Asiya*," the attendees repeated, with a depth of emotion Purpose felt to her transcendent core.

"Under the brilliant moon and starry sky, let us welcome Chief Magistrate Lela."

So they did, gathering around the new, untried leader until Purpose could no longer see a single coil on Lela's ivory head.

"Are you ready to depart?" Truth asked.

Purpose wasn't, nor was Truth's question limited to the physical plane. "She'll be lost without us."

"True, but only for a short while."

Flanked by Faith and Truth, they faded into the darkness, but not into nothingness. They would see Lela again.

4. Codes of Conduct

"I didn't think he would give it to you as part of the ceremony."

Lela had heard Ammon approach but only because he'd wanted her to. He may have been her tenderhearted poet, but he moved like the wind—sometimes gentle and silent, other times hard and biting. Making room on the bench for him, she shifted to her right.

Ammon sat beside her, closer than propriety dictated. Cool and strong, his hand found hers on the bench. "This is the perfect hideaway. I hope you don't mind that I followed you down here."

Turning her hand over, she pressed her palm against his. "Of course I don't. If you don't mind me borrowing your favorite place to meditate."

They'd sat on this bench many times, looking out at the oval pool, a family of white, long-neck geeth always in residence. The bowl-shaped lawn was surrounded by topiary geeth swimming atop yewroots, coniferous trees with red fruit berries.

"Only you and this part of the garden have made being under my father's watchful eye bearable." Ammon's shoulder rubbed against hers. "Geeth mate for life. They only take another mate, if at all, when their mate dies. If I didn't know better, I would say we modeled our mating beliefs after a species of waterfowl."

Lela didn't mind the silly idea, particularly since the humorous thought brought a smile to Ammon's face.

"Perhaps we did. Would you like for me to investigate your theory?"

Lela would soon depart Asiya, so she wouldn't have time for much, least of all indulging Ammon's playful theory. He understood the same, so a small smile was his only response.

"You're now a chief magistrate. How do you feel?"

Lela didn't quite know. Relieved, yes, but that descriptor felt incomplete. How could she explain that she felt the same yet forever changed by the experience? She'd done the will of her house and band. She'd made her parents and the regent happy. She had risen to the occasion the only way she knew how—with stubbornness. Lela would pray to the Fates, when she returned to her chamber, seeking their wisdom, strength, and guidance. She would also pray for Ammon, though he wouldn't wish it of her.

"Exhausted," she answered, when no better response to his question came to mind. "I feel as if I haven't slept in too many herns."

"You've earned your fatigue. If you so desire, we can begin the Light of Nurzhan tomorrow night instead of tonight as we planned."

Lela desired nothing more than to begin the courting rituals with Ammon. The Light of Nurzhan, also known as soul beholding, was the first of the courting rituals for Verity Band females. The purpose was for the female to look upon the true soul of the male, without the emotional shields one often wore during the bright light of day. If the soul revealed to her was pleasing, the female would invite the male to behold her soul. A successful Light of Nurzhan included three nights of soul beholding. After the courting rituals came the mating rituals, the first being the Unity of Hearts—a ritual that concluded with the physical consummation of the couple's relationship.

Resting her head on his shoulder and feeling the warmth of his hand over hers, she regretted the promise she'd made to her father.

"Ab'ba would like for us to wait to begin the courting rituals. I told him I would."

"You . . . I . . . for how long, Lela? Anulls?"

"That would be my father's preference, yes. But I only promised to wait." Lela peeked up at Ammon under long, dark lashes, an impish smile playing about the edges of her lips. "We planned on beginning our official courting tonight. If I am to honor my promise to my father, I cannot accept your invitation to behold your soul tomorrow night. I would accept, however, if you posed the question upon my return."

Ammon's laughter rippled through the chilly night air and straight into Lela's heart. "Just when I think I would have to practice more patience, you surprise me. You find strategy even in a daughter's truthful oath. Yes, we will honor your promise and wait to behold each other's souls until after you return from Lumeria. I am of a mind to offer my services as your personal High Star but wish not to provoke our parents any more than our hand-in-hand stroll already has."

A finger went to her chin and lifted for an imprudent but much-desired kiss. As always, Ammon's lips were as sweet as his spirit. Mouths sought forbidden enjoyment, but Lela remained alert to their surroundings. She heard no one nearing, not that she would've if Yusef had taken it upon himself to go in search of his youngest son.

Lela eased out of the kiss, recalling what Ammon had said when he'd first appeared behind her. *"I didn't think he would give it to you as part of the ceremony."* Had he been referring to . . .? Lela removed Yusef's gift from her cloak pocket. It was lightweight, so she'd forgotten the offering. It was a . . .

With sure fingers, Ammon plucked the item from her hand. "This is the tactical knife my father gave me when I turned fifteen anulls."

"At your Rite of Pala?"

"Yes. Sometimes, I think he forgets the rite proclaimed me a man and ready for Shielder combat and tactical training. I'm double that age now, but I love this knife as much today as I did when Ab'ba handed it to me." His fingers slid over a well-maintained custom-fitted sheath. "The weapon has three finger choils and contoured scales for a comfortable grip. It also comes with a neck paracord."

"Why?"

Combat and tactical knives were weapons of a bygone era. Lela had grasped Yusef's link to ancient Paladins when he'd proclaimed his band "blade and armor." But as she listened to the pride in Ammon's voice, as well as the expertise that came with being a well-trained soldier, her understanding expanded.

"The paracord is for inverted carry as a neck knife. It's small enough to be easily concealed under a blouse. If you will accept another gift from me, I also have a hunter's knife I'd like to give you. It has a fixed blade and a good grip."

"A fixed blade and a good grip," Lela repeated, the words rotten fruit in her mouth. "I'm not going off to war, Ammon. It's a peace negotiation."

"Among warring planets. That's why I'm giving you my Rite of Pala blade. I also hope you'll accept my hunter's knife. It's made of mor'up, which means it's sharp enough to gut anyone who may threaten to do you harm."

Lela gaped at Ammon, astounded into silence. She'd never thought him like his father, but it could've been Yusef speaking to her. True, regardless of the band, everyone received basic self-defense training from Paladin instructors. Only Paladins, however, received extensive training, their band responsible for regional law enforcement and planetary defense.

She should've objected when he slipped the paracord around her neck, the knife's tip touching the ver'ty. But she could do nothing other than stare at him, surprised by how casually he'd spoken of gutting an enemy. But Lela was also touched by Ammon's concern for her safety.

"The hunting knife can be hidden in a boot or in a sheath strapped to your thigh." A bright smile formed, and his eyes darted to her lap. "If you like, I could show you how to arrange the strap on your leg. You wouldn't want it falling off at an inopportune time."

"You're serious?"

"Yes, I could help you—"

Lela playfully pushed away the hand reaching for her cloak-covered thigh. "Not about that. I know we haven't begun the courting rituals, but I'm certain none of them involve the exchange of deadly weapons."

Ammon sobered. "My father and I may disagree more than we ought, but we take the safety of those we care about seriously. It says much that he turned what should've been a private gesture into a public offering. I'm unsure if you are aware, but mor'up, the natural resource the Affiq use to make many of our weapons and all of our transporter shields, is undetectable by any known scanner. Do you know what that means?"

"I cannot bring a weapon into peace talks."

"You sound quite appalled and very Verity, my sweet Lela."

"You're asking me to lie." She also didn't appreciate the criticism of her band, no matter how gently the comment was stated. "Do you know what will happen if I'm discovered with your Paladin weapons on my person?"

"You'll be alive, and the person who dared to harm you will be at your feet bleeding out," Ammon responded so matter-of-factly it took Lela's breath away.

"I . . . I . . ." There were no words. Well, there were plenty, but she couldn't get the image he had painted out of her mind to form them.

Ammon hugged her to him, his chin going to the top of her head. "I apologize. I should've been more thoughtful in my approach to this discussion. Ab'ba never liked the idea of chief magistrates going into potentially hostile negotiations unarmed, although they've done just that for anulls. Regent Etemaad refuses Ab'ba's pleas. He believes carrying a weapon into peace talks is dishonorable and a breach of trust."

"That's because it is."

"I don't disagree. But can you not see the more important truth?"

Despite her Verity training, Lela could. She pushed from him, standing when she desired nothing more than to return to her chamber for a long, uninterrupted rest. Instead of asking Ammon to escort her back to the hall, she found herself fingering the neck knife and posing a different question. "Will you show me how to use it?"

With a hand around her waist, he pulled her to stand between his parted legs, face upturned to hers. "If you hadn't asked, I would've offered. A weapon is only useful if the owner knows how to use it properly. Your goal won't be to overpower an attacker."

"You're speaking of the element of surprise."

"Ah, you do recall some of your Paladin training."

Lela quirked an eyebrow at Ammon. "Not some. All."

His pleased grin spread warmth through her. "Then I am most honored to add to your training. We have four doles before your departure. I will use that time to teach you how to fell an enemy twice your size."

Closing her eyes, she sighed. They were speaking of combat and tactical knife training so she could wound or kill a would-be attacker. Of all the conversations she'd thought she would have after her induction into the Council of Magistrates, arranging for private knife combat lessons in what was supposed to be a tranquil garden wasn't one of them. In fact, what they were plotting was even more improper than their romantic interludes.

Not only had Ammon agreed to teach a non-band member combat techniques reserved for Shielder trainees, Lela had, in all but deed, decided to violate the Inter Solar System Peace Mediators' Codes of Conduct.

If Lela was caught, it would be she on the receiving end of a deadly weapon, for the penalty for breaking the Codes of Conduct was death.

With a gentle tug, Ammon settled Lela on his leg. "I know what you're thinking. If it helps, I discussed this with Ab'ba before the ceremony and he agrees."

It did help. But Yusef would be solar systems away if the worst happened. The thought of it all churned her stomach.

Ammon's soft lips kissed her forehead. "Ab'ba believes in contingency plans, and so do I. Consider the knives a paranoid Paladin's bedtime tonic. Knowing you have them will help me sleep at night while you are on Lumeria. With Regent Etemaad by your side, you'll keep each other safe. The regent's personal High Stars will be there, as well as your own."

Lela had forgotten the new position came with bodyguards, a not so subtle reminder that the role of chief magistrate increased her visibility beyond Asiya.

Ammon placed another kiss to her forehead. "I know it's late and you're tired, but we can sit here as long as you want. I can only imagine how overwhelming but also wonderful this day must've been for you." Strong fingers caressed her scalp, while his other hand led her head to his shoulder. "I wrote a poem for the occasion."

"A gift other than your knife."

Ammon laughed. "One gift is pragmatic, a concession to my protective side, while the other feeds a much deeper emotion—a feeling I can no longer deny."

Without having proceeded through the Light of Nurzhan, Ammon was prohibited from speaking the words of his heart—a different code of conduct they were perilously close to breaking.

"A poem sounds lovely, Ammon, thank you."

Wrapped in his arms, Lela closed her eyes, her own feelings something she also could no longer deny.

"When the sun rises, and the dawn berry blooms . . ."

Four doles later, when Lela turned in for the night, her chief magistrate's cloak hanging on the closet door, her ver'ty necklace between her breasts, and a zot with files on the Lumerian

War on her nightstand, all she could dream about were the knives she'd packed and a dead body at her feet.

5. Opportunity Knocks

Earth
Human Homeworld
City of New York
International Congressional Office of Personnel Management
Eastern Headquarters

"Presidential Management Fellows Program, Department of Energy Research Program, The Volunteer Legal Recruitment Program." Susan Gideon peered at Zion from across her desk, giving him the full weight of her disapproval. "How many times are we going to do this, Mr. Grace?"

A long finger with chewed nails, a contrast to her flawless makeup, curly brown hair, and wrinkle-free blouse and skirt, Mrs. Gideon touched the floating, translucent screen in front of her in an upward movement. The suit jacket that hung on the back of her chair was more flexible than her attitude.

"I don't see a law school listed here, Mr. Grace."

For as many times as he'd been in her office, Mrs. Gideon probably had his résumé memorized.

"That's because I'm not in law school."

"Yesss," she said, drawing out the word in that paternalistic way of too many bureaucrats he'd met. "Yet you wish to apply for the Summer Law Intern Program?"

"I do."

"Three months ago, you applied for The Volunteer Legal Recruitment Program. You weren't enrolled in a law school then either." She pushed the screen twice and it disappeared, leaving nothing but stale space between them.

Zion had arrived at Mrs. Gideon's office, as he did every two or three months, in one of only two suits he owned. His father always told him to dress for the job he wanted. As of last year, he lived in his parents' basement apartment, commuting to New York International University instead of adding a room and board bill to an already expensive tuition. He still resided with his parents, although he spent most of his free time at his girlfriend's apartment—an overpriced flat that smelled of daisies and fresh baked chocolate cookies. The combined scents would forever remind him of Iman.

Mrs. Gideon's eyes lowered to the zot in his hand, a graduation gift from his girlfriend. "You graduated top of your class with a major in Planetary Relations. It's one of the most rigorous disciplines at NYIU, and they only accept one percent of their applicants."

She pointed to the window and the miles of green-blue sky outside the high-rise building. All her fingernails were chewed off, and he couldn't help but wonder if her disinterest in becoming a cannibal had caused her to stop when she'd reached the meaty part of her fingers or whether, belatedly, she'd realized nails didn't make for a healthy snack.

"With your degree and brains, why are you in my office again? There's nothing for you here, but there are plenty of jobs in the private sector for a person with your academic record."

His parents and girlfriend had asked him the same, especially after he'd graduated from college and turned down three lucrative job offers. The corporate world wasn't for him. That's not how he wanted to give back and to serve the people of New York and Earth.

"Internships, fellowships, and other work experience opportunities in the federal government," he said, referring to the document the United States government posted annually. Recruiters, like Mrs. Gideon, were frequent visitors on college campuses, which was how he'd met the fifty-something woman his junior year of college.

Lacing her fingers, she propped her elbows on her desk and leaned forward. "Listen, you're a good kid. Smart, like I said. But you don't have the requisite skills and knowledge for the programs you keep applying for. A degree in Planetary Relations isn't enough. Not here."

"Tell me what would be enough."

Zion's father, Elijah Grace, was a sentinel detective who hunted the vilest criminals. The job had left its mark on Elijah, but he gave each case everything he had. Elijah had once told Zion that the dead were too easily forgotten, and that the living were too easily ignored. Some people were less valued than others. It was that group Zion wanted to serve. Helping people was the role of government. He thought he could do it with a degree in Planetary Relations, but he'd been wrong. Which meant Zion in a suit and tie and his butt in Mrs. Gideon's chair, no matter how tired she was of seeing his smiling but determined face.

"How many languages do you speak?"

Now they were getting somewhere. "Six. English, Mandarin, Hindustani, Spanish, Arabic, and Malay."

Zion grinned at Mrs. Gideon, but she frowned in return, obviously unimpressed with what he considered one of his biggest assets.

"They're the topmost spoken languages in the world. Billions of people speak one of those languages."

"I know, and they're all languages spoken by humans. That's the problem with majors like Planetary Relations and schools like NYIU. They prepare students well to work and live in an international community but not for life beyond Earth and not with immigrants to our planet."

Mrs. Gideon's snort was as unattractive as her chewed fingernails but tinged with an ideological judgment he'd never heard from her before. For the first time since meeting her, two years ago, Zion felt as if he was seeing the real Susan Gideon. A part of Zion went on high alert, while the other part of him was intrigued when she turned on her screen again and gestured for him to move his chair to sit beside her.

She pushed a pink glowing box on her translucent screen, stopping at the international news show *Our Planet, Their Universe*. Zion rarely watched this show or the Intercontinental News Network because they gave too much airtime to xenophobic pundits. The pundits were planetists at their worst, arguing for strong border control policies and an end to interplanetary trade relations. Shortsighted and racist, INN and most of their guests were blind to the many benefits Earth gained from opening its borders to immigrants.

"The 2252 Immigration Bill will keep Earth from falling into the hands of aliens. We need your support. If you've ever lost a job to an alien or been an alien's crime victim then you know why this bill must pass. If their languages and strange customs have invaded your communities and schools, then support this bill. Enough of them already live among us, why invite more? This is Earth. Let's make it great again. Support the 2252 Immigration Bill and reclaim Earth for humans."

Mrs. Gideon all but growled at the host's opening of the news program. She muted her screen before he introduced his first guest. "What do you think?"

With the way her dark brown eyes stared at him, he sensed this unscheduled meeting had morphed into an unplanned and definitely unprepared-for job interview.

Zion cleared his throat and admitted, "I only know a little about the proposed bill. I haven't followed it closely."

Mrs. Gideon neither snorted nor growled. She simply stared at him. Her lack of a response, even a judgmental one, was somehow worse.

Zion cleared his throat again. "I have been to a couple of other planets. I speak, read, and write a little Khabir and Aadish." His accent for both was shit. Zion couldn't get the clicking sounds right. He didn't think it was possible for the human tongue to make the sounds properly. What he'd wanted to say to Mrs. Gideon was that the universal translator made it unnecessary for people to spend years learning world languages, much less languages of other races.

As if she'd plucked the thought from his mind, she pointed to the zot in his hand. "That's only as helpful as the planets and races our government has developed positive relations with. Each planet's ruling government controls what's uploaded to the Interplanetary Wide Web, from languages spoken on their planet to the foods they eat."

"I know. I also know planets don't stream the same information to every planet. Each planet, including Earth, is very selective about what they share and with whom. Due to the Our Earth movement, many planets have ended their bilateral exchanges with Earth."

"Very good, Mr. Grace. Can I then assume you know about the war between the people of Lumeria and Meleris?"

"The Lumerians are religious extremists, which wouldn't be so bad if they also weren't hell-bent on forcing their beliefs down the throats of their neighbors. How many Amakans do you think the Lumerians have killed in their so-called holy war?"

"Thousands, but not only Amakans of Meleris. You have—"

"The Yegoth of Wither and the Unbalk people of Shin," Zion interrupted. "They're small planets and not as technologically advanced as Lumeria. My mother and sister think the Lumerians are bullies on a small playground, and I agree."

"The Vargan Solar System isn't so small, but I also agree with your mother and sister. Have you seen the recent footage out of Lumeria?"

Zion was tempted to look around the office. He was in a government facility, after all, so it wouldn't surprise him if Mrs. Gideon's office had concealed security cameras. He damn sure knew the public areas did. If he were one of those conspiracy theorists INN loved showcasing, he would've avoided the men's room before seeking out Mrs. Gideon. He'd interrupted her lunch break, again. No wonder the woman was never pleased to see him.

"Come now, Mr. Grace. Nothing to say? I thought we were having an open and honest conversation."

He doubted they'd ever had either. At least not on Mrs. Gideon's end. In her "nice" bureaucratic way, she had just told him she knew what else students who majored in Planetary Relations were known for—accessing the deep web.

Zion shrugged. He was twenty-one, what in the hell did the government expect from his generation? "You mean the peace talks?"

For the first time since meeting Susan Gideon, she granted him a genuine smile. "What did you think of the footage?"

"The Lumerian prime minister talks too much and thinks too highly of himself."

"Again, I agree. But I wasn't asking about Prime Minister Drassul. What do you know of peace negotiations and Asiyans?"

"Some and a little."

"That's what I thought."

Mrs. Gideon pressed a square box on her screen. The same footage he'd found two days ago appeared, reinforcing his earlier thought about Mrs. Gideon being more than the recruiter she'd presented herself as when she'd participated in career day at his college.

They watched the five-minute reel of the Lumerian prime minister welcome two peace negotiators from Asiya—reading subtitles but also listening to the voice-over.

"Do you know which chief magistrate the Asiyans sent to broker a peace agreement between the Lumerians and the Amakans?"

Mrs. Gideon shifted her gaze from her screen to Zion. "I thought you said you know very little about Asiyans."

"Everyone knows they have a regent and five bands. Kind of like castes, I believe, but not quite."

"You're more or less right. It's a coup for Prime Minister Drassul to have secured the Asiyans in peace talks. They're highly sought after, but they don't go everywhere. The fact that they've involved themselves in the Lumerian-Amakan war speaks volumes."

Mrs. Gideon nodded to the screen. The footage had concluded. It stilled on images of two Asiyans, hooded cloaks covering them from head to ankles.

"This is where we need to be."

"What do you mean?" Zion returned his chair to its proper place, more comfortable with a desk between himself and Mrs. Gideon.

"If you want a career that'll make a difference and not an unpaid internship you hope will garner you an entry-level job with a senator you're likely already smarter than, then go home and study everything you can find on peace negotiations, beginning with the Inter Solar System Peace Mediators' Codes of Conduct. It also wouldn't hurt if you brushed up on all of Earth's accords with other planets."

That was a lot, and Zion was confused. "Are you offering me a job?"

"Better, I'm opening a window of opportunity. Earth is about to go into the peace negotiations business. That's what conservatives like INN and *Our Planet, Their Universe* will soon find out. We're expanding, Mr. Grace. We can't continue to favor certain immigrants while shunning others. But we need progressive voices all over the planet—young voices, like yours."

"Like mine?" he asked, head spinning from the strange direction the conversation had taken. "I have no idea what you're talking about."

"I'm talking about you becoming a peace negotiator."

"A what? I don't know anything about peace negotiations."

Interracial mediation wasn't remotely close to what he'd studied, although he could see a fair amount of overlap. Not in actual negotiation skills, but in having an appreciation for the culture of others and his experience working with and learning from immigrants.

"You'll learn. That's why I told you to go home and study." Mrs. Gideon pressed her screen a few more times. Seconds later, his zot alerted him to a message. "I sent you several documents to help get you started. Once you know the ins and outs of those documents and others, call my office. When you do, I'll have my assistant add you to the next scheduled government entrance exam rotation. We'll also talk about an internship. Make an appointment, though." Her eyes traveled from his face to his freshly pressed but well-worn black suit. "A paid internship. That should make your parents happy."

Zion smiled. *All my persistence is finally paying off. I knew it.* "With which branch?" Zion was partial to the legislative branch but, at this point, he'd take almost any branch and department.

Mrs. Gideon's grin couldn't have been more shit eating if she tried. Sitting back in her chair, she waited, her smile unwavering. It didn't take Zion long to catch on.

He groaned, and her smile broadened.

"You scouted me when I was a junior in college, didn't you?"

Mrs. Gideon opened the container to the lunch she'd abandoned when he'd arrived unannounced at her office. "No, that's when I made my presence known."

She played me, and the past two years have been one long-ass interview.

"You have patience and determination, two traits that will serve you well as a peace negotiator. Verity Band. You asked me which band the Asiyans are from. Based on our intelligence, they are both from the Verity Band. The larger of the two was Regent Etemaad. Only god knows why he would leave his planet to traipse all the way to Lumeria. That's what chief magistrates are for. They are the ones who are the peace negotiators."

"What about the petite one?"

Not that the regent was tall. The man couldn't have been more than five and a half feet tall.

"We don't know much about her, not even her name. If you noticed, not even Prime Minister Drassul called them by name. No doubt that was the Asiyans' doing. They are a tight-lipped race, especially concerning their leaders. But there are rumors the Chief Magistrate of the Verity Band stepped down."

"Retired?"

"I suppose that's what it could mean in their society. At any rate, we think there's been a change in leadership within the Verity Band and that the new chief magistrate is young and female."

"Young?"

"Another one-word question, Mr. Grace. If you're going to work for me, you'll need to expand your vocabulary and critical thinking skills."

She arched an eyebrow, and he remained silent and still, not taking her bait. If she wanted to rattle a kid from NYC, she'd have to throw more at him than a few rude words and a bushy brow.

"If you want to know the woman's exact age, we don't know. Asiyans live longer than us. They also have a longer calendar year. Beyond that, we don't know enough about them to calculate their physical and mental maturation. Regent Etemaad has served as the leader of his people for at least two decades. I've seen a few pictures of him without his cloak. Our government intelligence places him in his seventies, maybe early eighties. But I swear, he could easily pass as a man in his midfifties."

Zion whistled.

"Precisely. I'd love to have their slow aging. None of that really matters to the government of Earth beyond the fact that Asiya's new chief magistrate is unknown to us. If she is as young as we think, maybe early thirties, she'll be around for decades."

When Zion was a boy, he used to enjoy dressing up and pretending. More than once, his father had caught him wearing his police officer uniform, boots included. "Officer Grace," his father would say, "what are you up to?"

"I'm gonna catch bad guys."

"Sounds like a brave thing to do. Bad guys need to be caught."

Zion would smile, nod and then run around his backyard after imaginary bad guys. Zion had had fun, and his father never told him he couldn't catch the bad guys because he was too young or too small, or that his shoes and clothes were too big. All of that was obvious, just as it was also obvious that Zion would grow, not only into an adult body, but into any role he wished to chase down. Perhaps someone along the way had told the young chief magistrate the same.

"At some point," Mrs. Gideon said, unaware his mind had drifted, "Earth will have to deal more closely with other planets, especially powerful ones like Asiya. Most of what I've told you are unsubstantiated rumors from reliable as well as questionable sources. In time, you'll cultivate your own sources, learning which rumors to believe and take action on and which to ignore." She nodded to the screen in front of her. "This nameless, faceless chief magistrate is the future of Asiya. I can feel it in my bones. The fact that Asiyans have gone to greater lengths than usual to shield her identity makes me think I'm right."

Watching Mrs. Gideon push limp spring mix around with her fork reminded Zion he also hadn't eaten lunch. He made a mental note to bring lunch when he started working there, if her less than tasty-looking salad was the quality of food at the cafeteria.

"Earth is now paying close attention to what the Asiyans do and which wars they choose to offer assistance in ending."

"Because we want to be on the right side of a conflict?"

She shoved a forkful of salad into her mouth, swiftly followed by a napkin into which she spat the spring mix. Yup, Zion would steer clear of cafeteria food.

"The politically correct answer would be *yes*."

"What's the real answer?"

Into the trash can Mrs. Gideon's salad went. The poor woman. The next time Zion came, he would bring her a big bowl of his mother's spaghetti and meatballs. It was the least he could do.

"Read, study, research. That's my answer. Don't worry about the Lumerian-Amakan War or the Asiyans. That's political maneuverings above your pay grade."

He supposed it was. Not that he had a pay grade yet. Still, Zion couldn't help but be intrigued by the Asiyans. Could he do it? Did he have the chops to work in the interracial community at the level as the young chief magistrate? *I never thought that big before. Thanks to Mrs. Gideon, now I am.*

As soon as he was on the lift headed to the lobby, he used his zot to call Iman. He couldn't wait to tell her about his window of opportunity.

6. Watch and Listen

Lumeria
Lumerian Homeworld
Veer River Complex

Lela accepted the gloved hand of High Star Gayora, grateful for the strong support as she climbed from the river ferry. The Asiyan delegation had landed their shuttle at a spaceport located in a small province to the east of Veer where Prime Minister Drassul resided.

"Thank you, Gayora."

Lela would've preferred to have been given the option of selecting her own High Stars, but that decision fell within Yusef's domain. Her security team consisted of four bodyguards. Gayora, a dekull older than Lela, was the youngest but highest ranked of her High Stars. Lela didn't doubt Gayora's gender and age were taken into consideration when Yusef had assigned her as Lela's High Star Shadow.

High Star shadows followed their charge everywhere it was reasonable for them to go together. Shadows weren't meant to blend into the background. But they were unassuming to the point that, while in their presence, one could easily forget they were there. Forget until the shadow felt a need to remind an unfortunate soul that discreet didn't equate to passive.

In front of Lela walked Rahm, her High Star Shield and second-in-command. To her right was Orit. His observant green-gray eyes took in the wide, too-warm hallway the male Lumerian envoy led them down. High Star Waafir walked behind Lela. He and Orit held the same rank of besieger. Only two High Star ranks were above that of Gayora's shadow—High Star Chief of Regent Security and High Star Cleaver.

Walking in the same protective formation as her own High Stars, the regent's guards—Beres, Kondo, Gan, and Ramona—were men and women she'd known for anulls. She respected each of them. More, she liked them as individuals and valued them as professionals.

Taking in the regent's four cleavers, strong and proficient, Lela felt foolish for wearing Ammon's knives. Surely eight skilled Paladins would be ample protectors for Lela and Etemaad. Ammon's fears, though appreciated, had been groundless. Even the regent's security chief, Elan of the House of Blaz, hadn't accompanied Etemaad on this mission. Surely an experienced Paladin like Elan would've correctly assessed the level of danger to the regent. Elan's absence revealed much, so Lela released a slow breath, expelling unfounded tension that had gathered in her chest and at the back of her head.

In silence, the Asiyan delegation followed a male Lumerian down long hallways. The same envoy had met them at the spaceport when they'd arrived a day ago. Prime Minister Drassul and his entourage had been there too, along with a small group of what turned out to be interplanetary press.

"Do not remove your hood," Etemaad had told her, his voice betraying none of the irritation she'd known he'd felt about the unexpected presence of the media. "We will not allow Drassul to use our faces to support his religious cause to the interplanetary community."

Thus, for the entirety of the press conference, Lela and Etemaad neither spoke nor revealed their images to the cameras. Not that their silence mattered, for Prime Minister Drassul had spoken enough for three people.

They made a right. Strange, she hadn't heard or seen a Lumerian since entering the building. The envoy, bare chested with orange-red skin, wore skintight trousers and no shoes. His feet and hands were webbed. Black, geometric designs, clan markings, if Lela's research was correct, began at the envoy's shaved head and covered most of his forehead and his entire chin. His neck and chest, however, were unmarked, but his back was covered in interlocking black circles from shoulder blades to his trousers, where the design disappeared, presumably going down his buttocks, hips, and legs. Like his neck and chest, the envoy's feet and hands were design-free. To her knowledge, there were over fifty different Lumerian clans. Not all of them had webbed hands and feet like the envoy and the ferry captain, both of whom appeared as if they preferred swimming as their main mode of traveling.

The group stopped in front of a set of thick, closed doors—gray, flat, and smooth like every wall and door she'd seen since entering Prime Minister Drassul's complex. For Lumerians to be a physically colorful race with beautiful symbols decorating their bodies, their buildings were devoid of both. Yet, in the center of each door before Lela was a single eye. Two black irises surrounded by orange and red met the group's gazes. If Waafir weren't standing directly behind Lela, she would've stepped away from the eerie dark eyes.

They captivated her, not because the eyes were lovely paintings created by a skilled hand, but because her entire body tingled when she took them in. Her skin also heated the longer she gazed upon them.

Lela felt a pressure push against her forehead, like a finger trying to drill its way into her skull. It didn't hurt so much as it was an unpleasant intrusion that challenged her mental will for dominance. She conjured an image of the Fates of Asiya. Slowly, the pressure eased before receding completely, leaving her feeling nauseated.

She glanced at the Asiyan delegation. From their impassive expressions, she couldn't tell if they had experienced the same. When they were next alone, she would inquire. Even if no one else had felt the odd mental touch, Lela didn't question whether she'd imagined it. She could still feel where the finger had been on her forehead.

The envoy pushed a button on the wall to his left, causing the doors to part for the group. It was then, when the barrier was gone, Lela understood why they hadn't encountered anyone in the hallways. The Lumerians were inside a grand ballroom. At least five hundred Lumerians were in attendance. Some were bare chested, like the envoy, both males and females, while others wore either a thin layer of clothing on their bottom and top, open vests and tightly fitted trousers for the males, and multicolored tunic dresses for the females.

As if choreographed, everyone in the room stopped what they were doing and turned toward the Asiyans. An endless sea of glowing, bright blue eyes watched them enter from expressions that ranged from curious to cautious. The extreme color contrast of the hallways to the ballroom, drab to vibrant, was jarring. It wasn't only the people and their bold shades but the room itself. On the walls, floor, and ceiling were rows of pink, blue, and white lights against a dark brown background the same color of the river that brought them there on the ferry. The lights traveled like an arrow, dim at the shaft but increasing in brightness as it moved to the narrow tip. The unique display of light drew the eye, encouraging the viewer to follow the glimmering path in a single direction—the opposite side of the room. There, seated in front of a dark wall with an image of the same eye that was displayed on the doors to the ballroom was Prime Minister Drassul.

Again the Asiyans followed the envoy, as the crowd parted to let them through.

"I need you to watch and listen," Etemaad said to Lela in Katran, an ancient Verity language taught at Sagacity but rarely used beyond its hallowed halls.

Lela glanced around them seeing, for the first time, that many Lumerians wore wrist zots, including their envoy.

Asiyans spoke a multitude of languages, but only five were recognized as official languages of the planet—one language for each band and one, Giyan, that transcended the bands. At Lela's Luna of Analisia ceremony, everyone had spoken in Giyan. Now, the regent used a language never shared with anyone outside of Asiya, providing them a private moment amid a crowd.

"There is no need for you to speak while we're here, so watch and listen," Etemaad told Lela, in what could've either been a stern directive or a serious warning.

As regent, it was within his power to demand silence from a chief magistrate, although she wondered why he had done so. Now that they were on Lumeria, did Etemaad doubt Lela's ability to perform her duty as chief magistrate, thinking her incapable of competently aiding him in negotiating a peace agreement? She wouldn't have thought it of him, but he'd never revoked her right to verbal participation in any meeting, not even when she served as his disciple. Lela pushed away the pang of hurt and self-doubt and followed the envoy and Etemaad onto the dais where Prime Minister Drassul lounged, as if he were the King of Lumeria instead of an elected government official.

Perhaps he was more king than prime minister because Drassul reclined in a black throne chair framed in gold and decorated with the same clan markings on his face and chest—interlocking triangles. Between his markings were dark red circles of various sizes. His eyes glowed the brightest of all, accentuated by the motifs that traveled from under his eyes, up the bridge of his flat nose, and over his forehead where they ended in two curled horns. Like most of the Lumerian males in the ballroom, Drassul wore only fitted trousers.

The prime minister stood, lean, muscular, and a half foot taller than everyone in the Asiyan delegation. Drassul was also only three anulls older than Lela. She couldn't imagine leading a planet of billions of people, much less being responsible for having led them into an unnecessary war. Her conscience would plague her. Lela questioned whether Drassul had a conscience. If he didn't . . .

"Welcome, Regent Etemaad and Chief Magistrate Lela," Drassul said in Ereis, his received pronunciation typical of upper-class Lumerians. "We have waited for your arrival to begin the feast." He clapped his hands, and every Lumerian responded. Within seconds, the room had quieted with the Lumerians seated at a table. "Come, come, friends. As my honored guests, you will dine with me."

Lela watched as Lumerians appeared from a back room, carrying tables, chairs, and trays of food and drink. Moving quickly, they set three tables covered with linens, utensils, drinks, and platters of food. Despite Drassul's urgings for the High Stars to "sit and partake of this grand feast in your regent's honor," they did not. No Paladin would accept such an offer. In fact, if Yusef were there, he would've viewed the suggestion that a Paladin should place their comfort above their duty as an insult.

Lela and Etemaad sat at Drassul's table. Soon afterward, an older female Lumerian joined them. Her long, straight red hair and royal blue tunic dress flattered her lithe form, but the stony expression she wore was uninviting.

"Allow me to introduce my political advisor. Regent, Chief Magistrate, this is Lady Junoid. She will dine with us this evening. We Lumerians thank you for the service you will bring to the races of this great solar system."

"Thank you both for coming," Lady Junoid said, her cultured accent the same as Prime Minister Drassul's. Yet the political advisor had none of Drassul's feigned friendliness. Lela didn't know if that truth set her more or less at ease.

Throughout dinner, Prime Minister Drassul maintained a near-constant stream of conversation. The zot anklet she wore sent messages to her neural pathways, translating every word she heard. Not all zots interfaced with the body in such a way. The ones that did were expensive to make and to buy. They also required a physician to establish a neural link, a delicate and, if performed incorrectly, dangerous procedure.

The wrist zots the Lumerians wore, including Drassul's, had screens the wearer used to read the translation from whichever zot they were linked into. Zots communicated with each other, with each device user employing the Interplanetary Wide Web to download languages their planet could access. Each zot came with unique translation codes that could be deleted or changed. Zot users shared one of their translation codes with whomever they'd like to communicate with, such as Prime Minister Drassul with Lela and Etemaad. To prevent tracking or hacking, Asiyan-made zots were encrypted.

Staring down at the plate of food placed in front of Lela, she made sure not to frown in disgust. She glanced to Etemaad to her right, whose blank face revealed nothing. *This is supposed to be my dinner. I will have to eat it, some of it, anyway. The Fates help me, I'm uncertain if I'm capable of keeping it down.*

Lumerians seemed to be a people of opposites—plain buildings but multicolored bodies and clothing. The plate of food smelled delicious, mouthwatering in fact. But it moved. It all moved in some way, either slithering or twisting. By the amount of food heaped on their plates, Lela assumed they either thought Asiyans ate double their bodyweight or this was the normal quantity of food Lumerians consumed for dinner. Either way, there were green cylindrical tubelike portions and a pile of lumpy brown mush with crisp edges that all but shimmied when Lela touched it with her utensil.

"This bounty," Prime Minister Drassul said, his voice, for once, pitched to a conversational tone, "is all from the grace of Agala. He nourishes our minds and bodies. He provides." Drassul used his web-free but tribal-marked hand to gesture to the crowd enjoying their meal. "No one starves on Lumeria. Agala takes care of us all—his devoted servants. Our devotion guarantees our salvation," he proclaimed with as much certainty as Asiyans asserted the power and existence of their Fates.

"Everyone is entitled to their beliefs, Prime Minister Drassul."

The regent had spoken little since they had sat down for dinner. This informal meeting was a precursor to the opening of peace talks. As such, Etemaad would never have mentioned the crux of the issue between Lumeria and the surrounding planets, particularly Meleris. Yet, the prime minister's words were more than personal statements of fact. They were the basis for his religious and military incursions into sovereign territories.

"Yet you seek to deny me my Agala-given right to spread his teachings to the blind and lost. Is it not the duty of good, loving neighbors to show others the way to salvation? Is it not a sin to allow friends to starve their souls when they can feast on Agala's merciful light?"

"You are as much entitled to your beliefs as your neighbors are entitled to theirs. On that point, our perspectives do not diverge."

Obviously giving up on eating more of his dinner, Etemaad placed his utensil down but picked up and sipped from his glass of water.

"Lumerians live a life of obedience, Regent. We respect our elders, revere our instructors, and raise our young to have the same values. Your people also share such core ideals."

"Once more, I do not disagree."

Prime Minister Drassul clapped his hands again, and everyone stopped eating and talking. "Wonderful. It is a blessing to have Asiyans among us. You are a dignified and wise race. Surely, we will form the strongest of friendships." He pointed over his shoulder to the eye behind his throne chair. "Agala *sees* all, *knows* all, *is* all. Forever and always."

"Forever and always," the Lumerians echoed. Standing, they turned in the direction of Agala's all-seeing eye and repeated, "Forever and always."

They kept chanting, the sound growing louder after each recitation. Lela refused to look at the eye. Instead, she watched the enraptured crowd speaking in perfect unison, their undivided attention on Agala's eye.

Her pulse quickened, and her gaze darted to the High Stars. They stood at attention at the four points of the dinner table except for Gayora and High Star Cleaver Beres, who'd planted themselves directly behind Lela and Etemaad. Only Gayora moved, though. Her hand rose to Lela's high-neckline dress. With a single finger, she touched her neck where the paracord lay against her skin. A High Star Shadow, indeed. The Paladin watched Lela more than she knew. Later, she would speak to her chief of security about boundaries and privacy. For now, she had received Gayora's subtle message.

As abruptly as the chanting had begun, it ended, with the Lumerians retaking their seats. As if there hadn't been a break in their eating and socializing, they resumed. It was then Lela noticed the relaxing of shoulders of the High Stars, as well as the absence of Gayora's hand.

Lela drank from her glass of water, using the act to conceal her deep exhalation.

"Agala is the one and true God and prime ministers of Lumeria are his messengers. Agala created the Vargan Solar System first then Lumerians. We are the first people. The first civilization." Drassul held his arm in front of Etemaad, showing him the ventral side of his forearm. "Blood of Prime Minister Drassulk runs through my veins—the first prime minister of Lumeria and Agala's first messenger. It is my duty, as Agala's emissary, to spread his message."

"What is that message?" Regent Etemaad asked.

Etemaad could've been more direct with Prime Minister Drassul, reminding him that his father and grandfather, both of whom were also considered Agala's emissaries, hadn't sought to subjugate their neighbors. Such points, however, would be addressed during peace talks, not during an informal meal between sovereigns. Yet the meal was proving to be one of probing assessments in the guise of hospitality for Prime Minister Drassul, deftly met with strategic parrying by Regent Etemaad.

Prime Minister Drassul grinned, absolute in his beliefs, dogmatic even. While Asiyans didn't share the same opinion of how life came to be and who or what was responsible for its creation, they did hold firm to the notion of their correctness and the fallacy of other people's religious and spiritual beliefs. However, the obvious and significant differences between Lumerians' and Asiyans' treatment of people whose beliefs differed from their own couldn't be underscored, no matter how Drassul attempted to blur the lines between them.

Lela's attention drifted away from Drassul's ramblings. Throughout the course of the negotiation process, Drassul would learn that such monologues would yield him no leverage with a regent renowned for his patience, objectivity, and brutal honesty.

She surveyed the dinner party. They seemed to be enjoying themselves, focused on their meals and the friends or family who shared their table. Except for Lady Junoid, whose critical blue gaze shifted between Lela and Etemaad, no one stood out to her as a possible threat or impediment to the peace talks. Prime Minister Drassul would be the only barrier that mattered. From all he'd said, he either didn't see or didn't care that he had no right to force Empyreanism on his neighbors—death the sentence for refusal to convert.

Lela excused herself from the table. If the regent expected her to watch and listen, she couldn't effectively perform her duty from a stationary position. Before she'd taken more than three steps away from the table, Gayora was at her side. The High Star was dressed in black trousers and boots and a dark lavender shirt that matched the sash over her black tail jacket coat. Unlike male High Stars' long coats, the uniform coat of female High Stars had a stand V-neck collar, a center back split, and was adorned with silver studs on the front and ruffles on the cuffs and hemlines.

No one expected the High Stars to forego their weapons, not even for peace talks. But there were limits. The High Stars were permitted nonlethal laser guns while on Lumeria. Regent Etemaad had been directed to have the High Stars have their low-caliber weapons visible. For Gayora and the others that meant wearing a front chest holster over their Paladin coat.

They strolled around the ballroom, Lela nodding here and offering a greeting there. It felt awkward, disrespectful even, to be a guest and not engage in polite conversation.

"What are you looking for, Chief Magistrate?" Gayora asked in a whisper.

"I do not know. Perhaps nothing. What do you see?"

"Too many people for my comfort. If they decide to turn on us, it wouldn't end well."

"Are you saying they would slaughter us?" Lela stopped, stared at her chief of security, a woman who, with time, she would like to get to know better. Lela felt that way about all her High Stars. They would die for her. The least she could do was learn who they were beyond their duty as her blade and armor.

"You are Verity. I am not," Gayora replied, offering Lela no smile beyond the one she detected in her voice.

"So, you would lie to your chief magistrate?"

"If need be, yes."

Lela nodded. "I am most pleased to have your honesty."

"And I am most pleased to serve as your shadow."

They renewed their stroll, with Gayora on the inside and Lela closest to the wall.

As they rounded the room for a second time, Lela noticed a group seated in a corner, their bodies leaned forward around a circular table and engaged in what looked to be a serious conversation.

As subtly as she could, she made Gayora aware of the table of three men and two women.

"I see them. Have the regent and the Amakan president consented to the presence of the news correspondents?"

"Regent Etemaad has not. We were informed, by Prime Minister Drassul, that they are embedded journalists."

Gayora scoffed. "Except as a tool for propaganda, I've never understood the purpose of embedded reporters."

"When performed with honor, they relay the true nature of war to those far removed from the battlefields."

"The nature of war, Chief Magistrate, is violent and ugly. What is there not to understand? People kill, and people die."

"Quite true," she readily agreed with a short nod, her hands clasped behind her back as they strolled. "But there's so much truth that exists before, during, and after both. Killing and dying, while awful, are incomplete pieces of knowledge. Dates, locations, casualty reports, they tell only a portion of an intricate story of decisions, actions and reactions, regrets, triumphs, and sorrow. For every event, even a seemingly uncomplicated one, there are layers of truth if one takes the time to discover them."

Gayora halted, her red-brown eyes an eddy of contemplation as she observed Lela from a height a mere three inches above her own. Dark brown coils twisted high atop her head with gold strands intermixed. Gayora of the House of Vilmaris, was the kind of female Yusef would choose for Ammon. Honorable and self-assured, Lela doubted anyone questioned, including Gayora, her legitimacy to serve as High Star Shadow, certainly not whether she was granted a rank she hadn't earned or whether she could meet the demands of the position.

"Can Verity actually see the truth in every event?"

"Not in the way I believe you mean. There is no magic involved or a field of science only Verity are privy to." Lela resumed walking, with Gayora right beside her. "Verity search for and digest the known. We hunt for details and clues, knowing they are pieces to a much bigger puzzle. Sometimes, when we think the puzzle is finally complete, that we are beholding the fullness of an event, person, place, or concept, we may catch a glimmer we hadn't seen before."

"A glimmer?"

"Of an edge. Another side. A blank space we missed because we are imperfect. We approach situations and explorations from limited or tainted lenses. We draw conclusions from preconceived notions or force pieces into a puzzle because it's convenient, conforms to our logic, or simply because we're tired of the search for truth. Or worse, afraid of what we'll find."

Gayora pondered Lela's words, their pace slow but taking them in the direction of the table of embedded reporters.

"I can appreciate your perspective. You proclaimed yourself truth and wisdom. That was a bold statement to our people."

For Lela, it was less of a bold statement and more of a promise to Asiyans.

"Before the ceremony, my mother told me the Verity Band was wisdom made manifest. I could not dispute her claim. Considering she is the wisest person I know, I believed her."

"Mothers are a fountain of wisdom, no matter the band. Have you met my mother, Chief Magistrate?"

"I have not."

"Then I will be sure to introduce you to her, after our return. A'bra will boast she once defeated Chief Magistrate Yusef in a duel when they were Shielder trainees."

The thought of what would undoubtedly be an entertaining story settled, somewhat, her stomach. Lela should've chewed the food she'd eaten, but she hadn't wanted the squirming whatevers in her mouth longer than need be. She regretted her decision. Not swallowing without chewing but consuming the food at all.

When Lela and Gayora reached the table of embedded reporters, something made her stop, although she'd refrained from doing so at any other table.

From what Lela could see, none of the journalists wore zots. But the Grul, the only race at the table Lela recognized, had slid something from the table and onto the floor when she and Gayora had approached.

"You're quite far from home," Lela spoke in Vorcix.

The Grul stared at Lela through green reptilian eyes. Gruls were an evolutionary hybrid between upright reptiles and amphibians, with Gruls possessing a range of characteristics of each animal type. Besides the reptilian eyes that bore into Lela with barely suppressed shock at her having spoken to him in his native language, no zot required, he also seemed to have inherited bony external plates typical of many reptiles. The gray plates covered him from neck to his large clawed, webbed feet. Purple-green gills framed both sides of his green face, as well as the dorsal side of his forearms. Lips pulled back to reveal two rows of sharp, pointy teeth, in a threat or a Grul's version of a smile, Lela didn't know.

Gayora stepped in front of her, and she regretted going against the regent's order. He'd told her to watch and listen. He hadn't granted her permission to speak to anyone, least of all a Grul whose thick, whiplike tail was capable of severing heads and limbs.

"I am honored you know my tongue," the Grul said, his voice like sandpaper rubbing across her ears. He stood—six feet of pure muscle. "Very few races bother to learn Vorcix. They think it a guttural language of animals. But you, Chief Magistrate," he said, bowing deferentially low, "speak it as if born on Tsondelar."

Lela detected no mockery in the Grul's harsh-sounding voice, despite the lie he'd uttered. While Lela may have spoken Vorcix, the structure of Asiyans' oral cavity made it impossible for them to pronounce pharyngeal consonants in the same manner as a Grul with lungs and gills.

"You are quite kind."

With a nod, the Grul retook his seat. The other four reporters at the table remained quiet, but their eyes were on Gayora.

Lela backed away from the group's table, resuming her stroll. If she stayed longer, the group may have said or done something that would've required, by Paladin code of honor, a response from Gayora. So, Lela had retreated from the group.

Neither she nor Gayora spoke until they'd reached the opposite side of the room.

"They are an incestuous race of people."

Lela almost stumbled to a stop. "I was unaware of that fact about Gruls."

"Not Gruls."

Lela stared up at Gayora, brow furrowed.

"Ah, I see. You do not know of the Malcareon race?"

Lela had no idea who the other reporters were. It had taken great willpower not to gape at them. They were unlike any race she had met. When she'd seen them yesterday, they'd worn moonrulics, bodysuits with helmets that kept them protected from the Lumerian environment. With breathing and exposure to Lumeria's sun a nonissue while inside Prime Minister Drassul's stronghold, the Malcareons had foregone their moonrulics.

"Water, fire, earth, and air. Females are born as either air or water, while males are born as earth or fire. The females only birth quadruplets."

Fire had shocked Lela the most. His skin was pitch black except for the red, orange, and green swirl of flames over his entire body. They weren't tribal motifs like the Lumerians. The Malcareons' element was part of them, not just the vines and flowers that grew on Earth's body, or the blue, white, and pink frothy waves that made up Water's tall, slim frame, or the blue and white cloudy mixture of Air's form.

Lela placed a hand on Gayora's wrist, ushering her out of the way of a waiter carrying a tray laden with what Lela hoped was dessert. Not that she intended on eating the questionable food, but the delivery could signal the beginning of the end of the meal.

"Are you saying"—Lela attempted to locate the table of reporters in the sea of bodies, but they were too far away—"the siblings become lovers?"

Lela had noticed how they'd sat close to each other—touching in some way. A hand in hair, a shoulder against a shoulder, lips to an ear, all cues to their level of comfort with and affection for each other, but nothing untoward that would lead one to draw the kind of conclusion Gayora had stated.

"Yes," Gayora said, answering a question Lela had almost forgotten she'd posed because she had a more important question for her High Star.

"How long will it take for you to download and review the images your zot recorded from your occipital lobe?"

The Affiq Band had created a zot specifically for Paladins. Not every type of zot performed the same set of functions. Many features were basic, such as language translation and access to the Interplanetary Wide Web. But the zots that interfaced with the brain were limited to one or two special features. Too many demands on the brain risked it overloading and shutting down. Permanently. So, while Lela's and Etemaad's zots allowed their brains to translate any language linked to their zot, the High Stars' zots linked directly to their occipital lobes, enhancing that brain function while also pulling and storing images from the brain's visual processing center.

"I'll begin the process when we're back on the spaceship. A daily review of the data is protocol, for High Stars. When on a security detail, the download and review increase to twice a day, perhaps more, depending on the situation."

"I was unaware."

"You're a new chief magistrate. It would've been imprudent for Chief Magistrate Yusef to assign you inexperienced High Stars."

Gayora was kind and tactful, and Lela appreciated both traits.

Apparently, deciding they'd observed enough, Gayora led them back to their host and Lela's abandoned meal.

"Are you concerned about the embedded reporters, Chief Magistrate?"

"We'll speak of it later."

Lela possessed no strong feelings about the Grul and Malcareons, although she couldn't help but wonder how the group had come to serve in their current role on Lumeria. They did wear a press badge around their necks. The badges included their picture, name, and two stamps—one from Lumeria, the other from Meleris, the Amakan homeworld. The stamps depicted Agala's eye of Lumeria, and a golden sun with a blue jewel-eyed face in the center, which was the planetary symbol of Meleris. *That means the reporters are sanctioned by both warring parties to travel on and between their planets.*

Would the reporters be in attendance when the Asiyan peace delegation visited Meleris? If so, would Regent Etemaad permit her to speak with them, learning all she could about their presence there? Or would he make the same request, denying her a true role during this mission beyond that of silent witness?

7. Of Youth and Leadership

Vargan Solar System

Etemaad's hand settled on Lela's shoulder. "They're beautiful, aren't they?"

Lela and the regent were in the conference room aboard *Ibor Peace 01*, a medium-class cruiser with long-distance endurance, cloaking capability and firepower comparable to its size and purpose. Standing in front of a wide window, they took in the view of Vargan space.

"I've never seen anything like them. I read about the island planets during my research, but nothing compares to this firsthand experience. They are indeed beautiful."

The blue crystalline water of Wither Alpha looked refreshing enough to tempt any visitor into wanting to take a plunge. Such a decision, however, wouldn't result in a relaxing diversion from the day but in a painful death. Lela didn't know the composition of the liquid enticement, and she didn't care. That level of intellectual curiosity she would leave for Affiq scholars. Her truth came in the form of two repeated words from her research: acidic and death. Even the Yegoth weren't immune to their planet's protective liquid upper layer. The water of death comprised a third of the planet, forcing the Yegoth to reside in the coldest, rockiest part of the planet. The two islands that flanked Wither Alpha, Wither Beta and Omega, were devoid of a corrosive upper core.

If Etemaad approved, Lela would visit those two islands. At Sagacity, she'd learned long-distance research was an inadequate fountain from which to understand a people and their circumstances. The Yegoth were no less victims of the Lumerians than the Amakans. In fact, one could argue the Yegoth's position was worse because they had inferior technological and military capacity to defend themselves against Prime Minister Drassul's religious tyranny. Thanks to embedded reporters, perhaps the same ones she and Gayora had spoken with, races beyond the Vargan Solar System had seen the horrid faces of war. Those faces weren't only Amakans but Yegoth and every race in this solar system. Amakans may have spearheaded the war cause, but they'd done so with the support of their neighboring planets.

"Come sit with me."

Lela followed Etemaad to the rectangular table in the center of the room where they sat across from each other. In relaxed quarters, neither wore their cloaks. Lela hadn't fully accepted what the chief magistrate's cloak represented, not only to Asiyans but to people of other planets. To Etemaad, Lela was undoubtedly chief magistrate, but she was also herself. She even wore the induction gown gifted to her by his wife, Dariya. It was a lovely black, long-sleeved floor-length dress with a black and white striped blouse along with a square collar and ruffles around the collar and sleeves. The ver'ty necklace hung on the outside of her dress, while Ammon's knives—her knives—were hidden in her quarters.

While Lela took no pleasure in breaking the Inter Solar System Peace Mediators' Codes of Conduct, she couldn't deny the sense of rightness of her choice when she'd gazed into the hard, scrutinizing eyes of Lady Junoid. It mattered not whether Lela liked the other female, which she did not, but it mattered much that she found her untrustworthy. Lela had no basis for her opinion, so she had kept it to herself.

"What is your role during this mission?" Etemaad asked.

Lela paused before answering, careful not to sound petulant when she spoke. "To listen and to learn."

"That's correct. I do not trust Prime Minister Drassul or his sudden agreement to peace talks."

"Is that why you decided to accompany me on this mission?" Lela had to know, although she'd tried to convince herself that his decision had little to do with her.

As regent, Etemaad should be on Asiya and in the Hall of Concord. Chief magistrates negotiated peace agreements, even Yusef, but Etemaad hadn't been a chief magistrate in dekulls. He shouldn't be there, and she feared she knew why he'd made the unprecedented trip.

Etemaad stood from his chair and joined Lela on her side of the table. He took her hand in his.

Lela's warm skin met the smooth, cool band of Etemaad's signet ring. The Seal of Eternal Breath was the symbol of the regency. For as long as she'd known Etemaad, she'd never seen him without his ring. Where the band was dark as the universe, the flat bezel was an ever-moving swirl of pink, gold, orange, and lavender particles of energy and light. Created by the first chief magistrates for the first Regent of Asiya, a role intended to equalize the bands, the signet ring was designed to represent the Realm of Thuraya—the birthplace of all living beings. Asiyans believed life began in the Realm of Thuraya and, upon death, all beings returned there, their life energy reabsorbed back into Mother Cosmos. For Asiyans, the Realm of Thuraya held the mysteries of life and rebirth. It was there, in the heart of Mother Cosmos, where bound souls found each other, together forevermore.

"You are my best friend's daughter, but I love you as if you were my own. We're both Verity, so I'll grant you the truth you deserve as my daughter of the heart. The Council does not want you to fail as chief magistrate, but they fear the Verity Band's recommendation was motivated more by my affection for you than you being the best Verity to lead your band."

Etemaad's truth hurt, but it was no more than what Lela had already surmised. Asiyans were long-lived beings. Physically, they aged at a slower rate than many other races. On most other planets, thirty-two anulls would still be considered young but old enough to be viewed as credible and competent in one's chosen field. On Asiya, no one under fifty-five anulls held a planetary-level leadership position. No one until Lela. So yes, she understood why the Council would question her band's choice of leader. It was an insult, all the same.

Etemaad placed her hand on the table and his in his lap. "If Prime Minister Drassul continues to wage his religious war, this entire solar system will destabilize. Thousands of innocents have already perished, while I've worked with planetary leaders from nearby solar systems to alleviate the suffering of his victims.

We've offered humanitarian aid to the people of this solar system. The interplanetary task force has also initiated trade embargoes against Lumeria."

Lela listened as Etemaad explained every intervention his task force had used to encourage Prime Minister Drassul to cease and desist. The longer he spoke, the more she realized how much he hadn't shared with her in his briefing reports. Why had the regent withheld so much from her? Did he initially intend on having another chief magistrate broker the peace agreement? If so, had he changed his mind to provide Lela with an opportunity to prove herself to the Council and others who doubted her capability and readiness to serve as chief magistrate?

Rarely was Lela given to self-doubt. Of late, the emotion kept finding its way into her consciousness—an unpleasant development she didn't appreciate.

"No strategy the task force undertook stopped the Lumerians from their single-minded pursuit—the spread of Empyreanism." Etemaad's expression was bland but his tone was tinged with dissatisfaction.

The fact that Yusef hadn't been assigned this mission spoke to the one intervention Etemaad and his task force had refrained from using. Lela grasped the unspoken weight of the peace mission and why the Council thought her ill-equipped to persuade the Lumerians away from their oppressive approach to interracial relations in their solar system.

The stakes of the mission were too high to be used as a learning experience for a new chief magistrate. Reth or Mosi would've been better choices. If the regent had selected a more experienced chief magistrate, he wouldn't have felt inclined to also attend. As it was, the regent had allotted himself most of the responsibility for negotiating the peace agreement. He had already brokered a cease-fire before they'd arrived.

"I can see my truth has upset you. That wasn't my intention. I only wished for you to comprehend the full scope of our mission. Prime Minister Drassul would not have agreed to the cease-fire, if I didn't also concede to personally negotiate the talks. He viewed sending a new chief magistrate as an affront to his regional authority and image. Pure hubris, but I couldn't alter his erroneous opinion. But know, Lela, I have absolute faith in you."

She didn't see how that could be true. He hadn't asked her to perform a task beyond that of listening. While being an active listener was an important interpersonal skill, successful mediation involved far more than that singular trait. Lela knew she had much to learn. Her pride wasn't such that she wouldn't readily admit that truth. But the potential fate of an entire solar system shouldn't hinge on Regent Etemaad's ability to focus on training Lela while also engaged in delicate peace talks.

She stood, fists clenched at her sides and heart pounding from a discordant mix of insecurity and determination. "If you will excuse me, I must speak with Gayora." The High Star had assured Lela she would have the images recorded from her occipital lobe downloaded and organized into a report by midday. That time neared, and Lela was anxious to review the images. She'd already contacted Mosi, requesting the Affiq's assistance with information on Malcareons.

"They are an extinct race," Mosi had told Lela before correcting her statement. "Clearly, they are not extinct, if four of them are on Lumeria. I suppose a more accurate term for the Malcareons would be *endangered*. They are an endangered race of people, nearly all of them dead. One is more likely to discover a dwarf planet in their closet than see a Malcareon." Mosi had laughed, dark green and silver eyes twinkling with humor and curiosity, as they spoke via the audiovisual comm system in Lela's quarters. "Yet you've seen four, and in the most unlikely of places. I cannot fathom how those elementals have come to serve as embedded reporters to Lumeria and Meleris. But you are truth, and I am knowledge."

"Your knowledge will help me discover their truth. Once I've had an opportunity to reflect on Gayora's report, I'll have specific parameters for your research team."

"Very good. In the meantime, I'll have Binoba generate a preliminary report for you on the Malcareons and their homeworld of G4H Malcore. I must say, I am pleased they aren't all dead. Planets can die, Lela, and when they do so do its people. But not all. Survival instinct. If you learn nothing else from your first peace mission, you must understand the lengths people will go to survive and to maintain their way of life."

Lela had taken Mosi's words to heart.

"I'll be in my quarters, if you need me." Lela bowed to Etemaad, lower than her new rank demanded. But the additional level of reverence was but a small token for all he'd done for her. Lela intended to do as much for Etemaad, beginning with scouring through Gayora's report for any morsel of truth that could aid him during the negotiation process.

Lumeria
Lumerian Homeworld
Veer River Complex

"That's not part of the plan." Lady Junoid spun to face Drassul. As always, he lounged in his chair in the grand ballroom, carefree in the way of young, arrogant men with too much power and not enough good sense. "I may not be able to guarantee your safety, while on Meleris."

Nothing in his relaxed countenance altered, but Lady Junoid had served as advisor to two prime ministers prior to this one. And while Drassul was mostly unlike his father and grandfather, he possessed the same telltale signs of his disapproval—a subtle shift in his scent from water to green.

"No one would dare harm me," Drassul said, full of absolute certainty and utter naïveté. "Agala protects me wherever I walk, as does the Vedem and my bodyguards."

"Vedems will not be by your side while you're on Meleris. As for your guards, the Asiyans have brought eight Paladins. With this being a mission of peace, I didn't anticipate so many Paladin soldiers." Wiping surprisingly shaky hands over her brow, Junoid attributed the physical weakness to age and not to fear. The Asiyans of old would've been worthy of such trepidation, but the younger generation had exchanged war and might for prayers and peace.

"It doesn't matter how many Paladins will be there. We've used their honor against them. You saw their weapons yesterday—low-caliber guns, as we instructed. Such weapons will prove useless against our allies."

His devious smirk told her there was more to his plan than he'd revealed. How could she properly advise him if there were secrets between them?

"Do not concern yourself, for Agala sees and knows all. I have no fear in my heart because Agala protects the faithful."

"I believe that as well, but—"

"Look at yourself, Junoid. You've been stressed and angry ever since the Asiyans entered Vargan space. Trust the plan you've worked so hard to organize. The Grul and the Malcareons are here. Regent Etemaad and Chief Magistrate Lela are here. The leaders of Meleris, Wither, and Shin are willing to sit down in the same room with me for peace talks." A smiling Drassul sat up straight and pointed a steady finger at Junoid. "You did all of that, my lady. You are a credit to the Lumerian race. History will remember you well. Future generations of Lumerians will praise your name and sing songs in your honor."

"Not if I'm to blame for the death of their prime minister."

"As I told you, Agala protects, while the Vedems destroys all who do not claim Agala as the one and true God." Standing, Drassul walked from the dais to stand in front of Junoid. "Where did my unflappable political advisor go? You must know your plan would've died an early death if I insisted on having the negotiations here. No one would've agreed, least of all Theimos 105."

Drassul was correct. The Amakan president would've never consented to traveling to Lumeria for the peace talks. Knowing Theimos 105, he would've boycotted the talks, encouraging the Yegoth of Wither and the Unbalk of Shin to follow his lead. That truth didn't assuage Junoid's concerns. Some minds could be swayed, others manipulated or tricked, all of which benefitted Lumeria. There were races immune to the will of Agala, though. Fortunately, Asiyans weren't among them.

As he did when he was a boy eager to please an inattentive father but settled for a patient advisor, Drassul kissed her cheek. The prime minister was young enough to be her grandson. When she was as young as him, she had chosen God over family. To Junoid, love was God and God was love. Agala had provided and protected, giving Junoid three prime ministers to serve. While Drassul was the youngest and brashest of the three, he understood the power and importance of expanding the teachings of Agala.

"Father and Grandfather turned away from the old ways, my lady. Together, we will undo and right all that they got wrong. Agala demands absolute obedience, and I am his messenger. Father forgot why Lumerians exist. Only we are empowered by Agala to spread his word. Only we Lumerians know our true calling. Asiyans may believe themselves missionaries of peace but they are ministering to the wrong need. Religion, faith, order, that's what we offer our neighbors." Drassul kissed her other cheek. His hand on her shoulder was as steady and sure as his convictions. "Lumerians are the true missionaries. Asiyans are fake missionaries who will soon learn their true place in the cosmos. And that place, Lady Junoid"—Drassul raised a foot and slammed it to the floor with a hard *thud*—"is under our feet."

Finally, the long-awaited leader Lumerians deserved had ascended to the role of prime minister. Junoid's machinations were finally falling into place. Her goal of a Pax-Lumeria had been years in the making. She would achieve her ends, even if that meant collaborating with a racist Grul and assassinating planetary leaders.

"Once their regent is no more," Drassul said, glancing over his shoulder to the eye of Agala behind his chair before turning back to her, "the Asiyans will withdraw from our solar system. They think themselves untouchable. They think themselves better than the rest of the cosmos. They think their Fates real and Agala a false deity. They are wrong on all counts. Agala protects me. Let's see how well Etemaad's Fates protect him."

8. Betrayal

Meleris
Amakan Homeworld
City of Drutain

For the rest of her doles, Lela would never forget the acrid smell of blood, the rancid taste of fear, and the gurgling sound of death. Combined, they would rule her life for many anulls.

Regent Etemaad pushed Lela onto the floor and covered her with his heavy body. His forceful hand slammed over a mouth about to scream. "Stay quiet. Don't move," he whispered into her ear.

The hiss of laser fire blazed overhead. Lights in the temple flickered on and off, a deadly oscillation of darkness and illumination. Etemaad's heart hammered against Lela's pounding chest. People whimpered around her. Their cries were cut short by a pop and a sizzle.

"Make sure they're all dead. No one must be left alive."

She recognized that voice. At least she thought she did, but it was difficult to concentrate with the screams going off in her head.

Lela's eyes slammed shut and throat tightened.

Etemaad stiffened as a set of booted feet moved closer.

They needed to do something. They couldn't stay there, waiting to be discovered and then killed. *Fates help me, how many in the peace delegation are dead? Hurt?*

"Please, no, do not do this," Theimos 105 begged. The terror in his roughened voices resonated deeper than the triplicate of sound coming from his three heads. "We do not wish to die. We came here in good faith. We—"

Pop. Pop. Pop.

Lela fought against her tears. Fought to stay quiet and not to bellow her fury. Fought for calm while everything she believed to be true about this peace mission hissed away with each blast of laser fire.

Useless. Blind. She hadn't seen clearly. She hadn't listened well enough. She hadn't discovered the truth in time to save them. And now, cowering on the floor under Etemaad's protective body, Lela couldn't even shield her mentor from the approaching footfalls.

Ammon's induction gift taunted her. The neck knife was tucked under her cloak, the hunting knife strapped to her thigh.

Useless. So am I.

Needing to see her regent, she opened her eyes. But the lights no longer flickered, leaving the room in abject darkness.

The same familiar male voice spoke again but she also heard more than one set of footsteps. They moved steadily around the room, pausing then resuming.

Are they among the races who can see in the dark? Are they wearing night vision contact lenses? Can they see me and Etemaad?

The tip of a foot collided with Lela's head, sending white-hot pain through her. She refused to scream, though. Lela's and Etemaad's lives depended on the attackers believing them dead. The foot kicked her head again. This time, she didn't think it was an accident.

The booted foot shoved against her. Lela allowed her head to flop to the side, giving no resistance. The unseen figure shoved her over and again with his foot. She pretended to be dead, as did Etemaad.

Before Lela could process the attacker's shift in strategy, the weight atop her was gone, a quick dislodging that left her bereft. She shrieked, unable to remain silent a moment longer.

Eyes open and wide, she saw nothing, but heard everything.

"There you are, Regent," the same male voice said. "You're my big payday."

"I beg you, do not continue the path you've undertaken."

Later, Lela would interpret this moment differently, hear the true meaning behind Etemaad's words. Not a plea for his sur-vival. Not even a warning to the barbarian who held his life in his hands. No, Etemaad's thoughts were of his people and the soul-burning path into spiritual oblivion they would travel if he was murdered. On the brink of madness, Lela couldn't detect the calm in Etemaad's voice or the subtle message for her in his words.

Later, Lela would comprehend all she had missed. Until that day, however, war would become her truth and revenge her wis-dom.

"You're brave for an old man. I'll give you that."

"You won't escape. They won't let you. They'll come. Armor and blade. The old ways are never truly gone—only suppressed. I beg you, turn back before it's too late."

The male's guttural, unfeeling laughter was like another kick to the head.

Lela scrambled in the direction of the voices while also searching for the knife under her dress. Big hands grabbed a fistful of her long coils and yanked her backward. Blindly, she fought, twisting and kicking. Compared to most races, Asiyans were small of stature, but they were also quite strong. But so was the vile creature dragging her away from Etemaad and the male who intended on murdering him.

She had to do something. Had to get away. Had to find her knife and save the regent. Had to—

Pop. Pop.

"Noooo!"

Lela fought harder. Scream after scream burst from her quivering throat, deafening and all-consuming. Hands grabbed her by her shoulders and shook her with a force that had her head slamming against the hard floor.

Still, she screamed.

"Shut her up."

"I'm trying."

"Not hard enough. The Paladins are almost through the door. Kill her."

Big hands hit her in the face instead of shooting her. Over and again, fists connected with her face, chest, stomach, and still she screamed. Raged. Cursed.

Lela would see them all dead.

"I said kill the female. Stop toying with your prey."

She could see nothing. Nothing except for a sudden burst of red and orange fire. The fire hand reached for Lela again. His mistake. He should've shot her when he had the chance. He should've paid more attention to where her hand had been while his were assaulting her. He should've kept the gloves of his moonrulic suit on and not given her a glowing target.

Lela shoved Ammon's blade into the fire Malcareon's hand, pushing it through to the other side then forcing it to the wrist and the delicate tendons there.

It was his turn to scream, and he did.

"It's made of mor'up, which means it's sharp enough to gut anyone who may threaten to do you harm."

Ammon was right . . . about everything.

Holding the knife handle with a fierce grip, Lela dug the blade in deeper, using her considerable strength to slide the knife up his arm and across his left shoulder. With each deep cut through moonrulic and skin, she revealed more fire flesh and heated blood.

Orit's communicator crackled in her ear. Gayora's reassurance of, "We're almost to you, hold on," enraged Lela even more. They wouldn't arrive in time. Not for the peace delegates. Not for Regent Etemaad. Not for Lela.

The fire Malcareon hit her again. His unharmed hand swung, landing against the side of her face and breaking the communicator latched to her ear. Lela refused to relinquish hold of her knife. She wasn't a Paladin. She had neither armor nor shield to protect her regent. All she had was a sharp blade and a deadlier fury. She would hold on to both.

Lela drove her knife into the chest of her enemy.

He fell.

And she fell with him.

Two Hours Earlier

"I don't like it," High Star Beres complained.

Neither did Lela. Gayora had flown their shuttle over the City of Drutain before landing, allowing the Paladins to survey the city from the air. Even from the craft, she could see signs of war—bombed buildings, boarded-up homes and businesses, burned transporters, and more. From the look and smell of the city, the cease-fire was only doles old.

Upon their arrival at the Temple of Agala, a bland, stout structure reminiscent of the buildings found on Lumeria, not the tall, elegant buildings of Meleris, President Theimos 105's Deputy of Defense had escorted the Asiyan delegation into a private room. The room was bare except for a round table with chairs and the eye of Agala on the four walls. No matter where she moved, the eyes seemed to follow, generating a low-grade headache when she dared to look at them.

"We should leave," Beres recommended.

Regent Etemaad, the only one of their group seated at the table, nodded to his frowning High Star. "I understand your concern, Beres." The regent's gaze traveled to them all, including to Lela who stood between Gayora and Orit. "Look where President Theimos 105 decided to have the peace talks. In the middle of the chaos Drassul brought to this planet, he had the audacity to have a temple built in the name of a god the Amakans do not believe in. This temple is a deliberate reminder of a religion the Amakans have denounced."

"Prime Minister Drassul," Lela said and stepped in, divining the same truth as the regent, "wanted Amakans to know his god sees all, knows all, and is everywhere." She pointed to the eye on the wall across from her. "The Lumerians have built these temples on Wither and Shin too. Not only that, the eye of Agala marked most structures."

With the level of resistance of Amakans, Yegoth, and Unbalk to Lumeria's heavy religious hand, she didn't understand how the unguarded temples weren't destroyed by the locals. Like this temple, the others were in pristine condition. Unused, clearly, but free from any sign of attack.

Lela and her High Stars had traveled to Wither and Shin, accepting an invitation from the planets' leaders while Regent Etemaad had stayed aboard the spaceship, preparing for the first day of peace talks. The eye of Agala had indeed been everywhere—laser painted on windows, walls, bridges, even on the trunks of the revered trees of Shin. The Lumerian mark on the Vargan Solar System was far and wide. This temple was but another physical reminder of how deeply the Lumerians had infiltrated the planets they mockingly referred to as *neighbors*.

"This is insane." Perhaps Lela shouldn't have voiced her thoughts, but silence had yielded little. "So is Drassul. This is all a farce. For what end, I do not know."

"You would have us do what, Lela? Leave?" Regent Etemaad stood, one hand leaning on the table. "What will happen to the Amakans, Yegoth, and Unbalk, if we do? We saw the other half of this once great city. Immaculate, beautiful, but also a warning to those who would dare oppose Agala's missionary. Yes, the talks may very well prove to be a farce, but we are here, and we must do our best for the people of this solar system."

At what cost? Lela nodded, a respectful retreat from a position she would revisit when they were back on the spaceship and alone. *Now isn't the time to disagree with the regent, especially in front of the others.*

"I still do not like it," Beres protested again, as if they needed to be reminded of the untenable position in which they found themselves since arriving at the temple. "First, the Lumerians order us to carry nonlethal weapons. Now, the Amakans expect us to send our regent and chief magistrate into a room with only one Paladin as protector."

Etemaad lowered himself back into his chair. "We have no reason to distrust President Theimos 105. His request has less to do with us and more to do with the contingent of soldiers Prime Minister Drassul would surely bring with him, if not for President Theimos 105's demand of a single bodyguard for every leader participating in the talks. This is the one time the other planetary leaders have an advantage that Drassul does not. With us here, they can press that advantage. This is not the sword to fall on, Beres. You will be in the room with Lela and me. You will guarantee our safety."

High Star Beres pointed to the male next to him—High Star Kondo. She'd once heard Yusef refer to Kondo as "even-tempered and good-natured." She agreed, although she'd never been in a situation where her life had been in his hands. But it seemed, from the way Kondo moved to stand next to Lela, displacing her shadow for his cleaver, she would soon discover the truth for herself.

"One bodyguard for each leader. We have two leaders," Beres said, sounding pleased with himself but not at all happy with the concession. "Two leaders mean two High Stars. Kondo and I will take point."

The other two cleavers and Lela's High Stars stepped back, and Beres smiled his displeased smile.

"Stay on alert," he ordered. "If you hear or see anything you think will harm our regent and chief magistrate, let me know." Beres tapped his earpiece communicator.

Regent Etemaad rose again. "It is settled, but no one is pleased." Etemaad's deep sigh revealed what his words had not. "I do not wish more bloodshed, though I fear it may very well be inevitable. But violence breeds only more violence. If I allowed, Yusef would dispatch battleships to Vargan space, ready to wage a holy war on behalf of the Amakans, Yegoth, and Unbalk." He sighed again, as if the thought of Asiyans taking up arms against the Lumerians, even on behalf of three planets' worth of people, pained him.

Perhaps it does.

Most Verity were pacifists. Etemaad and Lela's father, Hasani, may have been best friends, but Hasani didn't share Etemaad's pacifism, and neither did Lela.

"We must be better than the likes of Drassul. We must pursue peace. We must trust, have faith, and hold fast to our purpose, even when others think us foolhardy and naïve."

Misplaced trust was indeed foolhardy and naïve, although she had never considered those words in relation to her mentor.

Do I now? What would be the price of a dishonorable retreat? Worse, what will be the price of us staying? Does Agala's all-seeing eye hold the truth of our fate?

Lela backed away from Etemaad, Beres, and Kondo. She didn't need to hear the Paladins' plan for checking the meeting room before permitting Lela and Etemaad to go inside. She joined her High Stars on the other side of the room, huddled in a circle that opened upon her approach.

"I know, I know," she said when four sets of disapproving eyes met hers. "The regent outranks me, and Beres outranks all of you."

"I'm your shadow." Gayora thumped her hand against her chest, and Lela was offended on the female's behalf.

High Star Beres, while technically correct in assigning the next highest ranked High Star to serve beside him, should've included Gayora in the discussion as how best to secure the safety of her charge.

"You are indeed my shadow, just as Rahm is my shield and Orit and Waafir are my besiegers. Nothing has changed. We are one." Lela held her hand, palm up, to Orit. "Since my shadow will be a room away, may I borrow your communicator?"

Orit's approving smile meant much to Lela, who permitted a mollified Gayora to secure the earpiece.

"When we return home," Gayora said, double-checking the placement of the communicator on the shell of Lela's ear, "I'll order you a personalized communicator for away missions. For now, Orit's will have to do."

Lela pulled several coils over her ear, hiding the communicator behind a sea of ivory. Again, Orit rewarded her with a pleased smile.

"Chief Magistrate," Waafir said, his deep voice conspiratorially low, his dark eyes serious, "I request permission to return to the shuttle."

"Why would you require my permission? What are you really asking of me?"

Her High Stars tightened the circle, and Rahm answered instead of Waafir. "We're asking your permission to countermand the regent's orders."

Of course, they were. Only Yusef could unknowingly form a High Star team willing to break the rules he held dear. Such an infraction could result in her High Stars losing their rank and status in Paladin society. Worse, their actions could embroil Asiyans in the very war they were charged with negotiating a peace agreement for.

They watched Lela with varying degrees of expectation, and she felt the full weight of what her response could mean for them all. She hadn't yet received Mosi's full report on the images she'd sent. Lela had read the chief magistrate's preliminary report. The report hadn't shed any greater light than what she'd already gathered on her own.

"Gayora, what do you recommend?"

"Have Rahm sweep the meeting room with Beres and Kondo, so we'll know the layout of the room in case the worst happens. Once you and Regent Etemaad are inside the meeting room, Waafir and I will return to the shuttle for real weapons."

This was not how Lela thought she would begin her tenure as chief magistrate. She had never been a rulebreaker. Yet beginning with Ammon, Lela had defied rules that stood between her and what she wanted. Was that not why regulations existed? To serve as an external guide when selfish desires tempted one into making decisions for the wrong reasons?

"Once you're back on the shuttle, use the Electron Migrator to send the weapons to this room's coordinates. I do not want the Meleris soldiers stationed at the spaceport and outside the

Temple of Agala to catch Asiyans in the act of a blatant rule violation."

Orit smiled at Lela for a third time, and her stomach clenched for how easily their five minds synchronized over a plan that could see them all disgraced, if not dead. She was supposed to be truth and wisdom, yet she was about to sanction a risky deception.

But as Lela sat beside Regent Etemaad and watched Prime Minister Drassul and four Lumerian bodyguards enter the meeting room, the eye of Agala painted into the intricate designs of their faces, she couldn't bring herself to think of her breaking of the rules as wrong.

9. Eyes of Agala

Meleris
Amakan Homeworld
Temple of Agala

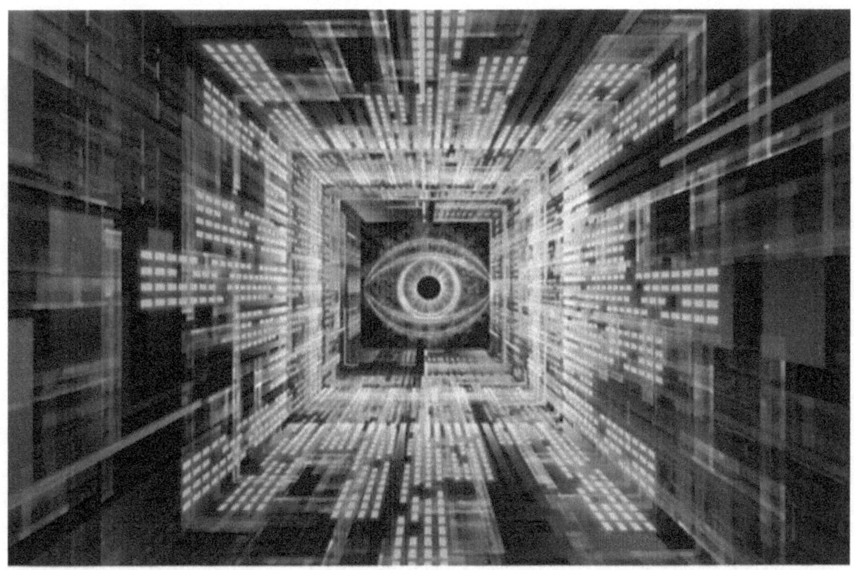

One Hour Earlier

Lela's headache worsened. She wasn't prone to having migraines, so she'd thought the discomfort would soon ease.

Perhaps it was the gory three-dimensional images of war victims President Theimos 105 insisted on displaying for the gathered delegates. Maybe it was listening to him speak about himself in the plural and through three simultaneously talking mouths. Or it could've been the overpowering floral scent of Alder Larchfern, Unbalk leader of Shin, a perennial race who worshipped a pantheon of tree gods collectively referred to as Silentwood. Whatever the reason for her headache, it was as stubborn as Prime Minister Drassul.

Drassul offered High Colonel Zirlat what Lela had come to recognize as a shallow smile that always preceded a narrow-minded or unyielding comment. "My father and grandfather have no bearing on these talks. They are the past. I am the present."

High Colonel Zirlat, Wither Alpha's representative, sat across from Drassul. His seven-foot muscular frame was covered in a black and blue moonrulic suit, including a helmet from which Lela could only see his pupilless white eyes, smooth, gray skin, ridged nose, and thin lips set in a permanent sneer whenever he looked at or spoke to Drassul.

The colonel's black-gloved hands balled into fists, and Lela tensed. Of the delegates who had convened for the peace talks, High Colonel Zirlat was the most visibly hostile. The Yegoth had every right to his anger. The images Theimos 105 had shared included not only Amakan casualties of war but also Yegoth and Unbalk. Alder Larchfern had lowered her head, the top a red mushroom that led downward to her tree bark textured body. Lela had made herself look at the images, despite wanting to avert her eyes too.

Drassul's bodyguards, dressed in far more clothing than she'd known Lumerians to wear—tactical body armor sans helmet—stepped closer to their prime minister.

If High Colonel Zirlat noticed the silent threat, he didn't show it, and his own guard made no move beyond shifting his gaze from Zirlat to the Lumerians.

"Your predecessors, while just as much of a believer in Agala as you are, had the decency to stop at messianism."

"Yet your people are no better off for their weakness as Agala's emissaries. You think them kind when, in fact, they left you to wallow in your spiritual barbarism. You are quite free to think of me as your messiah and savior, but I would rather you call me friend."

The high colonel's loud bark of laughter reverberated through the meeting room, a space that reminded Lela too much of Drassul's ballroom with its strange arrangement of colors on the floor and ceiling and the ever-present eyes of Agala on the walls.

Lela closed her eyes, seeking a brief respite from the unease of being surrounded by Agala's eyes evoked.

The delegates had already proceeded through the first two stages of the negotiation process—preparation and planning and definition of ground rules. Those steps had occurred prior to this meeting. They were in the clarification and justification stage, not that the Lumerians had shared evidence for their actions that any of the delegates had viewed as a valid justification. As it was, the more Drassul clarified his position, the more he antagonized the other leaders.

A warm, comforting hand took hold of Lela's underneath the table. "Are you unwell?" Etemaad inquired.

Lela did feel ill. Her head pounded mercilessly. The drilling finger sensation from the other day had returned. She felt as if the walls were closing in on her and that there wasn't enough air in the room to breathe.

I need fresh air. I want to leave this room and go outside.

But Lela couldn't leave. The group had established firm ground rules—among them being when and how long their breaks would occur.

She opened her eyes but wished she hadn't. The eyes on the walls fragmented into smaller eyes. They grew spiderlike legs and crawled away from the mother eye. Hundreds of them splintered off, forming gossamer webs of gold, red, and brown on the ceiling and walls. The spider eyes glided on the webs, landing on delegates and bodyguards.

Behind his helmet, High Colonel Zirlat's face froze. His mouth was open, prepared to respond to Prime Minister Drassul's insensitive statement, but no words came forth.

The room had gone silent, except for the spider eyes Lela could hear scurrying all over the room. She chanced a glance over her shoulder at Beres and Kondo; so too did Regent Etemaad. Like the others, they were frozen in place.

Lights flickered.

On. Off.

On. Off.

Spider eyes landed on Regent Etemaad, burrowing in his coils, swarming his ears, rimming his throat, and covering his mouth. Lela thought she would lose him to whatever had infected the others.

Coughing, he expunged spider legs. His eyes were wide with a strange awareness she glimpsed between the flickering of lights.

On. Off.

On. From the center of Agala's eyes, bodies emerged from the walls.

Off.

Regent Etemaad shoved Lela to the floor, and his hand immediately covered her mouth—preventing her scream of shock and fear.

The High Stars' reforged laser pistols had proven useless, leaving inconsequential dents in the meeting room doors that hadn't been closed the last time Gayora had checked.

"ETA?" Gayora yelled into her communicator.

Over their mobile comm system, she could hear Waafir's heavy breathing and thudding boots. Waafir and Gan had possessed no choice but to return to the shuttle for more firepower. The blasted doors weren't supposed to be closed. Yet there Gayora and her team stood, pistols laying siege to doors obviously built to withstand military-grade weapons.

None of this should be happening.

"Almost there," Waafir huffed out. "Almost."

It was taking too long to reach the peace delegates.

"Chief Magistrate," Gayora called out, hoping Lela would respond. She didn't but—

Pop. Pop.

Gunfire. Not from the High Stars but from inside the meeting room.

"Move it, Waafir. Move. It."

The sound of booted feet neared. Waafir and Gan bolted around the corner in a rush of tailcoats and anxiety. Waafir cradled a low-frequency meson cannon. Gan carried a self-guided thermal blaster. Both weapons would get the job done, but they could also kill the people inside the room, if Waafir and Gan weren't careful.

Gayora and the others moved away from the doors, giving a winded Waafir and Gan room to work.

Rahm pointed to the wall space above the doors. "The meeting room is large and has two levels. The table is located toward the center of the room, far enough away from the doors that, when they explode, they shouldn't hit anyone. To be safe, we should aim for level two. When I helped Beres and Kondo inspect the room, we were told the second floor wouldn't be used."

That was good enough for Gayora. "Gan, freeze the area Rahm suggested. Waafir, blast the wall to pieces afterward. There are innocents in there we need to rescue."

Gayora refused to think of their actions as a recovery. When she'd heard Regent Etemaad's quiet, distressed voice come through the chief magistrate's communicator, commanding her to, "Stay quiet" and "Don't move," Gayora had jumped to her feet. She'd rushed from the private room, weapon at the ready. The others had followed.

They scrambled out of the way of falling debris. Waafir's meson cannon had done what their pistols could not. A decent-size hole had been created. Paladins didn't need a better invitation.

Orit hoisted Gayora up. Her hands found purchase. Pulling herself upward, she slipped through the hole, boots crunching on debris. No light. No sound.

A beam of yellow appeared behind her, as did the rest of her team. Rahm took point. The tactical light on his pistol led them through the vacant upper level of the meeting room.

They couldn't rush in, no matter how Gayora's body twitched to run down the stairs and search for her regent and chief magistrate. Whoever had attacked the delegates was still in the room.

Biding their time for an opportunity to strike us down and make their escape. That won't happen. Not on my watch.

"One way in. One way out," Rahm had told them after his inspection of the meeting room.

Waafir had created a new exit. That left the sealed doors. Beyond the doors waited High Star Cleavers Gan and Ramona. If anyone tried to leave or enter by that route, they would have to deal with two skilled and battle-ready Paladins.

On silent, booted feet, Gayora's team, weapons at the ready, moved through the darkness and down the flight of stairs to the first level. Fanning out, they went on the hunt.

Laser gunfire had a distinct smell—burnt skin. So too did fresh blood—metallic. Both tainted the air, and Gayora feared what they would find.

The front doors exploded inward, smashing to the floor and letting in light from the hallway. Ramona held the meson cannon. Four Lumerians pulled weapons on Ramona and Gan. Prime Minister Drassul huddled behind his bodyguards, three more than every other peace delegate.

The male couldn't even respect the rules of his peers on the first day of peace talks.

Gayora didn't have time for a futile standoff, so she stepped forward. Her gaze quickly swept the room for the threat that had to be in there with them. But she saw nothing. No, she saw everything. Everything she'd feared. Everything she dared not think on too long lest she did exactly what Ramona and Gan had done, bursting into the meeting room without the stealth that was the Paladin trademark.

She saw. Fates no, she saw them all. Bodies. Silent, unmoving, dead—a recovery mission, not a rescue.

Rahm, Orit, and Waafir rushed past her, searching for what they would not find.

Survivors.

Gayora saw them. How hadn't she before? Blood tracks, as if someone had been dragged, led under the table and to the two forms she would recognize anywhere. Gayora ran to her regent and chief magistrate, but Orit and Waafir were already there, shoving the huge table out of their way.

"Lower your weapons," she heard Ramona yell to the Lumerian soldiers.

One of the males yelled a response, but none of the High Stars understood their language. The soldiers were only protecting their prime minister. If she were them, she wouldn't lower her weapon until she ensured her charge's safety. They'd done their duty. The High Stars had not.

"Let them go."

"But—"

"I said let them go, Ramona," she snapped, uncaring she'd pulled rank on a superior officer. They had something far more important to deal with than Drassul and his bodyguards.

Their beaten-up chief magistrate, for one, and, Fates help him, their dying regent.

Crouched beside the prone form of Regent Etemaad, hands pressed to his chest, blood seeping between her fingers, Lela appeared nothing short of a green Paladin who'd had her first taste of battle. The evidence was there—bruised and bloody face, torn and bloodstained cloak, and eyes of fury and grief.

Gayora dropped to her knees by Regent Etemaad's head. Several feet to her right were Beres and Kondo. Dead.

The others joined her, forming a circle around their regent and chief magistrate.

Gayora knew a fatal shot when she saw one, and she saw two on Regent Etemaad. Lela's efforts wouldn't stave off the inevitable.

Yet their regent still breathed—shallow and slow.

"I'm sorry," Lela whispered, her voice a broken tremor. "I'm so very sorry."

So was Gayora. They'd failed him. The High Stars had failed them both.

"Don't go."

Gayora wanted to utter the same hopeless plea. Lela had said there was much truth to be found between killing and dying. The somber expressions of her fellow High Stars, the executed bodies of the peace delegates, and her own raging heart screamed a truth greater than the list of fatalities that would appear in her High Star report.

Gan's steady hand touched Lela's shoulder. "We're losing him, Chief Magistrate. Give our regent something to take with him to the Realm of Thuraya."

Their chief magistrate, Lela, was traumatized, couldn't Gan see? While the High Stars' eyes glistened with tears, Lela's were red but dry.

"Lela," Regent Etemaad croaked.

"I'm here."

"Take." Fingers soaked in his blood, Etemaad removed his signet ring. "Yours."

"No." She shook her head and her body began to tremble.

Coughing up blood, the regent repeated, "Take. Yours."

"Chief Magistrate, please. You must help him transition to the other side," Gan pressed. "He doesn't have much time."

Lela's bloodstained hands fell to her sides, and her shaking worsened. Gayora thought she would collapse under the weight of the horror she'd lived through and the immense responsibility Regent Etemaad had bestowed on her.

But Chief Magistrate Lela did not fall apart. She did not succumb to whatever ghastly thoughts that lurked behind her shadowed gaze or the feelings that hid within her heart. What she did was reach her right hand out to Gan and her left to Orit, beginning the unity chain of family and friendship.

They held hands, a bond forged in blood, tears, and sorrow.

"We are the cosmos, living, breathing manifestations of energy, light, and life. When we die, when we breathe our last, blackness of space awaits our arrival. Stars we will become. Souls we are. Complete we will be, in a glorious place that birthed us all."

The final words Regent Etemaad would ever hear—the Realm of Thuraya his soul's destination.

10. Aftermath

Meleris
Amakan Homeworld
Temple of Agala

Amakan soldiers were everywhere, flooding the skies and the streets—
hunting. Their actions were the same as Paladins would have been if an assassin had entered their planet and murdered their leader.

An assassin had murdered their leader but there Gayora's team stood, arguing with the Amakan defense undersecretary. Along with President Theimos 105, the Amakan defense secretary had been among the casualties. The defense undersecretary may have had three heads and mouths, out of which he spoke at the same time, but none of them had uttered a word she was interested in hearing. Most sides had lost leaders that day. The Amakans' loss was no greater than anyone else's.

"We need to speak to Chief Magistrate Lela. As the only surviving delegate, we need a report from her. We need to understand what happened in the meeting room."

Gayora's team blocked the door to the private room assigned to the Asiyan delegation. They had escorted the chief magistrate back to the room after Gayora had convinced her to release the regent's hand so they could remove his body from the temple, along with Beres's and Kondo's. Gayora had wanted no images of their slain leader leaked to the news media, no more than she'd wanted Asiyans to learn of Regent Etemaad's death before Chief Magistrate Lela had an opportunity to contact the Council of Magistrates. Gayora didn't envy Lela that task, not that she seemed in the right frame of mind to think beyond the ugliness she'd endured.

"Our magistrate isn't the only survivor. Prime Minister Drassul and his bodyguards also survived."

"Even more reason for us to speak with your chief magistrate. Our president is dead. The man whose planet we are at war with lives. Do you not question that, Paladin?"

Of course Gayora did, but she wouldn't have this conversation with the Amakan. She needed to get Lela away from this temple and planet. The chief magistrate needed medical attention, which no one had offered, not that Gayora would permit a non-Asiyan to tend her. Not only was Lela her sworn responsibility, she was Asiya's new regent. They had lost one. They wouldn't lose another. The thought of Regent Etemaad sent a fresh wave of anger through Gayora.

"We Asiyans have our own way of handling such issues."

"What does that mean?"

The door creaked behind her, a cool burst of air on Gayora's back. Lela's hand, stained with dried blood, touched Gayora's shoulder. The four High Stars shifted, so their leader could stand between them.

"Mr. Defense Undersecretary, I am most sorry for your loss. As I am for all those whose lives were taken today. The Council of Magistrates will send a personal message of condolence to each family. Such sentiments, while sincere, cannot heal the wounds from this awful day. I will provide the Amakan, Yegoth, and Unbalk governments with a personal accounting of events inside the temple's meeting room, but not before I've had an opportunity to speak with my own government."

Lela didn't sound like herself, although she'd offered the right words as a diplomat. Her voice had lacked emotion and her tone had been stilted, even for a member of the Verity Band. Yet she'd spoken from a place of will and strength.

"Thank you, Chief Magistrate. We understand. However, time is of the essence. Our military is scouring the city for the assassin. We need to know who we are looking for. This should not have happened. We cannot fathom how it did. There are no obvious signs of entry, other than the damage done by your Paladins."

"Yes, I understand. About two herns into the peace talks, the lights began to flicker. Soon afterward, they went out and didn't come back on. The darkness left me blind, I'm afraid. I did not see the shooter. As I said, I'll forward your government my report as soon as I'm able."

If Gayora hadn't seen Lela's hunting knife next to a severed hand and unmarked gun, she would've believed her version of the truth. She hadn't lied. But the truth, when framed a certain way, could be its own form of deception. They'd taken the hand as evidence before local law enforcement arrived. Gayora had recognized the hand.

The fire Malcareon. We have a target. One, anyway. Were his siblings and the Grul involved? Probably.

Gayora spotted Ramona striding toward them, giving her the signal she'd been waiting for. "Regent Etemaad, Beres, and Kondo are secured in the shuttle," she whispered in Lela's ear. "Gan is at controls and ready to depart Meleris upon your command. Shall we leave now, Reg . . . Chief Magistrate?"

Gayora hadn't stopped soon enough, for Lela swung her head toward her, grief filling her eyes anew. Grief and anger. Lela had rejected Etemaad's regent's signet ring. But Lela's refusal did not make her any less Regent Etemaad's blood-chosen heir.

Gayora waited for the reprimand, but Lela only stared at her. The mix of brown, black, and gray of her eyes had dimmed, as if the shades had bled together to form a new color that had the word melancholy in its name.

"Chief Magistrate, I—"

"It's fine, Gayora. You're correct. It's time for our departure." Lela faced a displeased defense undersecretary. "We will speak again soon. We must return the deceased to their families."

"Yes, yes, of course. We will find the fiends who slayed our president."

"I'm sure you will do your best."

Before the Amakan could say another word or Gayora could interpret the undercurrent she'd detected in Lela's response, Lela had stepped around the Amakan and toward a waiting Ramona.

Waafir, Orit, and Rahm followed, nodding to the defense undersecretary as they made their leave.

Gayora glanced into the private room, making sure they'd left nothing behind. The High Stars hadn't, but Lela had. Gayora entered the room and stared at the left item before picking it up. Deceptively lightweight but no longer clean—literally and metaphorically—she dropped the garment onto the table. Blood stained the fabric—Etemaad's, Lela's, and the fire Malcareon her team would hunt to the end of the cosmos. They would find him and his co-conspirators before the Amakans did. That had been Lela's unspoken parting words to the defense undersecretary.

So much had changed since the first time Gayora had seen Lela wear her new chief magistrate's cloak. She'd worn it proudly during the Luna of Analisia induction ceremony. Now it lay discarded, blemished in more ways than the bloodstains.

So was Gayora. So too were the High Stars.

On the shuttle flight from Meleris to their spaceship, Lela didn't speak. Her eyes stayed on the door that led to the room where Gan and Ramona had placed their fallen brothers.

"Are we going home, Chief Magistrate?"

In the same emotionless tone Lela had used since they'd found her surrounded by the dead and dying, she answered Waafir's question with a soft but resolute, "No."

Lumeria
Lumerian Homeworld
Zeader Spaceport

"You shouldn't still be here." Lady Junoid scanned the spaceport. She'd had the foresight to call a planetary state of emergency as soon as Drassul's shuttle had landed in Veer. The prime minister had initiated an immediate curfew, broadcasting from his Veer River Complex for the people of Lumeria to "seek shelter and safety immediately." Drassul had to at least give the impression of taking precautions. After all, he'd just survived an assassination attempt. One would expect him to place his planet on high alert for an enemy cunning and strong enough to dispatch with members of the peace delegation.

Thanks to the state of emergency, the spaceport was uncharacteristically quiet. But Lumerian soldiers and Veer officers were on patrol. Any one of them could stumble upon Lady Junoid speaking with the Grul.

She slipped around the side of Quill's spacecraft, and the Grul followed. His whiplike tail was held up and to the side, as if he couldn't decide whether he wanted to add her life to the ones he'd already taken.

His voice, when he finally spoke, was as menacing as the male. The frightened elderly woman who lived inside the fierce political advisor trembled. With Quill so near, his anger palpable, the vacant spaceport no longer appealed. He could kill her, snapping her neck with his clawed hands, impaling her with his tail, or shooting her dead.

"Your presence here beyond the allotted time was not part of the plan."

"Neither was the old man and baby chief magistrate being unaffected by Agala's hypnotic eyes." A hand flew out and slammed against the hull of the spaceship, a breath from her head. "The female had a knife. A *knife*," Quill snarled, his incisors long and sharp. "We were the only ones who were supposed to have lethal weapons. But the female had a knife strong enough to cut through spacesuit, flesh, and bone. She would've taken Gronac's entire arm off, if she hadn't tried to kill him by stabbing him in his chest." The same hand smashed against the ship again, and she inhaled Quill's sour-smelling breath as he shifted closer. His face lowered to hers. "My crew getting hurt, now *that* wasn't part of the plan. Asiyans' immunity to your little mind warp concoction, *that* wasn't part of the plan. Almost getting caught by Paladins, *that*, Lumi, sure as fulk wasn't part of the plan."

If Lady Junoid wasn't afraid of what the Grul would do to her, she would've smacked him across his face, so much did she despise his vulgarity and racism. Reminding herself this was her planet and she was the second most powerful person on Lumeria, Lady Junoid squared her shoulders and stood tall. She may be afraid, but by the grace of Agala, she wouldn't allow the brute to see her cower in the face of his wrath.

"Per our agreement, I've wired the payment to your account."

"It all better be there," he gritted, spittle flying. "For the hassle, I should charge you more."

The mercenaries hadn't finished the job, so Lady Junoid had subtracted the fee he'd charged for the chief magistrate's death. Why should they incur the cost when the woman still breathed? After all, where was the fiscal responsibility in paying for a service not rendered? She would keep that detail to herself, however.

"Hassle?" She snorted. "Chief Magistrate Lela is child-size compared to you and the Malcareons. You came highly recommended. You're supposed to be the best." Quill's face hardened even more, but she wouldn't retreat from a point that pricked at the Grul's precious pride. "Thanks to my God, everyone in the room was immobilized. All you had to do was aim and shoot."

Because of Quill's incompetence, they had a witness. No one, except for Drassul and his bodyguards, was supposed to exit the Temple of Agala alive, not even the High Stars waiting in their assigned room. The Paladins' deaths had been part of Drassul's last-minute plan change. She also hadn't paid Quill for those incomplete missions either.

As long as her targets were in a room with Agala's eyes, their minds could be manipulated. Lady Junoid had no explanation as to how or why Regent Etemaad and Chief Magistrate Lela were unaffected but the High Stars in the meeting room with them had been. She did know why Theimos 105 had emerged from the spell when the others had not.

"I want him to know what is happening," Drassul had told her before he'd left his complex, giving Lady Junoid his final set of directions for executing their plan. "I want that three-headed pagan to know he's going to die. I want to hear him beg for his life in three voices. Make sure to pull him out of the illusion before that Grul heathen kills him."

"I could slice you open. Right here, right now. But I won't." Quill stepped away from her. Balled fists unclenched and tail lowered. "That Verity chief magistrate may be tiny and young, but she's far from a weak-kneed child. I'm male enough to admit I underestimated her and the old regent. She took Gronac by surprise, and he's paying for it. What will you do when she takes you and your pompous prime minister by surprise?"

Quill moved farther away from Lady Junoid. Apparently, their conversation was over. Good, she'd wasted too much time on the Grul. She needed him off her planet and away from Vargan space. She didn't care where he went, as long as he and the Malcareons were gone by the time Lela contacted Drassul.

Lady Junoid wasn't a fool. Of course, the chief magistrate would reach out to the only other survivor of what would surely be dubbed a massacre. She may even suspect the Lumerians were behind the plot to kill the peace delegates. No doubt, the people of Wither, Meleris, and Shin would think the same. With the deaths of their leaders, however, their planets would be in turmoil, leaving them vulnerable to Lumerian occupation. Her Pax-Lumeria would soon become a reality. With Agala's blessings, and the Vedems protection, Lumerians would be an unstoppable force.

"The Asiyans have no proof of our involvement," she yelled at Quill's retreating form. "They won't make a move against Lumeria without proof. Paladins are honorable warriors. They would never wage a war based on an unsubstantiated accusation of a woman-child."

Quill disappeared inside his ship.

With haste, Lady Junoid moved to safety inside the terminal. From a section of a window-wall, she watched Quill's spaceship lift into the air and fly away. It wouldn't take him long to reach the upper atmosphere and Lumerian space.

There goes the only evidence of Lumeria's role in the assassination of four planetary leaders. Chief Magistrate Lela may have taken Quill and that strange fire Malcareon by surprise, but the girl would do well to lick her wounds and go home. If she doesn't

. . .

11. Show and Tell

Ibor Peace 01

Lela had never been one for a loss of words, even when she had little to say. She wasn't shy or an introvert. Nor was she prone to performance anxiety. Yet, standing in front of the comm system in her quarters aboard *Ibor Peace 01*, the Council of Magistrates gaping at her, their anguish in every line of their shocked features, Lela fought not to stumble over her words or to melt into a puddle of tears.

The chief magistrates were no longer in Khatra at the Hall of Concord in Northeast Asiya. Each had returned to their respective region soon after the Luna of Analisia ceremony. Only the regent resided at the Hall of Concord where the High Stars' headquarters and ambassadorial offices were located.

They had responded to her emergency meeting request, filling her living quarters with their three-dimensional holographic images. Reth and Mosi were in their offices and seated behind their desks, while Yusef paced in tight circles in his home library and Chiku appeared as if she hadn't yet been to bed. They were in different time zones, including Lela, who'd interrupted what should've been the chief magistrates' uneventful day with unspeakable news.

"I do not understand." Mosi had uttered the same statement of disbelief three times. Taking deep breaths, she refocused dark green eyes that had stared off into the distance upon the somber telling of Etemaad's execution. "Why would someone kill our regent? You were there on a mission of peace. We only wanted to help save lives. Yet someone dared to take our regent from his people."

Yusef stopped pacing. Lela had seen many brewing thunderstorms but never in a male's eyes. "Have you permitted Orit to tend to your wounds?" He stepped forward, sweeping observant, stormy eyes over her. "No, it doesn't appear as if you have."

With the way the chief magistrates watched her, taking in the bruises she couldn't conceal with clothing, Lela felt inspected and judged.

"My dear girl," Chiku said in a voice that was one part worried mother but two parts warrior queen. "Did you make the beast regret laying hands on you?"

Throat tight at the memory of fighting for her life, Lela nodded her reply.

"Good. Is he dead or in custody?"

"Neither."

"More's the pity."

"I'll speak with your parents," Yusef interjected, as if Nenet and Hasani had been the topic of conversation. "A parent shouldn't have to see the aftermath of their child's assault. No more than a female should have to experience the pain of learning of her mate's murder."

An image of Dariya, Regent Etemaad's mate, sitting beside a six-anulls-old Lela while drinking iced t'urin and conversing with Nenet, settled in her mind and over her heart. More images came of Etemaad and Dariya over the anulls—smiling and laughing—the couple an integral part of Lela's childhood and young adult life. Images of Beres and Kondo blended with those of her uncle and aunt of the heart. She'd known the High Stars for anulls.

In battle, Paladins were hard because they had to be. But in day-to-day life, they were the most caring of people. Beres and Kondo had given their lives in the line of duty. They'd been denied a future, and their families a mate and a father. When Lela slept, she knew she would dream of the three males—their faces of death forever burned in her memory.

No, Lela did not want to burden her parents' hearts with news of Etemaad's death and her escape from the same fate. But Nenet, no matter how close Lela had come to dying, still had a daughter to hold on to; whereas, Dariya no longer had a mate to laugh with her when joy overflowed her heart or to embrace her when sadness dimmed her spirit. Nenet, Dariya's friend of four dekulls, would know how best to help her cope with her sudden loss.

Chiku spoke again. Her words reminded Lela that women, regardless of their age differences, often thought along the same lines. "I'll speak with Dariya. There's no ideal approach to deliver such heartbreaking news but there are countless ways to mishandle the sensitive moment. Lela, dear, take Yusef's advice.

Nenet will be on the first warship to the Vargan Solar System if she sees your bruised and swollen face. I'm of a mind to come there myself. When I gaze upon you, I must remind myself you are on this council for a reason. That you were chosen by your band for a reason."

"But it's easy for us to forget," Reth broke in, snow-white coils falling down his chest and disappearing behind his desk. "Especially when we see you thus: angry, hurt, and grieving. We grieve with you. We also share your anger. We need to know more. We need to learn the truth. Come home, Chief Magistrate. We will handle the regent's assassination."

Yusef, who'd stepped away from his comm system, speaking to someone Lela couldn't hear or see, returned. "Yes, return home, Lela. By the time you arrive at the Hall of Concord, the Council will be there to meet you. We'll begin hunting for the killers then."

Lela knew who the killers were, and she wouldn't give them time to find a hiding hole.

"Mosi, have your scholars completed the report on the Grul and Malcareons?"

"Almost. With the death of planet G4H Malcore, it has been difficult to obtain accurate information on four specific Malcareons. So far, Binoba and the researchers I assigned to assist my disciple haven't located any records of the names listed on the press badges. Since their names cannot be verified, it's impossible to trace the reporters' movements. Our next step is face recognition research. Do you suspect the reporters were involved in the massacre?"

"I do." Lela pointed to her face. "The fire Malcareon is the one who attacked me. I also recognized the Grul's voice. Gayora and I spoke to him only two doles prior. I think he may have been the person who shot and killed Regent Etemaad."

Silence from the Council then a barrage of questions Lela couldn't begin to answer because they talked at once—heated and ready to take action.

"Are you positive about the Grul and Malcareons?" Yusef demanded. "You need to be absolutely sure. We'll understand if you aren't. Many people, even trained Paladins, confuse suppositions with facts when under duress."

Acknowledging Gayora's entry into Lela's quarters, she mouthed "Thank you," accepting the two items she handed her. Gayora had stored both items in vacuum-sealed evidence bags. Holding one in each hand, Lela showed them to the Council.

Mosi gasped, and Yusef swore.

Reth pushed to his feet, sending his chair spinning. "Yusef, you recognize the gun?"

Yusef moved forward, as if he could step from his private library into Lela's living quarters to get a closer look at what she held. "It's a high-speed fusion pistol. Tell me, Gayora, is it the same kind of weapon used against Regent Etemaad and High Stars Beres and Kondo?"

"I can't be certain, Chief Magistrate, but I believe so. The wounds are consistent with the damage done by this type and caliber of gun. We'll have to wait until a forensic pathologist has examined the bodies before we can safely draw that conclusion."

"Upon your return, we *will* speak on this matter further. I want an explanation as to how eight Paladins failed to protect their regent and chief magistrate." Yusef's voice rose, as did his index finger, pointing it at Gayora. "I want a complete accounting of what happened from every member of your team, including from Gan and Ramona."

When Yusef's voice rose higher still, Lela turned her back to him and stepped in front of her shadow.

"You may be excused, Gayora. I only needed you to bring me the evidence you collected." She handed her back the sealed bags. "Return these to the storage locker. Tell Gan and Ramona to prepare the shuttle and the cargo."

"Lela, what are you . . ."

She ignored Yusef's angry commands. Lela may not have been able to save Etemaad, but she could protect Gayora from Yusef's misplaced fury and his need to punish someone for the deaths of his Paladins and the regent. His target, however, was aimed at the wrong person.

Lowering her voice, she asked, "Has the information from Beres's and Kondo's zots been downloaded?"

"Yes."

"Good. Make a copy for the Council and send the data crystal with Gan and Ramona. Has the other ship detected our presence?"

"I don't believe so."

"Do what you must to ensure it doesn't."

"Of course, Chief Magistrate." Gayora's formal bearing softened, and she squeezed Lela's hand with an older sister's tender understanding but a Paladin's harsh self-reproach. "You cannot stand between your High Stars and our earned castigation."

What of my own castigation? I'd been too ill to see potential signs that something was amiss. I hadn't even noticed when the doors to the meeting room had closed—locking us inside.

Everyone wanted a report from Lela, and while she had no intention of divulging all to the other governments, she needed to formulate a detailed and accurate report for the Council. But how could she write such a document when her mind kept conjuring images of eyes with spider legs?

"We'll speak later, Gayora."

Bowing to Lela, Gayora left.

Lela turned to the Council and immediately held her hand up to silence Yusef. "You may have formed my security team, but they are not yours to reprimand. They saved my life today."

"And lost our regent his. I will have Elan revoke their High Star insignias."

"It is, of course, the Chief of Regent Security's right to make such a decision. But I have six High Stars under my command,

and they are the only reason we are now following what I believe to be a ship carrying the Grul and Malcareons."

Yusef calmed, while the others perked at the revelation.

Reth reclaimed his seat behind his desk. "Explain."

"On our flight to the Vargan Solar System, my security team determined optimal locations to leave our long-range surveillance drones. Regent Etemaad's cleavers were tasked with daily footage review."

The use of cloaked surveillance drones was protocol for all Asiyan peace missions involving disputes between two or more planets. While many planetary leaders liked to claim they "owned" the space around their planet, to Asiyans, the cosmos belonged to everyone. For them, planetary rules of privacy and sovereignty could not extend to a free and open Mother Cosmos.

"Have the High Stars reviewed today's feeds?" Yusef asked, a glint of vicious anticipation in his eyes.

"We all have. Until today, no ships had ventured beyond their homeworld. That's likely due to the brokered cease-fire."

"I assume," Reth said, "the drones picked up the shuttles leaving from their respective planet to attend the peace talks on Meleris."

"They did. One shuttle left Lumeria, Wither Alpha, and Shin. We have a date and time stamp for each departure from the planets, as well as their arrival on Meleris."

Lela paused, recalling that Prime Minister Drassul had been the last to enter the meeting room but his ship had been the first to reach Meleris. The Asiyan delegation had arrived an hern early so the Paladins could scout the area. They hadn't seen the Lumerian shuttle at the spaceport. They hadn't even known they should've seen the shuttle and prime minister until they'd viewed the video feed. Where had the Lumerians been and what had Drassul being doing that had caused him to enter the meeting room last, although he'd been the first to arrive on the planet?

So many unanswered questions. Her head hurt from them all.

"The Lumerian shuttle left Meleris before ours."

Lela paused again, waiting to see if Yusef would inquire as to why the High Stars hadn't detained Drassul for questioning. Thankfully, the chief magistrate said nothing. With Yusef, however, rarely did his silence mean what one hoped. He would revisit the issue. The only unknown was when. It wouldn't matter that the High Stars had no authority or basis to question, much less detain Drassul. He wasn't a person of interest in the assassinations, even if Lela and the defense undersecretary shared the same suspicion of the male. Similar thoughts had to be percolating in Yusef's mind.

"Two herns after we arrived back on our ship, an unmarked gunboat left Lumeria."

"Gunboats don't carry as many passengers or hold as much cargo as the average shuttle," Yusef said. "What gunboats sacrifice in those two areas, as well as in speed, they make up for in heavy armaments."

"Tough armor and shielding, Waafir had explained."

"He's correct."

"Can this cruiser class of Ibor ship defeat the gunboat in battle?"

Lela had asked the same question of the High Stars. They'd given her a reply she believed, but none of them had Yusef's wealth of knowledge and combat experience. If he possessed a counterposition, she needed to know.

"Perhaps. Peace ships are formidable, but they weren't built for rugged battles. Without knowing what you're up against, the unknown is too risky. You wouldn't have posed that question if you weren't following them from a safe distance and using the ship's cloaking ability. My advice is for you to maintain cloaking and not to engage until it is safe to do so. I assume that's your plan."

Plan might be too big of a word for the unsettling thoughts swirling about Lela's mind. She didn't wish to utter them aloud, much less explain her muddled thought process.

"I am Verity," she said instead, falling back on old training. "I will learn the truth of today."

"That is all we can ask of you," Reth said, voice soft and eyes considering. "But it is too large of a request."

"Much too large," Chiku agreed. "But I see no other way."

"Neither do I," Mosi concurred with a shake of her head. "The burden of tracking Etemaad's assassins should not be on your young shoulders. Yet it is, and there is little we can do to assist you."

"Lela," Yusef said, "the gun you showed us is one of many sold on the black market to mercenaries and others of their ilk. If the gunboat does indeed carry the Grul and Malcareons, interrogate them first."

First. Yes, Lela knew what would come second. They all did. No trial but a sanctioned execution. Even if the Lumerians proved innocent, the Grul and Malcareons were not.

"Yes." Lela could say more, but she neither had the inclination nor the energy. Her head felt like it was in a vise, and she stank of blood and sweat. She needed to shower and to sleep but only one appealed.

The chief magistrates stared at her, but none gave voice to the truth that existed in the solar systems that separated Lela from her homeworld. She and the High Stars might not return to Asiya. They all knew, but not a single chief magistrate tried to stop her. Even if they'd objected, she wouldn't have been swayed by their arguments. Perhaps they saw that truth on her face more so than her bruises.

Chiku reached out a hand to Lela, the same way she'd done at the induction ceremony. The older female couldn't touch her, of course, and Lela didn't have to kneel, but she bent her knees anyway. Her head lowered, eyes closed, and heart twisted in sorrow but not in fear of the unknown.

"Be safe, Lela. May the Fates walk in front of you, lighting your path so it will never know darkness and uncertainty. May the Fates hold your hand, guiding but not leading. May they offer insight, when you think none exists. Our prayers are with you, Chief Magistrate. Be safe and return to us."

Northwest Asiya
Paladin Region of Khomi
Shielder Hall

"When are we departing?" Ammon moved fully into his father's library. It wouldn't take him long to pack and be ready to board the next warship.

"Doors close for a reason. They are meant to offer the person inside the room privacy. You're old enough to know what a closed door means and how to knock before entering."

Yusef was grumpier than normal, and Ammon understood what he must be feeling. He had entered his father's library only after his series of knocks had gone unanswered.

"Regent Etemaad was shot and killed," Ammon had heard Lela say in a sullen, detached voice that had threatened to break his heart. He'd wanted to rush into the room and interrupt a private meeting of the Council of Magistrates, so he could see for himself Lela was unharmed. She hadn't been murdered, like Regent Etemaad, thank the Fates, but she had been far from untouched. Ammon hadn't needed to see the bruises the elders had talked about to know Lela was in pain. Surely he hadn't been the only one to detect the fury and anguish in her voice. He felt no different. He wanted to destroy everyone involved in the regent's assassination.

"When are you leaving to rendezvous with Lela's ship?"

"I'm not." Yusef finally turned away from the comm system. The anger he thought he would see on his father's face wasn't present. But tears were. His eyes were full of them. "He's dead."

"I know." Ammon drew closer, standing in front of Yusef. "We'll make them suffer, Ab'ba."

"Of that, I am certain." Yusef's hand rose to Ammon's face, wiping away his own tears. "Lela is too far away for us to reach her in time to be of assistance."

"But—"

"For once, heed my words." Yusef lowered his hand to Ammon's shoulder, squeezing before allowing it to fall to his side. "Lela's ship is several solar systems from our Bazlorian system. Even if we left now and used faster-than-light travel, we wouldn't catch her ship. There are also no wormholes between us and her that would reduce our travel time. Lela and her security team are right where they need to be."

"Following the gunboat."

"That's not the mission they're on. If it were, you wouldn't be frothing at the mouth to rush after Lela, and I wouldn't be cursing myself for not demanding she return home."

Ammon opened his mouth to yell, "Why didn't you?" but stopped when Yusef stepped away, returned to the comm system, and typed in a code. A recorded holographic image of Lela appeared. He stared. Ammon had thought seeing her bruised and battered face would send him into a rage. The sight did boil his insides. A hurt Lela ignited the protective Paladin that hadn't had a restful night's sleep since she'd left on her peace mission. Yet it was Lela's unyielding stare, looking out from red, puffy eyes that nearly undid Ammon. "She's terrified."

"Terrified, yes, but also Ibor-level stubborn. I couldn't have stopped her pursuit, even if I had been so inclined. I do not wish further harm to come to Lela. I am grateful that I do not have to sit the Rite of Sephtis for four stolen lives. But I am what I am, Ammon, and that is Chief Magistrate of the Paladin Band. I would not have chosen Lela for the Lumerian-Amakan peace mission. I opposed the regent's decision. In hindsight, I should've also objected to him accompanying her. It simply isn't done. But Etemaad was determined to guide Lela through her first peace mission, and Elan and I had no reason to believe their lives would be in danger. That gross miscalculation will haunt me to the end of my days."

Ammon stopped Yusef's hand when his fingers reached for the icon that would close the image file of Lela. He disliked seeing her thus but not seeing her was worse. Per their agreement, they hadn't contacted each other since the day of her departure. Ammon had left the Hall of Concord with his parents, content to begin working with Shielder trainees while waiting for Lela to return home and for them to begin the courting rituals.

"Ammon, I did not show you the saved image of Lela for you to obsess over what that brute did to her or what she must do next."

"Why then?"

"Because you cannot save Lela. She doesn't wish to be saved."

"You don't know her the way I do. She's scared and hurt and trying to prove her worth to you and the entire Council. Do you actually believe she doesn't know what you think of her? That she doesn't know what you all see when you look at her?"

Yusef snatched his hand away from Ammon's, clicking the close icon before Ammon could stop him again.

The image of Lela winked out.

"Let me tell you what I see. I see a young woman who doesn't comprehend the depth of her power or the reach of her influence. She follows but also leads, blending the two so seamlessly she doesn't realize the significance of what she's doing, no more than she comprehends how rare that natural skill of hers is . . . or even how dangerous. Lela's an idealist who is willing to become a martyr for a belief larger than herself. She isn't wholly Verity. Nor is she Paladin, Devdas, Affiq, or Euridice. Lela is all the bands. That truth makes her actions and thoughts unpredictable beyond comfort."

"For all that you've said, much of which is true, you still don't know Lela's heart."

"Perhaps not her heart, but I do know her, son. I know if she thinks the Grul and Malcareons were the ones who killed the peace delegates, she's correct. I know Lela will send Gan and Ramona home in the shuttle with our fallen because she's sensitive and thoughtful, like her parents. She cannot spare the families their pain, but she can return their loved ones to them, so they can proceed with the Rite of Sephtis. Finally, I know Lela won't stop until she's satisfied that she has learned every wretched truth, including who hired the Grul and Malcareons. Lela is precisely where she needs to be, and not at all where the Council would've sent her."

Ammon reached around Yusef to the comm system. With a single touch, the holographic image of Lela reappeared. She'd survived, while many others had perished at the unforgiving hands of mercenaries. No government-sanctioned soldiers carried high-speed fusion pistols and certainly no legitimate embedded reporters did either.

"There aren't many pistols made that can pierce the body armor of a Paladin." Eyes still on Lela, Ammon asked Yusef, "Do you know whether Beres and Kondo wore their Einar?"

"It's protocol."

Ammon took that as a yes.

"Then they came prepared to kill High Stars."

"I've concluded the same. We will have our chance to avenge our regent and brothers."

"War with the Lumerians?" Ammon reached out his hand to Lela. Irrational disappointment washed over him when it passed through the hologram.

"The thought of war does not appeal, but the rage inside will not be loosed until those responsible for the regent's death are dead."

"I feel the same. She's not a child, you know?"

"No, she is not. But Lela is so very young." A steady hand settled on his shoulder. "So are you. But, as you've reminded me time and again, you are a man. As such, I need you for what is to come. All Paladins will be needed. Can I count on my youngest son?"

Yusef's question was an unintended insult. Was Ammon not Paladin enough in his father's eyes that the chief magistrate couldn't assume he would be the first in line to defend the honor of their people? Did Yusef think Ammon so weak of warrior spirit he would have to ask him to stand beside his brothers and sisters in mortal combat? Obviously, he did. Ammon's pride was pricked far less than his heart was hurt by his father's low opinion of him.

"I am Paladin. I am blade and armor. I know my duty, Ab'ba."

"Good."

The hand on his shoulder slid away, and Yusef's footsteps tracked across the library and toward the open door. "I have much to do, so does Lela."

"Your point?"

"She too is blade and armor. That's also what I see when I look at that image you're agonizing over. Lela needs her armor, Ammon. She cannot afford to remove it until her new mission is complete."

"Even if it crushes her heart, scars her soul, and dulls her spirit?"

"She's a chief magistrate," Yusef said, as if his reply was an adequate response. It was not. "Leave Lela to her mission. Do not interfere. Do not weaken her with your sorrowful eyes and bleeding heart."

"Any other insults, Ab'ba?"

"As I said, you're so very young, Ammon. What you feel is precisely how every male who loves would feel if the female of his heart had been hurt and was actively pursuing deadly villains. It's how I would feel if it was your mother aboard *Ibor Peace 01* instead of Lela. But sometimes, son, love can be a weakness. If you love Lela, do not weaken her with it. Have faith. Have faith and trust Lela to return with her High Stars."

Again, Yusef spoke as if he comprehended Lela and Ammon better than they did themselves. He wouldn't contradict him. When it came to Ammon, the only opinion that ever mattered to Yusef was his own.

"I'll be ready when you leave for the Hall of Concord."

"I know you will be."

As quietly as Ammon had entered, Yusef exited the library, leaving him alone with the still image of Lela.

Taking advantage of the empty library and open comm system, Ammon called Lela's quarters. Three attempts and an hern later, a female answered, but not the one he expected.

"Good evening, Ammon."

"Hello, Gayora. Where's Lela?"

Shifting to her side, the room behind the High Star Shadow came into view. Lela slept on the bed behind Gayora. In this vulnerable state, one could easily miss the quiet might that was this special Asiyan female. Ammon did not wish to disturb her but not for the reason Yusef had given.

Love could never be a weakness.

"She looks exhausted."

"We all are, but none more than the chief magistrate. If it's important, I will wake her."

"No need, but thank you, Gayora. Lela has more than earned her rest." Although, with the furrow he could see on her forehead, he doubted it was a peaceful slumber. "If I promise not to be long, will you permit me to stay?"

"To behold Lela's soul? I cannot sanction—"

"Again, no, Gayora. I am not requesting such a breach in decorum. I only wish to watch over her for a little while. Now is not the time for the Light of Nurzhan ritual."

"I shouldn't." Gayora glanced from a hopeful Ammon to a sleeping Lela. Then she cursed when Lela rolled over, whispering Ammon's name in her sleep.

He smiled.

"First Yusef, and now you. Except for your brother, the males of the House of Eetu will be the end of my High Star career."

"I would never dishonor my Lela."

"*Your* Lela. If I hadn't seen the strange hand holding display myself, I would be shocked by your claim. Knowing you, and now having spent time with her, the pairing makes too much sense."

Gayora exited Lela's bedroom. As Lela's shadow, she wouldn't have gone far—probably to the living quarters. He was grateful for the limited privacy she had granted him.

Ammon wished he could see Lela better, move closer, touch her. But he would have to settle for watching her sleep, knowing, at least for now, she was safe.

12. The Cost of Failure

Earth
Human Homeworld
City of New York

"Oh, no you don't. Come back here." Zion wrapped an arm around Iman's waist and tumbled them back into bed.

Iman laughed, squirmed, and Zion held her tighter.

"Let me go."

"Nope. You're mine, remember? You agreed to marry me."

"You're underemployed, you leave your socks on my bedroom floor, and you failed your government entrance exam."

"You wound me, Private Adeusi." Zion rolled onto his back and then balled a fist and mock stabbed a knife into his heart.

"Wound you? I doubt it. Your skin is as thick as those peanut butter sandwiches you make." Rising onto her elbows, as naked as him, Iman smiled down at Zion. "If that's all you plan on eating after we're married, it'll be cheap to keep you."

"Yeah, well, one of us should probably learn how to cook. I'm leaning toward that one being you."

Zion wasn't surprised when a finger poked him in his side. He was surprised, however, and pleased, when Iman straddled his hips.

Holding up her left hand, catching it in the light streaming in through the open window of her bedroom, Iman admired her engagement ring. "It really is beautiful. Whoever said diamonds were a girl's best friend knew what they were talking about. Thank you."

"Thank Grandma Grace."

She poked his side again, but not with the hand still lifted to the sunlight. "I meant thank you for not waiting until you passed the government entrance exam and started your internship before asking me to marry you."

"You're going off to war, and Sage has a big mouth."

"Your sister is sixteen, what did you expect? And stop being melodramatic. I'm going to basic training."

"What else?"

"What else is there to say?"

"That you lowered your standards and agreed to marry a failure."

"Don't talk about yourself like that. You've never failed at anything."

"Do you want me to show you the email again? It's still in my zot's inbox. The entrance exam was harder than I thought it would be. By the way, I stopped by Mrs. Gideon's office today."

Iman made to move off Zion, but he placed his hands on her thighs, a silent request for her to stay.

"I have to shower and dress for work."

"I know."

Iman stretched her sexy, lean body atop him. Her head settled on his shoulder and her eyes lifted to his.

Zion wrapped his arms around her, enjoying the creamy softness of her skin and the earthy scent from their lovemaking.

"What did Mrs. Gideon say about the test?"

"She told me if I showed up at her office again without having passed the exam, she would build a machine so she could travel back in time to give my mother an Oviduct birth control injection because, and I quote, 'If you can't pass a simple entrance exam, your parents' sperm and egg were wasted on you.'"

"Ouch."

"Yeah."

"And you want that woman as your boss?"

"Hell no, but I think I can learn a lot from her."

"If you want to learn how to bust balls, maybe. If that's your new thing, you might as well sign up and we can go to basic together." Warm, soft lips kissed his jaw. "I'll be back, you know."

"I know. You leaving for basic isn't why I proposed."

"Are you sure?" Leaning up from his chest, she quirked a brow at him.

"It's not," Zion protested with too much vehemence to convince himself of his lie, let alone her. "Okay, maybe it is."

Zion lowered his gaze, feeling more like a loser than he had when he'd opened the email with his test results. Technically, Zion had failed only one section of the three-part exam. As Mrs. Gideon had told him, "All or nothing, Mr. Grace. Two-thirds is unacceptable. Better you learn that now than out in the field when sides are relying on you to broker a deal that'll save lives. Unless you plan on only caring about the safety of two-thirds of the people."

Now that had been true melodrama.

He lifted his eyes to meet hers again. "What if you meet another guy?"

"I'll meet plenty of guys in basic. So what?"

"What if you like one of them better than me?"

She laughed and kissed his jaw again. "I would kick you out of my bed and send your pouting ass home to your mother, if I believed a word you just said. One thing Zion Grace is not is insecure . . . or a quitter. Stop sulking, suck it up, and study harder."

This time, when Iman made to slide off him, he let her go. "I'll be gone for four months. Use that time to focus on your studies."

His eyes dropped from her pretty face to her tantalizing breasts.

Iman rolled her eyes and crossed her arms over her chest. "And you've just made my point."

"I study when I visit."

"We have sex when you visit." Her eyes fell to his lap. "Lots of sex. Then you make the biggest peanut butter sandwich I've ever seen, turn on a sports channel, and then study whatever books and documents you've downloaded to your zot."

Zion reached for Iman again, but she jumped away.

"Study. I have faith in you."

Faith. That five-letter word shouldn't have jolted him like a bucket of ice water to his libido, but it had.

Iman has faith in me? Why? What have I done to earn that level of trust?

Sure, she had agreed to marry him, but they both knew their parents would push for them to wait. Their parents would argue they were too young. Hell, his mother had already started in on him when he'd asked for Grandma Grace's engagement ring. Zion would be fine with waiting. He wasn't in a rush. But he also wasn't a fool. He may not be the insecure type, but he was the forward-thinking kind of man. Did that mean he had less faith in a future with Iman than she had in him?

Or maybe I am insecure in my relationship and about my career choice. Shit, is this new feeling of self-doubt the cost of failure?

"Want to join me in the shower?" Iman asked from the doorway.

Grinning, Zion jumped from the bed, confident he wouldn't let her or himself down in this area. "I thought you didn't want to be late."

"Quickie," Iman said, darting out of the bedroom and into the hallway with a playful giggle.

He ran after her but stopped when he stepped on the remote to her telecommunication unit. The two-dimensional display came to life. An image of a temple appeared behind a news correspondent. *She's Amakan.* Picking up the remote, he unmuted the unit but still had to read the translation at the bottom of the screen to understand what was going on.

Zion sank to the foot of the bed. The more he read, the tighter he gripped the remote.

"What's taking you so long . . .?" Iman stopped, read. "Oh my god. That's awful."

Even if Zion hadn't spent the last few weeks studying interplanetary relations and interracial politics, he would've recognized the prelude to an unstoppable wave of violence and bloodshed.

Iman joined him, holding the hand not strangling the remote. "What kind of monsters would do something like that? And in a temple of all places."

Schools, buildings of worship, hospitals, venues where one would think people could gather and be safe, shouldn't be the site of a mass murder. Yet human history had proven, time and again, that no locale was sacred to the violent, misguided, and depraved. Obviously, such deviance wasn't limited to humans and Earth.

The more Zion read, the more he realized he was waiting for the reporter to provide an update on the young chief magistrate from Asiya. All the Amakan had noted was that the Asiyan leader, Regent Etemaad of the House of Sanna, had been among the dead peace delegates. For obvious reasons, the reporter focused more on the death of the Amakan president—Theimos 105—than on any of the other casualties.

Zion turned to other news channels. Sure enough, the massacre was breaking news everywhere, although the bloody event had occurred days earlier. No matter the advanced technology, there was a communication lag between planets, especially when, like between Earth and Meleris, the distance was great.

"This is what you want to do, Zion? My god, your job was supposed to be safer than mine. At least there's no war our planet will send me off to fight when I finish basic training. Even if they did, as a chaplain assistant, I will carry a weapon. As a peace negotiator, you will have to rely on someone like me to protect you. I hope peace negotiators are at least provided protective vests."

Iman lurched forward as if she would vomit, then slapped a hand over her mouth.

Considering Iman's reaction to the reporter's vivid descriptions of the fatalities, she may want to think long and hard about a military career.

"Shots to the head . . . Shots to the upper torso . . . Execution-style kills . . ."

Zion couldn't wrap his head around that kind of unprovoked violence.

"Peace talks ended . . ."

"I can't . . . I can't watch any more of this. It's sick, and now I'm definitely going to be late."

Absently, Zion nodded. He kept switching channels. He'd found broadcasts streamed from Shin, Meleris, and Wither Alpha and Beta, but nothing from Asiya. No matter how many different channels he turned to, no one shared news footage or a written statement from the Asiyan government. It was as if their regent hadn't been murdered along with the others. Not even planets in the Bazlorian Solar System discussed Regent Etemaad's murder. Zion had experienced media blackouts before, but he had never seen one so thoroughly executed.

That's real power. No wonder Earth wants to be in the same sandbox as Asiya.

A familiar image appeared on the screen. Zion had seen the same man before and, each time he did, his voice grated. He didn't need to understand Ereis to know he disliked the man and the sound of his voice.

Zion read the closed captions.

"I barely escaped. Agala watches over his servants. He provides. He protects, and he was with me in his temple home. There is no other explanation as to why I was spared, and the others were killed. Agala knows the hearts of the righteous. Our God is wise. It was not yet my time to join my ancestors."

"Pompous zealot asshole."

The broadcast wasn't an interview, but a replay of a planetwide address given on Lumeria by Prime Minister Drassul hours after the assassinations.

"Our hearts go out to those who've lost loved ones this day. Agala will watch over them." With an orange finger, he pointed as if speaking to someone in front of him. "The criminals who shed blood on what was supposed to be a day of peace and reconciliation will be found and punished. I will personally lead the efforts. No one is beyond the reach of Lumeria and Agala's eyes. They will be caught and brought to justice. I promise you, citizens of Lumeria, we are blessed. Our God will never forsake us." Arms held wide, Prime Minister Drassul spun in a circle. "I'm proof Agala protects those who honor and serve him."

Zion clicked off the telecommunicator, tossing the remote on the bed. He wanted to throw it, and his fist, in Prime Minister Drassul's arrogant face. How stupid did a person have to be to swallow that man's bullshit?

Zion didn't know why he cared about the fate of the young chief magistrate, beyond the fact that he wanted to believe that not everyone who'd gone to Meleris to help stop a war had found themselves on the other end of some sicko's gun. Maybe he cared because the chief magistrate was a woman and, like his detective father, Zion hated to see a person hurt, especially women and children. Or his concern could've stemmed from the thought of how terrified the chief magistrate must've been when confronted with her own mortality. He would like to think she survived.

Zion grabbed the remote again and turned on the unit. Five channels later, his persistence paid off. The video footage was taken from behind a group of quickly walking Asiyans. Surrounded by four bodyguards—High Stars— was the Asiyan chief magistrate. Unlike the last time he'd seen her, she didn't wear her cloak. She was petite. Tiny, compared to Iman, who was nearly six feet tall. If the chief magistrate's hair was height, the Asiyan would be eight feet tall. Whether her hair was silver or gray, he couldn't tell from the awkward angle of the recording and the angry male Asiyan bodyguard who shoved the reporting crew away from his chief magistrate.

Anyone who watched the video footage knew exactly what the bodyguard had said, even without the use of a translating zot or closed captioning—Get the hell away from her. She's been through enough.

The chief magistrate turned, a subtle shift to nod at the female bodyguard to her left. The High Star slipped from her black coat and held it over her chief magistrate's head.

A subtle shift and for only seconds, but Zion had glimpsed the woman's face. *If that chief magistrate is in her early thirties then I am as old as Methuselah. She could be one of Sage's tenth-grade girlfriends. No way is that the same person who was hidden under the chief magistrate's cloak. Yet it must be her.*

In a room of twenty people—delegates, bodyguards, aides, and secretaries, only two had exited alive.

Lumerian.

Asiyan.

Zion slipped into his boxers and undershirt then pulled up the Inter Solar System Peace Mediators' Codes of Conduct on his zot.

Iman is right. I need to focus. If the chief magistrate, as young as she is, can survive an assassination attempt then I can damn well pass all three parts of an exam.

Apion Solar System
Nikogeus Moonbase

Ochill's moonrulic covered his fragrant green skin and the starry night sky design that ran from his face and down his body. Lorracon, a water Malcareon, also wore her moonrulic. The tight suit fit her curvy form to distracting perfection.

"We shouldn't have stopped," Ochill complained.

"We need supplies, fuel, and a doctor for your brother."

"You expect to find all of that in here?" Ochill waved a hand, a wide gesture that took in the crowded bar. "We're more likely to catch a disease in here than find a healer who can help Gronac."

Lorracon had already found a mark. At a table across from where Quill and Ochill stood at the bar, Lorracon flirted with a small group of humans. *Lust and desire, so easy for her to entice*

*the fools with the blackness of her eyes, the blue sparkles of her
face, and the milky white of her full lips.*

Every time Quill came to this bar, he saw more humans there.
The scrawny race wasn't good for much, but their eyes were delicious, and they could be great sources of information. Lorracon
would find out what she could from them.

In the meantime, Quill could use a quick drink. They may have
had to stop, but Quill had worked in this business too long not to
trust his instincts. He'd felt followed ever since leaving Lumeria.
The gunboat's sensors had detected nothing, no more than his
eyes had seen another ship. But his tail itched, a sure sign that
something wasn't right.

Taking the drink from the bartender, Quill slid a Nova Silver
coin to the Bhorant, the payment much more than the price of
the ale. He watched as one of the bartender's cephalopod limbs
hovered over the coin, while the other seven limbs continued to
make drinks for other customers. Quill had eaten a Bhorant or
two in the past. When dipped in hot but'aon, their limbs were
worth the hassle of killing one.

"We need a doctor, healer, anyone who knows how to tend
to knife wounds without killing the patient while doing it."

The limb over the coin lowered but didn't take the money.

Bhorants were the rare race who, while they had a head, possessed no mouth. They were telepaths, who instantly learned
the language of any mind they touched with their telepathy. So,
Quill knew the mollusk understood him.

"We don't want trouble. Go. Now."

"We don't want trouble either." Quill downed his drink and
slammed the glass onto the scarred wood surface of the bar
when he finished. "We'll go when we're ready. I said we're in
need of a doctor. Point one out to us, and we'll leave your bar in
the same condition we found it."

Quill sensed an impatient Ochill at his back. They'd left
Derian, the air Malcareon, in the gunboat with Gronac. She'd
tended to his wounds as best she could, but none of them knew

much about caring for the sick and wounded. The first aid kit on the ship had been better than nothing. The meager contents were good enough for Derian to stop her brother's bleeding, cauterize his wound and minimize his pain. Ironically, perhaps even humorously, the fire Malcareon had a fever. He'd been feverish for days. So while no one had wanted to stop until they'd put many more solar systems between them and Meleris, Gronac wouldn't last another five days without medical help.

Not for the first time, Quill cursed having gotten involved with Lumis. Not only had their mission not gone according to plan, the old batchul had stiffed him on his payment. His fault for not checking the electronic transfer before leaving Lumeria. That was fine. Once Gronac was back on his feet, Quill would pay Lady Junoid a visit she would never forget.

"Fuel, food, doctor. That's all we need."

"Go. Now. We want no trouble."

"What did he say?" Ochill asked.

"He wants us to leave." To the Bhorant, Quill asked, "Why do you keep saying you don't want trouble? There won't be any, if you help us. I have another Nova Silver coin for your trouble."

White, bulbous eyes lifted to the second floor. Quill turned, his hand immediately going to the gun strapped to his thigh. Scanning the balcony, he saw nothing out of the ordinary. People gyrated against each other to the hard, pounding beat of technotronic music.

Quill and Ochill moved to stand back-to-back. They searched the bar, looking for whatever frightened the bartender because he sure as fulk knew it wasn't them. But he saw nothing to justify the itching of his tail or the thudding of his heart.

"Lorracon," Ochill called to his sister.

One of the human's hands was on her waist, while the other was on a part of her body that would've cost him his life had Gronac been there.

"They're no help. Leave them."

Peeling herself from the frowning human, Lorracon strolled away from her admirers, a smile on her face and several Celestial Gold cards fisted in her hand. Depending on how much money was on each card, it may be enough to buy a doctor's services and whatever else they needed while on the moonbase. One thing was for sure, they would have to go to the more upscale parts of Nikogeus, if they hoped to find someone to help Gronac.

Quill had assumed he could find a doctor slumming it in Lower Nikogeus. Normally, that would've been the case. The rich and pompous, like Drassul and Junoid, thought themselves better than everyone else. When it came down to it, though, the likes of the Lumis and those who lived in Upper Nikogeus, were no different from Quill and his crew. They all stank of sewer water.

The music screeched to a halt. People on both levels rushed toward the exit. They didn't run but the impromptu evacuation had been swift. So fast and unexpected, it took Quill, Lorracon, and Ochill precious minutes to respond.

Lorracon sidled up to Ochill. "What's going on? Why did they leave?"

"I don't know." Ochill grabbed his sister's hand. "And I don't intend on staying around here long enough to find out. Let's go."

Ochill ran with Lorracon to the heavy-duty metal doors. "Let's go, Quill," Ochill yelled. "We need to get out of here. I have a bad feeling about this."

Quill's tail itched to the point of pain. He hadn't moved, but he did grip his gun harder.

"Fulk, the door is locked. I need your help, Quill. Get over here."

That got Quill moving. Throwing his weight into doors that should open automatically, he pushed with all his strength.

Nothing.

"Stand back." Quill pulled his gun from his shoulder holster and shot at the closed doors. "Fulk, that's not working. We need more firepower."

"Together then." Lorracon let loose a round of laser fire into the doors.

Quill and Ochill added theirs to hers. They kept firing.

"Guns on max. Don't stop until we bring these doors down." No matter what, Quill would get out of there, even if he had to drain the energy in his weapon to zero.

Something above them creaked . . . moved.

"Get out of the way," Lorracon yelled.

Quill dove to the side.

Something loud dropped from the ceiling.

Quill turned over to see what had nearly crushed him. He stared at a security gate. One of the reasons Quill was an assassin instead of a burglar, like his two older sisters, was gates like this one. They were used in prisons and in the homes of the rich and pompous. The bar wasn't either, but it was owned by a notorious drug dealer.

Quill watched as Lorracon clutched shaking hands to her chest and took deep breaths. "I'll call Derian. She can get us out of here."

"With what? Unless she levels this place with the gunboat, there's nothing we have on our ship that can get through the doors or the gate."

"I'm calling her anyway. We must do something. We have to . . ." Lorracon's hand dropped from where she'd been searching for her mobile zot in her boot, and her eyes traveled upward to the balcony.

Quill followed her gaze. In an instant, he was on his feet and his weapon aimed at three figures on the balcony. In the same way he had recognized the Pavise 5.0 security gate, Quill had known the itching of his tail had been a warning. It no longer itched, though.

Why should it? The danger has finally revealed itself.

The last time he'd seen them, they had been preoccupied with their dying regent. Walking past a group of trained killers hadn't been the escape he'd planned, but the Paladins had blown the doors open. So, he and his crew had taken advantage of Drassul's illusion one more time.

Gone was the black body armor he'd last seen them wearing. Quill aimed at the High Star in the center—the biggest target among a group whose small stature made them no less deadly. The high-speed fusion pistol in his hand had left a spray of brains and blood on the meeting room floor when he'd shot the two High Stars. He had known he would have to be quick. But he needn't have worried about the Paladins. The eyes of Agala had done their job well. All Quill had to do was point and shoot at the unmoving and vulnerable targets.

But there were no Agala's eyes in the bar, no more than the High Stars wore the black body armor his gun could slice through with ease. Instead, they wore robot-like armor. Sharp-looking claws extended from a metal body, onto which a gravity equalizer gun was attached. On the forearm of the other hand was a fusion laser shooter, glowing white from a full charge. A bird's face marked their metal helmets and their long hair was protected by the same robotic armor.

Pistol on max, Quill shot at the Paladins. Ochill and Lorracon followed his lead.

Hits landed, so they kept firing.

The Paladins took everything Quill, Ochill, and Lorracon threw at them. It still wasn't enough.

"Fulk," he roared.

"We need to get out of here." Ochill grabbed Lorracon's hand. "We'll find us another exit."

They took off running.

Quill kept up the assault. Over and again, he shot at the High Stars, while they stood looking down at him but doing nothing to defend themselves. They didn't have to, since Quill's weapon had proven useless against their full-body armor. Useless but also out of energy.

He dropped the powerless gun to the floor and raised his arms in surrender.

Quill smiled. "Honorable warriors of Asiya," he yelled up to them, hoping their armor was equipped with a translating zot. "Why fight, when we can be allies? Why fight, when I'm only a hired gun?"

Quill wouldn't lie for the Lumis, not when telling the truth was a better strategy for escaping this bar with his life. The Paladins' presence on Nikogeus was proof enough they knew he and his crew had killed their regent. Gronac should've taken care of the baby chief magistrate when he'd had the chance. If not for her, the Paladins wouldn't have known who to look for. As soon as the chief magistrate had walked up to his table in Drassul's ball-room, the specs of the Temple of Agala on the zot in front of him, he knew she would be trouble. He'd barely had time to remove the zot out of view before she'd stopped and spoken.

"In exchange for letting us go, I'll tell you everything you want to know. I'm unarmed." Quill turned in a complete circuit, letting them see he had no other weapon.

He kept a knife in his right boot and a small gun in his left, neither of which would do him any good.

Quill heard approaching footsteps, but he didn't dare turn his back on the Paladins.

"No back door," Ochill said from behind him. "There are a few windows on the east and west sides of the bar and in the bathrooms, but they're too small to climb through. No way out other than the front door. I hope you have a plan. If not, we're fulked."

Gruls knew how to wiggle themselves out of tight spots. The difference between Asiyans, especially Paladins, and Gruls was a matter of honor. Gruls had none, while Asiyans possessed too much.

Quill stepped forward, making sure to keep his hands where the Paladins could see them. "I'm unarmed. And my associates' weapons can't harm you. If you shoot us, it'll be murder. Paladins fight for innocents. They only kill enemies. We're no threat to you. But we could be of use. We'll tell you all about the plot to kill the Amakan leader and the others."

Quill glanced over his shoulder at Lorracon. He nodded in the direction of the bar. The Bhorant had to have a release mechanism behind the bar that controlled the security gate and doors. He wished he would've thought of it sooner.

When Lorracon didn't immediately move, he thought she may not have understood. But when he nodded to the bar again, her eyes widened with dawning clarity. Slowly, she backed away from Quill and Ochill, her arms, like his, held high.

He turned back to the Paladins. Just as he'd thought, they hadn't moved to stop Lorracon.

Fools. The woman is a killer. If given a chance, she would slit your throats and drink ale from your skulls.

There was no place in this hard, unforgiving universe for honorable warriors. It was either kill or be killed. *Survival of the fittest.* Smirking, Quill opened his mouth to repeat his offer. First and foremost, Asiyans were peacekeepers. Paladins followed strict codes of military engagement.

The security gate began its ascent. Lorracon had found the release switch. All Quill had to do was keep talking, keep reminding the Paladins he and the others weren't a threat and could provide them with enough evidence on the Lumis' involvement in the assassination plot to send them back to Lumeria and after Drassul and Junoid.

I can do this. I can get us safely out of here. "In exchange for letting us go—"

Pop.

Thud.

"No, Lorra . . ." Ochill screamed and took off toward his sister.

Pop.

Thud.

What the fulk? No, this can't be happening. Paladins don't kill in cold blood. They don't . . . Quill reached for the gun in his boot. *I won't die in this bar. Not like this. Not—*

Pop. Pop. Pop.

13. Truth and Lies

Two Days Earlier

Lela sat at the conference room table aboard the peace cruiser. The High Stars occupied the seats across from her. Each held a hard copy of Mosi's updated report. The printout had been a waste of paper, but the too-fleeting act had taken her mind off bloody truths.

"I don't know what I was thinking when I let you leave the Temple of Agala without your cloak as covering. Regent Etemaad told me . . ." Gayora trailed off, frowning.

They hadn't spoken the regent's name in days, although his murder had driven them from Vargan space into the vast cosmos and after dangerous criminals.

Closing her eyes for a moment, Lela massaged her temples, feeling a shallow thrum of pain. "What did he tell you?"

"He told us all," Orit replied instead of Gayora, "to protect your identity. Banou told us the same."

Her hands dropped from her temples and she focused on Orit. "You spoke with the former chief magistrate. When? Why?"

Orit looked to Waafir, who sat next to each other. The besiegers then turned to Gayora and Rahm to their right.

"I don't care which of you answers my question, as long as someone does."

Turning over the report and placing it on the table in front of her, Gayora cleared her throat. "After we were assigned as your High Stars, Banou and Regent Etemaad summoned us to the Council of Magistrates' Ruling Chamber."

"We didn't question the order. We simply complied," Rahm said, and the other three High Stars nodded.

Lela understood such blind, trusting obedience. It was the way of their people. They were critical thinkers, but they relied on, perhaps they were even controlled by, adherence to strict rules and procedures. Order undergirded their lifestyle, almost as much as they were driven by their core values of purpose, faith, and truth.

Another value drove them now—a deadly purpose unbecoming of peacekeepers. It lurked within them, parasites feasting off blood curdled from the sickening sight of Beres's and Kondo's bodies. The top half of their heads had been reduced to unspeakable bits and pieces. The Paladins had transported the bodies back to the shuttle, but they'd had to leave parts of their friends behind.

Lela despised leaving any part of Beres and Kondo in that wretched temple on Meleris. She couldn't change the past. But she would discover the truth from the miasma of lies that had been the peace talks.

First, she needed to listen and understand her High Stars' truth.

"Banou and Regent Etemaad stressed the importance of maintaining a low profile." Gayora inclined her head toward Lela. "Even for an Asiyan, you appear younger than your anulls. Regent Etemaad wanted to reduce the preconceived notions that often accompany thoughts of youth."

Orit, who had tended to Lela's wounds, leaned his forearms on the table, shoulders hunched. "No one who has ever spoken to you, Chief Magistrate, would think your thought process anything other than that of a fully formed adult. We certainly do. But Banou and Regent Etemaad were correct. Naïve, innocent, and sweet, those words came to mind when I first saw you at the Hall of Concord."

Lela searched the faces of each Paladin, concluding they shared Orit's opinion. Unless this mission went terribly wrong or Yusef followed through on his threat to have their High Star insignias revoked, the five of them would be together for many anulls. So, she granted her High Stars a rare privilege—an opportunity to speak openly, honestly, and without offense or punishment.

"Speak your truth of your opinion of your chief magistrate." The insecure girl within asked: Have I proven to be a disappointment? Do you view me as a failure? Am I worthy of your loyalty and trust?

Again, they looked to each other before one of them deigned to respond to a statement posed to Orit but was an implied question intended for them all.

Unsurprisingly, Gayora led. "We are all more than we appear, Chief Magistrate. Sometimes, we are also less. Whether those two points are positive or negative depends on the person, the perception, and the circumstances. We should not be seated at this table with you. I admit, it makes us uncomfortable."

"It was not my intention to create discomfort."

Waafir, who smiled more than any of her other High Stars, granted her one that reached his eyes and touched her heart. "This is the kind of discomfort we gladly accept. Every chief magistrate and their security team forms their bond in their own way. Apparently, this is yours."

Lela didn't have a calculated method of forming bonds. How she treated the Paladins wasn't a strategic plan executed to yield the greatest effect. Lela cared little for arbitrary barriers, such as rank, not when such divisions stifled creativity and minimized participation.

"I neither have all the answers nor can I complete this mission on my own. Paladin or Verity, Chief Magistrate or High Star, none of those distinctions matter, not when the Fates call us home. Or when you are a killer's next target."

Lela lowered her hands from the table to her lap, where she could hide the small tremors in her hands that came whenever she talked about or thought of her near-death experience.

"None of us knows all, but what we do know, thanks to Chief Magistrate Mosi's researchers, is the name and long illegal career of the Grul."

While Mosi's research team had yet to find image matches of the Malcareons, they had little trouble finding a match for Quill Machelete Nomont of Tsondelar, age forty-six. His father had been killed trying to escape from a workhouse prison. His mother still lived on Tsondelar, as did two of Quill's younger brothers. His older sisters, like their brother, had an extensive criminal record that spanned several planets. The siblings were on the Interplanetary Most Wanted List, an astronomical bounty on their heads—Quill's the most.

"We know where Quill was last seen."

"Nikogeus Moonbase," Orit said. "With a wounded Malcareon, they'll have to stop soon, unless they don't intend on seeking medical assistance."

Lela recalled the Malcareons' physical closeness in the ballroom of Prime Minister Drassul's complex. She had no idea whether Gayora was correct about them having an incestuous relationship, and she didn't need to know. Such knowledge wouldn't change the conclusion she'd drawn about them the evening she'd seen them huddled together.

They love each other. That's the one truth I detected at a table of liars.

"Even if the Grul doesn't care about the fire Malcareon, his siblings do. I agree, Orit, I believe, after several days of flying through space, they'll land soon."

Gayora activated the flux visualizer in the center of the conference table. A three-dimensional holographic image of the current solar system beamed from the clear rectangular prism.

Gayora changed the brightness, saturation, and tint of the flux visualizer, helping to bring the ship they followed and the surrounding space into clearer focus.

"I'm concerned," Rahm said, "if we follow them for much longer, they'll detect our presence. We've been lucky they haven't already."

"Old gunboat, old tech. Gayora," Waafir said, "how far away from Nikogeus Moonbase are we?"

"At the speed we're going, two days. If we execute Chief Magistrate Lela's plan, we can reach the Apion Solar System in half that time."

Gayora minimized the projection, and the High Stars shifted their focus to Lela.

"I know it's a risk," she said, giving voice to their unspoken concern. "If I'm wrong, we may never find Quill and the Malcareons again."

And that was assuming the gunboat carried the group of five.

"Rushing ahead to Nikogeus is a huge risk," Rahm agreed. "So would be getting into a firefight with an armored gunboat. If we're right, we'll have the element of surprise."

"But if we're wrong," Gayora said, fingers laced in front of her, "we'll never forgive ourselves for letting the killers of our regent and friends escape what is due them."

What was due them. Funny how the mind sought to protect self-created delusions, even for Paladins.

Lela ignored her own self-delusions. Instead, she concentrated on ending this mission without losing anyone at the table. Her security team saw to her safety. But did she not owe Gayora, Orit, Rahm, and Waafir the same? Their families? Yusef?

She could command them to execute her plan. They would consent, if she demanded it of them. Yusef would've done so, if he was there, as would have Regent Etemaad. Urges of all kinds lived inside Lela, but none of them would have her denying the Paladins the right to choose their fate. So, without interference from her, she permitted them to debate her plan.

Nenet had once told Lela that there was a kind of wisdom found in silence. From Lela's experience, that could indeed be the case, if silence was also accompanied by listening.

"Watch and listen," Regent Etemaad had told Lela. She hadn't done either enough. Watch and listen. She was listening now—too late. Watch and listen. What had she observed, since leaving Asiya? What could she still not see?

"This is not how it's done, Chief Magistrate." Gayora pulled up the flux visualizer again. "Display Nikogeus Moonbase."

The visual appeared, and they stared at the still image. Prefect Norcana governed the moonbase. Lela had full confidence she could coordinate efforts with the government official. Together, they could ensure the Grul and Malcareons paid for their crimes. Prefect Norcana would have five fewer criminals who used her region as a safe harbor.

"You'll allow Prefect Norcana to take credit for what we'll do?" Gayora asked.

"Yes. We neither want the recognition nor need the bounties. The prefect can claim both. They will make for fine bargaining tools."

"I agree." Gayora stood, as did the others. "I mean *we* agree. You do not owe this to us, Chief Magistrate. We are responsible for reclaiming our pride and honor."

"There can be neither, for any of us, as long as those who trespassed against Asiya are free to kill again. We will not allow that to happen. You will have your justice, and I will have my truth. Are we agreed then?"

"Yes," they answered in unison.

"Good. Thank you. If you'll excuse me, I need to introduce myself to Prefect Norcana."

"And we have our Ibor armor to prepare." Gayora followed the procession of High Stars toward the conference room door, stopping when it opened and everyone else filed out. "Voice only, no video," Gayora reminded Lela.

"Yes, I know."

"It was stained with blood, that's why I didn't return your cloak. I assume that was the same reason you left it behind."

"Among others, yes."

Lela grasped Banou's and Etemaad's concern about perceptions, as well as their intention to minimize Lela's exposure to those who would seek to manipulate or harm her. Despite their best efforts, she had still been targeted. Hiding hadn't stopped someone from wanting her dead.

Lela hadn't been thinking clearly when she'd left the temple. Reporters, soldiers, and onlookers had swarmed the area. It was then she had realized how exposed she'd left herself. Thanks to Gayora's quick thinking and black coat, Lela had been able to conceal her identity the rest of the route to the shuttle.

Gayora's presence in the threshold kept the automatic door from closing and Lela from using the telecommunication system to contact Prefect Norcana. They had a short window of opportunity to act on her plan, meaning whatever was on her shadow's mind needed addressing before they could proceed.

"You may speak freely."

Gayora stepped inside, and the door closed. She remained where she was, though, shoulders squared and back straight.

"You dream."

Gayora had spoken the two-word sentence with the reverence Lela had sought to avoid her entire life. Few people knew she was a dreamer. Lela would like to keep it that way, not that she feared Gayora would speak of it to anyone else. She was her shadow. At this point, Lela doubted she had any secrets Gayora hadn't discovered. Thanks to Ammon, Gayora even knew how close they had become.

The thought of Ammon warmed Lela, as much as it saddened her. She couldn't display weakness in front of her High Stars. But, oh, Lela craved Ammon's loving, assured touch. She desired nothing more than to cast aside her mask and fall into his strong embrace. Ammon would understand. He wouldn't judge. With him, Lela could be her authentic self. That Lela, however, wasn't who was required to accomplish the task she'd given herself . . . the task the Council expected her to successfully complete.

Naïve, innocent, and sweet. Perhaps there had been more than a shred of truth to Waafir's first impression of Lela.

"I can tell you have more to say. Proceed."

Apparently, Gayora required no additional prompting. "Do the Fates come to you in your dreams?"

"Yes." Lela wouldn't elaborate, even if Gayora probed further.

"We had to put everything in our reports to the Council."

"As well you should have." Lela had as well, including Regent Etemaad's dying wish. But . . . "We will not speak of it. Now is not the time."

Gayora parted her lips but didn't utter a word. She needn't have, though, for her action delivered the same message.

High Star Gayora of the House of Vilmaris lowered her head and torso before turning on her booted heels and exiting the conference room. Not the customary head bow to a chief magistrate but a half-body bow to a regent.

Another must be chosen as Regent Etemaad's successor, perhaps Reth or Chiku. Maybe even Yusef. Any of the chief magistrates would make a fine Regent of Asiya. Any of them except for Lela.

I am not Etemaad's blood-chosen heir.

A self-delusion—the lie she told herself because the truth was so much more frightening to accept.

Apion Solar System
Nikogeus Detention Center

"This is your doing, isn't it?"

The air Malcareon pressed midnight blue palms to a clear wall that separated her from Lela. White swirls of electrical energy sparked from those hands, leaping from fingers to neck. The energy ignited the white swirls on her cheeks and forehead that framed a blue-black face and white lips set in a tense, flat line.

"You were behind the raid on our gunboat by Nikogeus constables. They're never around when anyone needs them. But they stormed our ship, took me and Gronac in custody, like they knew to expect our arrival on the moonbase. They came right after the others left. Not a coincidence, but your doing. Isn't that right?"

The white swirls on the air Malcareon's face and hands darkened, flowing like a leaf blowing in the wind. Her hand slammed against the cell wall, over and again. White tears formed in black eyes, dripped onto the blue-black canvas of her face and created thick pink lines between the white swirls.

"Don't just stand there hiding under your cloak." *Slam.* "You're the reason I'm in this cell." *Slam.* "No one else is in this section with me." *Slam.* "Cell after cell. Empty." *Slam.* "There's bright light everywhere. You can see me, but I can't see you." *Slam.* "Say something. Don't just stand there. Say something, you fulking batchul."

Lela touched the wall of the see-through cell but said nothing, not even when the air Malcareon manifested a likeness of the fire Malcareon in the palm of her hand—his lower torso submerged in flickering flames. The air Malcareon stared at her creation. More pink blossomed on the parts of the Malcareon's body Lela could see—her face and hands, although she didn't doubt the color was the same under her moonrulic suit. The pink on her lips added soft layers to her face.

"Where did those constables take Gronac? Tell me!"

Lela lowered her hand from the cell wall, while using the other to remove her hood. She may have left her chief magistrate's robe on Meleris, but cloaks were essential to every Asiyan wardrobe. After the incident with the Drutain news reporters, she had promised Gayora to wear a cloak in public.

"No one else is in this detention center. For the time we are on Nikogeus, this building belongs to Asiya."

"You mean it belongs to you and your High Stars." The air Malcareon blew on the image of Gronac, extinguishing his likeness. Shifting pupilless eyes to Lela, she crinkled her nose and twisted her lips in a sneer. "Gronac should've blown your brains out when he had the chance. He thought you a doll. A doll he wanted to break with his bare hands before setting on fire."

That was his mistake. He should've left his glove on. If he had, neither of us would be here.

"I'm not a doll, although, if you wish, we can spend time discussing toys of our youth or," Lela began then walked away from the cell and sat in an observation chair ten feet away to continue, "you can tell me about the plot to kill the peace delegates."

"Fulk you. I'm not telling you anything. Where's Gronac? What have you done with my brother? Where's Lorracon and Ochill?"

"I believe we have information the other wants."

"This isn't a game. Gronac is dying." A hand came up and slammed into the wall again. "You took his hand and nearly his arm."

Lela had also stabbed him in the chest. From the sound he'd made, it must've hurt worse than the hand she hadn't, at the time, realized she'd sliced off.

"The hand that wanted to break a doll." Lela nodded, more to herself than to the female shifting from dark blue to black. "Yes, I defended myself the way any sane person would have. The way you would have, if someone tried to kill you. Self-preservation. I believe you and your siblings are the last of your race."

"Are you threatening me?"

"No, I was merely stating a fact. An unfortunate truth, but a truth all the same. The final memory of a race should not hinge on the violent actions of four individuals. Yet you and your siblings have ensured that fate."

"Shut up!"

Now that they'd found the mercenaries, the sense of urgency that had driven Lela for over a welk began to subside. Her tension headache remained, as did her grief and anger. Yet, with this Malcareon, she could afford patience. The truth would eventually find its way to the light.

"If you're going to have your High Stars torture me, then get on with it."

"Your calm voice doesn't betray your fear at the prospect of torture, but your face and hands do. Pink is such a lovely color, although I prefer purple. On you, Derian . . ." Lela paused. "May I call you Derian? That is your name, isn't it? I heard the fire Malcareon . . . I mean . . . I heard Gronac yell your name when Prefect

Norcana's constables dragged him from the gunboat. He's quite the protective male, even when weak." Lela leaned forward in the chair and returned Derian's unyielding stare. "Paladins are honorable warriors. They do not torture. They hunt. They fight. They kill. But they do not torture."

"Then you might as well leave, Asiyan, because I have nothing to say to you."

Derian glanced around the empty holding cell, turning in a complete circle before locking her eyes on Lela again.

"It's only the two of us. I have nothing but time. Gronac does not."

"Is that a threat? Are you planning on killing him, if I don't cooperate? You're of the Verity Band, tell me the truth. You can't lie."

That was a typical off-worlder's interpretation of what it meant to be Verity. Members of her band could lie. There was nothing physical, technological, or otherwise that prevented them from doing so. Verity chose to live a life of truth. Couldn't and wouldn't weren't synonymous. The difference was significant to Lela. If Derian understood what it meant to be Verity, the distinction would be significant to her as well.

"We Verity do believe in the truth. We also believe in a fair exchange of truths. Truths are our currency. They are free but also costly. Costly to share and costly to keep." Relaxing her back against the chair's rails, hands in her lap, Lela spoke the absolute truth. "No, I do not plan on killing Gronac as a punishment for your lack of cooperation."

Light pink lines formed on Derian's hands. "Do you plan on killing me whether I cooperate or not?"

"Those are two questions framed as one, although a single word, if the answers are the same, could satisfy both." Closing her eyes, Lela took stock of her breathing. Measured. Her heart. Steady. Her mind. Focused.

"What else? Why are you just sitting there?"

"Truths as currency," Lela said, opening her eyes. "I've given you a truth, but you've yet to enter into a fair exchange. Until you do, you'll receive no other truths from me."

The faint lines of pink disappeared, leaving only ashen swirls and a dull blue-black. The longer Lela observed the air Malcareon, fists balled and nostrils flared, the more she wondered about the use of the moonrulic. She'd assumed the Malcareons wore the suits to protect their elemental bodies from whatever existed in foreign environments that could harm them. While that may be true for Malcareons, as it was for every race at some point, depending on the planet they visited, Lela formed a hypothesis in need of testing.

She stood but didn't move closer to the cell. With the bright lights, she could see the blue, black, and white of the air Malcareon perfectly fine. But there was no pink.

"Are you a Malcareon?"

Derian halted her pacing. "What kind of stupid question is that?"

Not an answer to Lela's question but a data point. A slither of pink had appeared on Derian's lips, even before she'd responded to her question.

"Are you currently locked in a cell in a detention center on Nikogeus?"

"Have you lost your senses, Asiyan?"

Another blush of pink and a second data point.

"Are you a fire Malcareon like Gronac?"

This time, the female stomped to the wall, slammed her palms against it, and glared at her.

Lela searched Derian's face and hands. *No pink.*

"Even when a person doesn't wish to answer a question posed to them," her father had once told her, "the answer will come to their mind. For most races, the brain's natural tendency is to seek answers we know we possess. It's our default. Unless we are trained to suppress that part of ourselves, we have little control over that function of our brain. What we do have control over, Lela, is what we choose to do with the information our mind retrieves. Ask and they will answer, even if only to themselves. Ask, and the truth will be revealed."

Quite true. But the right type of question was required. Open-ended ones wouldn't yield results, not with the Malcareon. As Lela told her, Paladins did not use torture as a strategy for punishment or interrogation. While torture contradicted Paladins' moral code, they had a more practical reason for not employing torture as a method of soliciting truthful responses. Quite simply, information gained from torture was unreliable. When under duress, one was equally as likely to tell the truth as to tell a lie to stop the source of pain.

Lela retook her seat. "Gayora," she said, knowing her shadow was listening to everything from the security office, "turn off the lights in holding cell 48A but leave on the audio translator."

"Who are you talking to? Don't turn off the light. Don't—"

Darkness descended.

"Turn them back on."

"You sound afraid. I think I even heard a tremor in your voice. If I'm not mistaken, Malcareons can see in the dark."

There it is. A pink line appeared between a white swirl on Derian's forehead. With the lights off, Lela could better see Derian's colorful body, especially her pink lines. *Pink, the color of her truth.*

"Were you hired to kill President Theimos 105?"

No answer. Pink line.

"Were you hired to kill Alder Larchfern, Unbalk leader of Shin?"

"No."

Another pink line appeared on her forehead.

"Were you hired to kill High Colonel Zirlat of Wither?"

"No. I wasn't hired to kill anyone. I'm not a killer."

Yet another pink line formed. *Hypothesis confirmed.* Lela only needed to pose the right questions, and she would have her answers. Her father was correct. The mouth lied but the mind told the truth.

"Were you hired to kill Regent Etemaad of Asiya?"

"No."

"Were you hired to kill Chief Magistrate Lela of Asiya?"

"No. I told you, I'm not a killer."

Two negative responses, more pink lines.

"Turn on the lights." Spittle flew and fists pounded against the see-through wall. "Turn them on now."

"Why? So you can hide in the light?"

"I'm not hiding, and you have no right to keep me here. Where's my family?"

"I'll tell you after you answer all of my questions."

"I have nothing else to say to you." The female stomped to the other side of the cell.

The security cameras would pick up every angle of the female, so her position in the cell mattered not. All Lela had to do was ask yes or no questions. The air Malcareon's anatomy would do the rest.

Lela took a deep breath then released it slowly. She had a mental list of questions she needed to reframe into closed-ended questions.

"Are you a hired assassin? Do you work with your siblings to kill people for money? Do you work with Quill Machelete Nomont of Tsondelar to kill people for money?"

After each question, Lela paused, giving the air Malcareon's body time to physically react and the cameras an opportunity to record her colorful responses.

The female slumped to the floor, her back to Lela and blue hair pulled atop her head.

"I can hide my hands and face, so you can't see them."

"You can try, but I wouldn't recommend that course of action."

"I thought you said Paladins don't torture people."

"They don't. But Gayora will strip that moonrulic off you, if she must. I suggest you not give my High Star a reason to join you in there. You are, after all, partly responsible for the deaths of our regent and two Paladins. By Asiyan law, you've forfeited your life, as did the Grul and your siblings."

"Y-you k-killed them?" She stumbled to her feet, dark face awash in bright white swirls intermixed with dark pink lines. "Tell me the truth."

"I have. I've spoken only truthfully while you've spewed lie after lie."

"No, you sit there all high and mighty, questioning me about a dead old man all the while knowing you killed my family."

Lela pushed to her feet, maintaining eye contact with the pink-blossomed face of the Malcareon. If anger was air, the room would be filled with Lela's.

"Confess your sins, Derian."

"Confess yours."

Eleven steps placed Lela in front of the holding cell. She pressed her hand to the cell wall and revealed her soul to a person undeserving of her honesty. "I've committed the sins of disobedience, impure thoughts, pride, selfishness . . ." Raising her other hand to the wall, Lela added in a whisper, "And hatred."

The Council could do with her confession what they would. Their reactions didn't quicken her pulse. The thought of committing more sins, worse than the ones she'd shared, plagued her sleeping and waking mind.

"I've confessed my sins. It's time you confessed yours."

"We should've killed you."

"Yes."

Midnight blue palms lifted. Blowing onto her right hand, the same image of the fire Malcareon . . . Gronac appeared. When she blew into her left hand, two images manifested in her palm—the earth and water Malcareons.

"If they are all dead, I have nothing left to live for. I'd rather die at the hand of your High Star than have you turn me over to Prefect Norcana. I don't want to spend the remainder of my life in a penitentiary crammed with the vilest criminals from every corner of the universe. Promise me, Chief Magistrate Lela of the Verity Band, that my death will be quick and that you'll bury me with my brothers and sister. I want your word."

Lela had promised Prefect Norcana the bounty on the Grul. She assumed there were similar bounties on the Malcareons, but the siblings, other than removing them from Nikogeus, weren't included in her agreement with the prefect.

"You have my vow."

The Malcareon's head fell forward, her hands dropped to her sides, the images disappearing, and she wept through her confession.

"We were hired by Prime Minister Drassul, via Lady Junoid, to kill everyone in the peace delegation. He used Regent Etemaad's desire to end the Lumerian-Amakan War to get close enough to the Amakan leader to kill him. Drassul also wanted to kill Regent

Etemaad to prevent Asiyans from further interfering in Lumerian affairs. To send a message to your people, Quill told us. Without your leader, Drassul thought Asiyans would retreat from the Vargan Solar System and never return."

Hands that had still been pressed against the wall, suddenly slipped with the buckling of Lela's knees. Like a flower wilting, she slid to the floor. Unlike Derian, Lela didn't cry. She wanted to, though. Fates help her, she wanted to sob and scream.

"It's those fulking eyes of Agala. They hypnotize. I don't know how or for how long. But they do. We were already in the temple meeting room when the delegates arrived. On the second floor. No one saw us, not even the guards who swept the room. They looked at but through us, as if we weren't there. That's the power of the hypnotic eyes. But you and Regent Etemaad weren't affected. I don't know why. Lady Junoid assured us that wasn't possible."

The Malcareon continued speaking, the hidden cameras catching her every word. But Lela had stopped listening. She barely noticed when Gayora entered the section.

"Come." Gayora took her by her elbow and helped her to her feet. "The others are waiting for you upstairs, Chief Magistrate. What comes next is not meant for your eyes. I do not wish you to see."

Death, the ultimate punishment.

Their eyes locked and two undeniable truths existed between them. One, Gayora would kill the air Malcareon, as she had Gronac. Two, Lela had sanctioned the deaths of the five mercenaries before she'd contacted the Council.

"Are you planning on killing him, if I don't cooperate?" Derian had asked Lela. She had answered in the negative. Lela hadn't lied. Verity did not lie. They also did not correct faulty thinking. The Malcareon had posed the wrong question.

A sad, unfortunate truth.

"Do you plan on killing me whether I cooperate or not?"

A much better question. Lela had deflected, although the truth to the Malcareon's query had been in other statements Lela had made. But fear blinded, just as hatred did.

Lela walked away from Gayora and Derian. She had five burial arrangements to make, a video to send to the Council, and the contents of her stomach to expel.

14. Five Votes, One Decision

Northeast Asiya
Regent Center of Khatra
Hall of Concord

"I've never seen the ruling chamber so full of people," Ammon whispered to his brother Gurion.

From his location on the viewing platform, with over two dozen Asiyans crammed on there with him, Ammon could see the entire chamber below. The Council hadn't yet arrived, but they were the only ones who hadn't.

"Neither have I. Elan and all of his High Star Cleavers are here." Gurion nodded in the direction of the Chief of Regent Security, standing at attention in his black Paladin-in-Arms uniform. Elan's cleavers formed a line along the perimeter of the room. "Luminaries and regional leaders. They're all here. The last time we all gathered like this it was for Lela's induction ceremony."

"You're right. This gathering is too much but also nothing like the night Lela was inducted into the Council."

Gurion's voice lowered. "Did you have an opportunity to read the report I gave you?"

"Yes." Ammon kept his response as vague as Gurion's question had been. Neither brother should've had access to Lela's official report to the Council, including the video confession from the air Malcareon and the footage of her security team's execution of the mercenaries.

"Can you feel it? The heat? The rage?"

Ammon nodded. His hands gripped the platform's railing, helping to remind him to stay rooted instead of dashing off to meet Lela's shuttle.

Gurion shifted, making room as more Asiyans joined them on the viewing platform. "Everything is changing so fast. Too fast. The Council should've waited to have this meeting. I know why they didn't, but . . . Lela's been gone for welks. An additional dole or two wouldn't have changed anything. Sometimes, Father is so focused on his goal he doesn't consider the ramifications of his decisions on others."

Lela's peace cruiser had landed in the Khatra spaceport a mere two herns ago. No doubt, Elan and Yusef had arranged for a shuttle to transport Lela and her High Stars to the Hall of Concord immediately, giving her no time to decompress from her ordeal before being thrown into the spotlight.

"Lela was informed about today's meeting, if you were wondering. Chiku made sure of it."

"Father shares everything with you but tells me next to nothing."

"No, Father tells me what he wants me to know. The rest I learn from hacking his computer and reading his encrypted files."

Ammon smiled. "And here Father thinks I'm the disobedient one."

"Father's insight is as amazing as his blindness is infuriating. Tread carefully, Ammon. The Council, no matter how they may appear from the outside, are experiencing a great upheaval."

"Because of Lela?"

"Because of Regent Etemaad. Lela is the center of the storm, but not for anything she has done. The Council will rally around her because to do otherwise would dishonor the regent's dying wish. You said you read the report, so you know of what I speak."

Lela had always been Etemaad's preferred successor, but the power to select the next Regent of Asiya did not fall to the current regent.

"The Rite of Rayla," Ammon said. "A Paladin blood oath ritual. Guardian, protector, that's what a regent is to our people."

"Lela sent the signet ring back with Gan and Ramona."

"I was unaware."

"We're on the cusp of war, and we have a chief magistrate who doesn't wish to be regent, and a Council torn over the right actions to take to ensure the future of Asiya."

The low hum of chatter filling the chamber receded to silence. The opening doors to the chamber had drawn everyone's attention.

"Take care, Ammon, Lela is not who she was when she left home. She is more. She is also less."

Gurion's final whispered words, spoken as Reth entered the chamber, caught Ammon off guard, not because he'd said them so close to his ear, but because he'd voiced his private fears.

Mosi, Chiku, and Yusef followed Reth into the chamber, wearing their purple and black robes but having foregone donning their hoods. One by one, the chief magistrates claimed their seat at the Table of Wisdom and Guidance. Two chairs remained.

Ammon recalled the last time he'd been in this room. Yusef had claimed his customary seat, while Regent Etemaad had sat in the chair reserved for the Chief Magistrate of the Verity Band, leaving his own vacant. Now, both of those chairs were empty.

No one spoke or moved. They all stared at the closed doors, including members of the Council.

Ammon felt unaccountably nervous—afraid even—though he had no idea why. Lela had survived. More, she had brought the murderous fiends to justice. Yet as the doors opened again, a disquieting sense of foreboding settled over him. It felt like a warning but one that came with the sad knowledge that the future could not be altered to produce a different result.

The doors opened fully.

Hands still on the railing, Ammon leaned forward, his sight unobstructed. If he hadn't known the assigned positions of Lela's High Stars, he wouldn't have been able to tell one from the other. Front, Rahm, High Star Shield. Back, Waafir, High Star Besieger. Right, Orit, High Star Besieger. Left, Gayora, High Star Shadow.

The Council stood, the only people in the room not stunned into immobility and silence.

Whereas the Council donned their chief magistrates' robes, a symbol of their position in Asiyan society, Lela wore a black full-length dress with a lavender cloak tied around her neck. Lavender, the same shade as the streaks in Regent Etemaad's coils but not the shade of purple worn by the Regent of Asiya.

Ammon glanced at the band around his right arm. The material was the same shade as Lela's cloak—pink lavender. Every other Asiyan in attendance wore the same shade of lavender somewhere on their person, for pink lavender was the color of mourning. But when combined with black, as in Lela's dress, it sent a deeper message.

Love and war.

Unsurprisingly, Yusef spoke first. "Welcome home, Chief Magistrate Lela."

Lela inclined her head, a respectful bow to her elder.

Her High Stars, despite being home, in the Hall of Concord and surrounded by friends and allies, maintained their protective shield around Lela. Their stance was made worse by their chosen attire.

Chief of Regent Security Elan strolled up to Rahm and placed a hand on his armored shoulder. "You do not need to wear the Ibor in here. You have served as the chief magistrate's shield well. She is safe."

When Rahm and the others failed to disengage their helmets, Ammon thought Elan would shift his attention to Gayora. He didn't. Instead, he backed away from the group. His gaze traveled to Yusef as he made his retreat.

Once more, the chamber descended into silence.

Lela stood in the center of her High Stars, face and eyes devoid of emotion. Ammon wished he could go to her, grab her in his arms and whisk her away from there. He couldn't, of course, but his heart raced and his skin heated at all she hid behind her mask.

"See what I mean," Gurion whispered. "She's more and less. Her High Stars have chosen her, and they've just let everyone know who they will fight and die for. If Lela doesn't accept the regency or the Council her, we could have a civil war on our hands. Look."

Ammon's gaze followed Gurion's pointing finger. Gan and Ramona, who'd been in the line of cleavers, left their posts. He watched, eyes wide, as the females strolled past Elan to join

Rahm. They flanked the High Star Shield, a silent but powerful pledge of allegiance.

Lela's head lowered. Despite her entrance, this moment wasn't about her, which she seemed to grasp when she said, "Chief Magistrate Chiku, would you and your Devdas Band lead us in a prayer for Regent Etemaad, High Star Beres, and High Star Kondo?"

"Of course."

Seven members of the Devdas Band stepped forward. Like Lela, everyone lowered their heads while Chiku and the seven Devdas recited an old, beloved prayer. When they finished, the strange tension in the room had subsided.

Lela's security team recalled their Ibor helmets then joined the line of cleavers. But few watched where the High Stars went. Most everyone's attention was focused on Lela as she approached the Table of Wisdom and Guidance.

Without a glance in the direction of the regent's chair, Lela strolled past it, seating herself in the chair reserved for the leader of the Verity Band.

Ammon sighed, unsure what the vacuum of space left by Regent Etemaad would mean for Lela, for him, indeed, for all of Asiya.

Without preamble, Reth said, "When Regent Etemaad was murdered our lives were forever changed. We wanted answers. Why? Who? Thanks to Chief Magistrate Lela and her High Stars, we have our answers. They are difficult truths to swallow and to keep down. But we've never feared the truth, or the actions needed to address them. And we won't now."

Reth reached over and covered Mosi's hand with his own. In turn, she patted his hand with her other.

Mosi's voice was no less firm when she spoke than Reth's had been. "What we will show is a confession from one of the mercenaries responsible for the deaths of our regent and Paladin brothers. We will not share this footage again or beyond this chamber. You will take the message of the Council back to your regions. Soon, all of Asiya will know what you will see this day."

Ammon couldn't see who turned on the telecommunication system, not that it mattered. Images appeared in front of the Council's table, a three-dimensional display of an air Malcareon in a see-through cell. A cloaked figure stood outside the cell. He had known it was Lela the moment he'd seen Gurion's stolen copy of the detention center's security footage. He hadn't needed the voice confirmation, although he'd smiled at hearing the familiar soft voice of his beloved.

Instead of watching the video again, Ammon observed Lela. While she sat facing his direction, her eyes remained downcast, hands folded on the table. Again, the urge to protect and comfort her warred with his common sense. His eyes fell to Hasani and Nenet, seated in the front rows of chairs at the end of the Council's table. Like Ammon, they only had eyes for Lela. They at least saw her the way he did, and the utter insensitivity of having this meeting so soon after her return. At most, she'd had time to go to her chamber and change before being escorted there.

"They edited the footage," Gurion said.

Ammon hadn't paid enough attention to notice.

"Lela's confession. Gayora's kill shot. Both were removed. This is a sanitized version of the truth."

Those two omissions didn't alter the essence of the footage. One deletion protected a female's honor, while the other spared the audience the grisly details of what it meant to be a Paladin warrior.

The temperature in the room, warm for all the bodies crammed within, seemed to decrease, degree by degree, as the air Malcareon described, in vivid detail, Prime Minister Drassul and Lady Junoid's assassination plan. With each truth revealed, the once silent audience was no longer quiet, no longer passive observers.

It began with the High Stars stomping their feet in a fast, rough cadence of soldiers marching onto a battlefield, their war cries echoed by Ammon and Gurion then all the Paladins in the chamber. Members of the other bands joined in. Their bellows bounced off the walls and back to them.

The Council stood. Everyone quieted, but nothing could quiet Ammon's surging heart.

An image of the regent appeared on the telecommunication system. In his purple and black robe and full of life, Regent Etemaad stared back at them.

In unison, the Council bowed deeply to their fallen leader. All around him Asiyans sobbed, and he wasn't surprised he did too.

Yusef was the first to rise from his bow. "I, Yusef of the Paladin Band, vote for war against the Lumerians. I am blade and armor."

Reth rose. "I, Reth of the Euridice Band, vote for war against the Lumerians. I am justice and law."

Mosi stood tall. "I, Mosi of the Affiq Band, vote for war against the Lumerians. I am knowledge and creativity."

Chiku straightened. "I, Chiku of the Devdas Band, vote for war against the Lumerians. I am fealty and faith."

Only Lela remained bowed at the waist. They waited, but she neither spoke nor moved.

Nenet pushed from her chair, but Hasani's hand halted her movement toward their daughter. Gayora appeared as if she too wanted to rush to Lela's side. Ammon certainly did, but Gurion's strong grip on his arm gave him pause.

"Lela will not break. Look at her. Really look at her. She's not shattering. She's angrier than anyone in this room."

At whom, though?

With a slowness contrary to her youth, Lela rose. In a booming voice Ammon hadn't known existed within her, she spoke. "I, Lela of the Verity Band, vote for war against the Lumerians. I am truth and wisdom." Stepping away from the table, she approached the image of Regent Etemaad. Once more, Lela bowed. Not her head and torso, no. Lela dropped to her hands and knees, her lavender cloak spilling around her like a winged beast of prey. Forehead to the floor and at Regent Etemaad's holographic feet, Lela screamed, "I am truth and death. Justice will be ours."

15. Broken Propriety

"Thank you, Gayora. You needn't have escorted me to my chamber. You and the others have more than made your point."

Gayora keyed in the code to Lela's chamber, permitting her to enter first. It shouldn't have surprised her that she knew her security code, yet it did.

The door slid closed behind them, leaving the females in darkness.

"Lights at fifty percent," Gayora said, looking at Lela, a question in her eyes.

"Fifty percent is fine. Anything brighter will only add to my stubborn headache, while dimmer will have me crawling into bed before undressing and bathing." Untying her cloak from around her neck, Lela dropped it onto a chair. "That armor is frightening to behold."

"It's supposed to be."

"Not at home. Not with our people."

"Especially with our people. Asiyans respect strength."

"That's not all we respect, and not all strength is defined by the threat of violence."

"Perhaps not, but perception of the opposite is the reason the Lumerians thought us easy prey . . . thought us weak."

"Because we're peacekeepers?"

"For some, civility will always be viewed as a weakness open to exploitation. You could've commanded us not to wear the Ibor armor, if it bothered you."

Lela's mind had been so preoccupied with the upcoming Council meeting, she hadn't given her High Stars' attire much notice. It wasn't until they stood before the Council, the chamber silent, all eyes on them, that she'd realized how they must've appeared to others. *Like we had returned home to stage a coup.*

She sank into the same cushioned chair with her cloak, noticing the weapon on the table in front of her. A weapon that didn't belong to her. She sighed. "I am grateful to have you by my side, Gayora. Indeed, I don't know what I would've done on Meleris and Nikogeus without the support of your team."

An armored finger pushed the laser gun toward Lela. "I may be the highest-ranked High Star on the team but Rahm, Orit, and Waafir aren't mine. We are yours. And so is this."

"I don't want it."

"A double meaning I would've missed before I became your shadow. The position of regent is yours, whether you wish it or not, as is this weapon I've gifted you."

"I didn't ask for it."

"Another double meaning. I left the gun here when you changed for the meeting. It's a symbol."

"Of what?"

The same armor-covered finger slid the laser gun even closer to Lela. "That's for you to figure out."

"You're not helping my headache, Gayora, and I'm tired of Paladins gifting me with weapons."

"This tired, grumpy side of you is new. You want to be left to your solitude, don't you?"

"Very much. I need to think . . . meditate . . . if I can. Sleep." *Cry. Scream. Fall apart without an audience.*

"When you're ready, I'll train you on that weapon. Being a proficient markswoman involves more than aiming and shooting. Part of my training will also entail how to prevent an attacker from disarming and overpowering you."

"What if I'm never ready?" Lela stared up at Gayora, waiting.

The High Star shook her head. "Three in a row. You said that one purposefully. I'm not taking your bait. Even exhausted, I don't like my odds in your Verity wordplay. I'll show you how to shoot, whether you think you're ready or not. You're proof chief magistrates should carry weapons and learn more than rudimentary self-defense."

Except for Yusef, of course, Lela couldn't envision any of the other chief magistrates submitting themselves to hand-to-hand combat and weapons training, especially Chiku. Devdas were the least physically inclined of the bands. They would rather pray than fight their way out of a dangerous situation.

"I have no interest in learning how to use that weapon." Forcing herself to stand, one hand on the table, the other on the arm of the chair, a chill started in her fingers.

"But you'll permit me to teach you, anyway."

"You'll have to be here for that to happen." Seeking warmth, Lela wrapped her hands in the folds of her dress, careful not to tremble in front of Gayora.

"Are you asking me to stay here instead of attaching myself to a battleship division?"

"Your duty is that of my shadow. Rahm, Orit, Waafir, none of you are active military." *Fingers, hands, wrists, arms, so cold. What is happening to me?*

"A chief magistrate cannot obstruct a change of assignment, but a regent can."

Lela glared at Gayora, her heated anger not enough to warm all the places the cold attempted to freeze.

"Suit yourself. Return to Lumeria. Fight, kill, but don't you dare die."

"Is that an order from my regent?"

"Besides Yusef, you are the least tactful person I know. You are excused. I would tell you to take your laser gun with you, but you'll refuse for the sole purpose of testing my resolve. You're exhausting."

"A'bra says the same." Gayora smiled, her features softening with the gesture. "I thought you said you never met my mother."

With more energy than it should've taken, Lela backed away from Gayora, whose eyes lowered to the hands still fisted in her dress.

"You're about to implode. Your pupils are dilated, you're shivering, and you're probably cold but also hot. Let me . . ." Gayora stepped forward, hand reaching for Lela, but she backed away, nearly stumbling. "Regent Le—"

"I told you not to call me that. I also said you were excused. Since you think giving orders is a critical leadership skill then I command you to leave my quarters and not to return until you are summoned."

"Chief Mag—"

"So we are clear, Gayora, issuing orders, particularly to those used to receiving and following them, requires little from the person in charge. What is difficult to accept and to live with are the ramifications of your decrees."

"You will never know the potential result of every decision you make. No one can. That's why we have faith."

"Faith doesn't heal the wounded, no more than it can resurrect the dead." Lela retreated deeper into her chamber, leaving Gayora next to the table with the gun she didn't want but would learn how to use because no honor or truth existed in the realm between helplessness and survival. "If I'm going to implode, as you seem to believe, I'd rather you not be here to witness my fall."

For all that Gayora expected Lela to ascend to the rank of regent, as if the transition, so soon after Etemaad's murder and Lela's induction into the Council, would be a straightforward matter, the High Star's expressive eyes questioned her more than she ought. If anyone other than Yusef had assigned Gayora as chief of her security team, she would've thought the person had done so as an indirect method of encouraging Lela to take a more authoritarian approach to leadership.

As intelligent as Yusef may be, the Paladin lacked the patience and trust required to form such a security team with no guarantee his plan would work.

"You're neither my moral compass nor my leadership advisor. Leave me."

Shuffling into her bedroom, Lela removed her shoes and clothing, exhaling deeply when she heard the door to her chamber hiss open then close. Later, she would regret her harsh words to Gayora. For now, she welcomed the silence and solitude.

As cold as an ice cap, Lela submerged herself into hot bathwater, barely feeling the heat through her frigid skin.

Unable to hold her emotions in any longer, the dam burst.

She cried.

Remembered.

Blood and brain splatter were everywhere—the walls, the floor, the bodies. Contorted mouths screamed, horrified eyes cried, and leaked wounds purged blood and hope.

Etemaad.

Beres.

Kondo.

They appeared in the bathroom with Lela. White, soulless eyes stared down at her. Scrambling from the tub and slipping on the wet floor, she reached for them. They backed away. Ethereal in form, their blood . . . their anguished wails were knife wounds to her heart.

Falling to her knees, sobs broke free. "I'm sorry. I'm so sorry I failed you."

Beres and Kondo frowned. The parts of them they'd had to leave on Meleris materialized in their decomposing hands, bloody, putrid chunks that should never be seen outside of a person's body. They tried to fill the gaping hole in their heads, managing only to smear chunks of flesh and brain matter over their faces.

She wanted to close her eyes, to look away, to protect herself from the macabre sight. But her gaze stayed fixed on the murdered High Stars, their lost souls in her bedroom instead of at peace in the Realm of Thuraya.

I failed them. I failed him.

Etemaad held one hand to his stomach, the other outstretched to Lela. Those white, soulless eyes of his saw into her. She could feel them dissecting every organ of her shivering body, disappointed at her flaws, her utter inadequacy.

How could Lela ever be for Asiya what Regent Etemaad had been to them all? He'd given his life to protect hers. What did she have of equal value to give in return?

Not enough. Not nearly enough.

Dragging herself to her bed, she collapsed upon it. Lela squeezed her eyes shut, willing away her waking nightmare. Time passed, herns maybe, but Lela didn't sleep, didn't open her eyes, didn't do anything other than hold her knees to her chest and choke on her sobs.

Beep. Beep.

Lela didn't respond to the intrusive sound, her mind caught in a bloody loop of gunfire and death.

Beep. Beep.

Gayora had her security code. The High Star could let herself in, if she was so determined to disobey Lela's orders and had returned. The thought had Lela jumping out of bed, crashing to the floor when her knees buckled and gave.

She struggled to her feet.

Beep. Beep. Beep.

Finding her robe at the foot of the bed, Lela shrugged it on, belting it around her waist.

Beep.

Lela stumbled into her living room, the space darker than it had last been. Gayora thought she knew better than Lela even in that, she thought with irrational ingratitude.

Beep.

Blindly searching on the table for the laser gun she knew her shadow hadn't taken with her, Lela grimaced when her fingers settled on the weapon. She held it in her hand. Its weight was insignificant but the damage it could inflict was all the courage she needed to face whoever was on the other side of her door.

Had the Lumerians followed them to Asiya? Rage heated Lela's core. How dare they come for her. Who had they hurt to reach her chamber untouched?

Gayora?

Rahm?

Ammon?

No, no, not Ammon. She would kill them, if they had harmed him.

The snarled command of "Open," ripped through her, heart pounding, hands sweaty but resolve firm. She wouldn't be any-one else's victim.

Room dark and eyes tear filled, she raised the laser gun, pre-pared to defend herself to the brutal, bloody end.

"No, Lela, it's me."

Lela's finger stilled against the trigger. "Ammon?"

"Yes, love, it's me." He peeked from behind raised hands as she lowered her gun, allowing it to fall from her hand and to the floor.

"Ammon. They k-k-k-illed him. They . . . they . . . killed Etemaad."

Lela started to follow the path of the fallen gun. But Ammon caught her up in his strong arms, carried her to her couch and sat, her on his lap and cradled against him.

"They killed him," she cried into his shoulder. "The Lumerians said they wanted the regent to help negotiate a peace treaty be-tween them and the Amakans. He agreed in good faith. But the Lumerians used him to reach the Amakan leader."

"I know, love. I know." Stroking her damp coils and shivering back, his body heat and voice soothed her. "Those Lumerians will pay. We will make them all pay. That I promise."

Somewhere in her delirium, Lela could hear the veracity of Ammon's words, feel the power of his intention, of his own righteous madness.

"We all heard your war call, and the Paladin Band will make it so. I will avenge him for you, for us all. Please don't cry, love, I can't bear it." Ammon wiped away tears from both of their faces. "I vow, in the name of the Fates, Regent Etemaad will be avenged."

He kissed her, lips tender.

Lela had dreamed of Ammon—even more after Etemaad's death. She'd confessed to impure thoughts. They were all of Ammon. His lips. His hands. His body. Sinful thoughts for an unmated female.

Lela straddled Ammon's hips, careful not to lose contact with his mouth. Yes, she'd dreamed of him, desperate for his comfort, the potency of his nearness.

"Lela," he moaned into her mouth. "I was afraid I'd lost you."

"You haven't. I'm right here."

They kissed more—longer, deeper, hungrier. Hands wandered to uncharted territory, no longer careful, no longer concerned about propriety.

What do courting rituals matter, anyway? What are we saving ourselves for, if a power-hungry leader can hire killers to take away everything we cherish? What purpose does restraint serve when death can claim us when we least expect?

Lela slipped from Ammon's lap. Turning her back to him, she walked toward her bedroom, not looking behind her to see if he followed.

When she reached her rumpled bed, the lighting in there marginally brighter than in the living room, Lela turned to find Ammon in her doorway, breathing as if he'd run a marnil. Lela untied her belt, letting the robe slide from her body.

Ammon's eyes darkened, tongue licked lips, and breath caught. "Are you sure?"

Lela nodded.

"We cannot take this back. No one else will know what will happen between us this night. But I need to hear the words. Tell me what you want."

"I want to curl into a ball and cry until I'm dehydrated and have no more tears left to shed. I want to hide in my closet, the way I did when I was a child after a nightmare. I want to curse the Fates for not making me strong enough to protect Regent Etemaad. And I want to hurt Prime Minister Drassul and Lady Junoid as much as they've hurt all of us."

"Lela . . ." Ammon rushed toward her, and she crashed into him, wrapping her arms around his waist and sobbing into his black long coat. "I should've come earlier. I knew you needed me. I shouldn't have made you wait so long, but I wanted to make sure Gayora didn't return. When I saw her leave, she looked upset and concerned, so I thought she might soon return."

Picking her up again, Ammon settled them in the center of her bed. Face close, hand caressing the soft skin of her hip, Ammon breathed her in.

She shivered, and not because her skin felt like she stood atop Salah Mountain on a snow cornice in her bare feet.

"Tell me what you want. Anything, Lela. If it's within my power to grant it to you, I'll make it so."

Hand rose to his cheek. Rising to brush her lips against his, she whispered, "I want you, Ammon. For as long as we can have each other."

Lela refused to think about Ammon going off to war, although his Paladin honor wouldn't have him making any other choice.

"Do you want the same?"

Leaning in, his lower body pressed against her side—his manhood's reaction a rewarding and humbling response.

"I'll always want you," he said, turning his head to kiss the palm of her hand. Then his full lips were on hers again, kissing her with none of the restraint they'd once practiced.

Helping him undress, marveling at each hard, masculine plane she uncovered, Lela could only stare up at him when he settled atop her and between her legs.

Lela watched Ammon watch her as he entered her for the first time. They moaned at the joining—perfect, sweet, forbidden. She would never, no matter the unknown journey before them, regret taking this leap of love.

Two herns after Ammon had fallen asleep, Lela still hadn't found her own slumber. Sitting up, the sheet falling to her naked waist, Lela couldn't help taking in the male she'd given her body and heart. For so long, she'd wanted to see him thus—his face in repose and him in her bed. The urge to recite the words to the Light of Nurzhan warred within Lela. They had broken many rules of propriety since beginning their secret relationship, but none more than the act of lovemaking without having progressed through the Light of Nurzhan and Unity of Hearts rituals.

Lela needed no more sins on her conscience. But . . . Ammon was there, body bare and soul calling to hers.

What would his soul reveal? Surely, it would be as bright and beautiful as the male. A sun in my cloudy world.

The palm of Lela's hand covered Ammon's heart. Closing her eyes, she recited the prayer that would draw an echo of his soul to the surface. If he loved her, the way she believed, the echo would follow the path of her coaxing voice. But her love had to match his, her affection for him a rhythmic lure. So, Lela repeated her prayer, pouring all she felt for Ammon of the House of Eetu into each word.

Ammon expelled a breath, and Lela opened her eyes, sensing her success. She couldn't wait to see his soul's echo.

Her hand fell away from his chest.

No, this can't be right. Did I recite the prayer incorrectly? Surely not. I studied the ritual in anticipation of this moment. But . . . but . . . I must've done something terribly wrong.

The dripping, gray cloud above Ammon's head, shrunken in on itself and coarse to the eye, gave off an aura of moroseness.

Did I do this to him? Did my call for war taint Ammon's soul?

Lela made to slip from the bed, confused by the sight of Ammon's tarnished soul, but she halted when he awoke. The echo of Ammon's soul splashed onto his forehead like a rain droplet to the desert floor, reabsorbed as if it had never been.

"Where are you going?"

"I . . . umm . . ."

"It doesn't matter. Come here." Patting his chest, where Lela had tried to find sleep earlier, Ammon grinned up at her, no signs of a tainted soul in the eyes that beheld hers. "Come back here. I'm not ready for our time together to end."

"Neither am I, but you must return to your chamber before dawn." Lela found the perfect spot on Ammon's brawny chest, snuggling into the warmth of his sturdy body and sighing, almost convinced his shrunken soul had been a figment of her fatigued mind.

She kissed his chest. His nipples. His neck. By the time she reached his mouth, all thoughts of the improper Light of Nurzhan ritual had vanished under a female's renewed desire.

Despite their earlier lovemaking, Lela wouldn't conceive. They would have to make love dozens of times before their bodies synchronized enough to make procreation possible. For Asiyans, it was nature's way of ensuring the male and female belonged together before bringing a child into the world.

"I love the way you feel." Big hands held her breasts, exploring fingers circled her nipples, and adoration spread from Ammon's heart to the aching heat between Lela's thighs. "I love the way we feel together."

So did she. "Ammon . . ."

Rolling Lela onto her back, Ammon smothered her with delicious kisses, his hands still covering her breasts—squeezing and caressing.

The ache blossomed into an incessant throb. She spread her legs to accommodate him, his thick erection at her center. Grabbing a fistful of his gray-black coils, she pulled him down into a hungry kiss, her mouth anxious for the taste of him, her body eager to have him join them again.

They kissed. Ammon caressed her with his unyielding erection—teasing them both with the hard, wet friction. He glided over her sensitive bundle of nerves, over and again.

Lela ripped her mouth from his, ragged moans and raised knees nonverbal pleas for Ammon to join them once more. He did, driving into her with a force that shook the bed.

She moaned her pleasure. Legs wrapped around him and drew him in deeper.

"So good," Ammon groaned against her ear, a rumble of masculine enjoyment she wanted to hear over and again.

So she met him thrust for thrust, her craving for him no less than his for her. Lela took and gave, learning his body while ignoring the very real possibility they wouldn't have more stolen moments like this one. Worse, the cosmos would conspire against them, denying Lela and Ammon a happy ending.

"Stay with me, Lela."

"I'm here."

"So am I. Right here. Always."

16. The War Council

While Lela may have slept in, permitting Ammon to stay in her bed and chamber longer than he ought, she neither confused the time of the Council meeting nor was she late. Yet when she'd entered the chamber, the entire Council present, including former Chief Magistrate Banou seated in Lela's chair, she had known the real meeting had occurred prior to her arrival.

Worse, the only vacant chair at the table belonged to Regent Etemaad.

Jaw clenched. Shoulders stiffened. Lela fought not to frown.

"Ah, there you are," Banou said, smiling at Lela. "Right on time as always."

"On time, yes, but also quite late." Her displeasure found its way into her voice.

Banou winced.

"I thought I was an equal member of this Council."

Reth stood. "Of course, you are." Walking to the head of the table, Reth pulled out Regent Etemaad's chair. "Now that you've arrived, the meeting can officially begin. Here you are, Lela, please sit."

Lela glanced from the chair to Reth, whose calculated smile she disliked. He'd left her with two distasteful choices.

"If I refuse your offer, I'll dishonor myself and disrespect you. This meeting is supposed to be about the upcoming war with Lumeria, not about me."

"One and the same," Yusef said. "But no dishonor or disrespect, Lela."

"But manipulation."

Reth nodded. "Perhaps a little. Forgive me. I thought to expedite the matter. If you aren't quite ready to claim this seat, you may have mine for this meeting since your former one is in use by our guest."

Choosing silence over confrontation, Lela accepted Reth's offer. She joined the others at the table, lacing her fingers in front of her. Tension radiated from her shoulders and down her back in tingling sparks, undoing the relaxed satiation she'd found with Ammon.

Mosi, who sat beside Lela, patted her hand, observant eyes traveling over her face. "We should've scheduled this meeting later in the day, so you could sleep more." Lifting her hand to Lela's cheek, she caressed, her touch heartfelt. "You've had an awful ordeal. Your wounds have nearly healed . . . the ones we can see. Don't be cross with us. We needed to speak with Banou before you arrived."

"Why?"

Mosi withdrew her hand, but the comfort it offered remained in the eyes that held Lela's. "We need to understand why Agala's eyes did not affect you and Etemaad. Before we can send Paladins to fight a war so far away from home, the mystery of the illusions must be solved. We cannot permit what happened to Beres and Kondo to claim more of our Paladins."

"I agree, but I still do not understand."

"Lela," Yusef said, "think through this with us. I know you're still tired, but we need you fully present."

Eyes narrowed at the Paladin. What made him think her mind was any less on the meeting than his or the others?

Yusef grinned Ammon's lovely smile. "There you are. That's the spark we need. You're awake."

"You take too much pleasure in annoying me."

"He thinks it's a gift," Chiku said. "But only he agrees. Returning to Mosi and Yusef's point, after reading your report, we discussed the lack of effect of Agala's eyes on you and Etemaad."

"If you read my report, then you know I wasn't unaffected. Something happened to me. I saw . . . saw . . . spider eyes." Lifting her hands, she "walked" her fingers on the table, simulating how the spiders moved on the walls and from one person to the next.

Mosi imitated Lela's movement, as if the replication would help her better understand what Lela could not. "But Etemaad had neither your headache nor your visions, is that correct?"

"I believe so. He wasn't frozen in place like the others. When I was insensible from my headache, unsure of what was happening around me, he was cognizant. As I wrote in my report, Regent Etemaad got us both to the floor and away from the gunfire."

"So," Yusef began, "the question we must ask ourselves is what you and Etemaad had in common that minimized the effect of the hypnotic images on the two of you."

Ah, that's why Banou was there. "You think our resistance, though mine was minimal, had something to do with us both being Verity?"

"Yes," Yusef answered.

"An interesting theory, if band membership involved genetics. There is nothing biologically unique about being Verity, any more than there is for any of the other bands. We are simply five subcultures of a larger Asiyan culture. Choice, not heredities."

Banou, seated across from Lela, nodded. "Quite true. Not genetics, but culture, as you said. As such, we have different learning and practical experiences. The Council asked me here to assist them in brainstorming points of convergence between you and Etemaad that would be unique to Verity. Similarities the two of you shared with each other but not with Beres and Kondo."

Five sets of eyes settled on Lela. How long had they been in the chamber discussing her and Regent Etemaad? Yusef said he'd wanted Lela to help them "think through" the situation. From the way they stared at her, they didn't require her assistance but her confirmation.

"I thought," Lela said, her voice a low timbre of anger, "that Yusef recommended Gayora as my shadow to Chief Elan. That, in a rare moment of sensitivity, he thought it important for me to have a female High Star close to my age as my security chief. But it was you." She shoved to her feet, Reth's chair tumbling backward and crashing to the floor. "It was you. My parents would never betray my trust. But my shadow, a female I've begun to think of as a friend, she betrayed me to you."

Banou also stood, palms on the table. The older woman leaned forward, as if she would fall from her accusation. "I did suggest Gayora to Elan and Yusef, but she is loyal to you."

"Until today, I would've believed you."

"Lela, please . . ."

"The relationship between a chief magistrate and their High Stars is supposed to be sacrosanct. You had no right."

"You're a dreamer," Banou said. "You and Etemaad, both dreamers. Rare. Beautiful. Divine."

"Lela . . ." Mosi reached for her hand, but Lela avoided her touch, backing away from the table and the fallen chair.

Past conversations she'd had with Etemaad and Banou flitted through her mind. They'd taken notice of Lela at a young age. Etemaad and Hasani were friends. Banou and Etemaad had served on the Council for dekulls. They'd trained and mentored Lela, creating a leader, even a young one, palatable to their band.

Lela swallowed a sob. "My father told Regent Etemaad. Apparently, he, at some point, told you. When you had an opportunity, with Gayora, to confirm what you've known for only the Fates know how long, you took it."

"The Fates speak to you in your dreams. Why conceal such a blessed gift?"

"Because of this." A hand swung out, gesturing to the open-mouthed Council members. "See how you all look at me. I'm *not* divine. I'm *not* blessed by the Fates."

"But they protected you. They revealed enough of Agala's hypnotic eyes to keep you from drowning under their weight."

"Do you hear yourself?" Lela backed farther away, a headache forming, her pulse quickening. "You five are still a Council. I see that now. You claim I'm one of you, that you trust me, but that's untrue."

"We do trust you," Chiku said. "Lela, I know how this must appear, but—"

"It's not about appearances but the truth. I haven't misinterpreted your actions. If anything, you've misinterpreted mine. I had every intention of discussing my thoughts on Agala's eyes with you all today. Was I also planning on sharing my status as a dreamer? No, because frankly, it's none of your business. More importantly, I've had the entire flight from Nikogeus to ask the same question of myself you all discussed without me this morning."

Yusef stood, righted Reth's fallen chair and remained standing, his back to the table, his front to Lela. "You said my 'rare moment of sensitivity.'" Arms folded over broad chest. If Paladins were given to pouting, surely Yusef would've worn such an expression. "We truly do not understand each other. Something else you and my son have in common. But I digress. Please return to your seat. I know we've upset you. For that, I offer my humblest apology on behalf of the Council. Now is not the time for us to wage war against each other."

Lela didn't disagree, but she took issue with the calm, slightly rebuking way Yusef had made his statement, as if she was a child throwing a temper tantrum and the Council long-suffering parents.

So many thoughts tumbled about her head in response to Yusef. Lela ignored each one that would've had her expressing too many built-up emotions—some hers, the others Ammon's.

Continuing, as if Yusef hadn't interrupted, Lela said, "Regent Etemaad's dreams could be prophetic, as is also often the case with Devdas dreamers. That has never been the case with my dreams, however." She had directed the sentence to Banou, who held her gaze with a strength of character she had always respected. "As long as I can remember, the Fates have come to me in my dreams. They don't speak to me. Nor do they reveal images."

"I . . . I . . . don't understand," Banou managed to get out. "If they reveal nothing to you, why then do they enter your dreams?"

"I have no answer to your question."

Chiku, who hadn't ceased staring at Lela with wide eyes, said simply, "Explain what happens when they come to you."

Lela reflected on the last time the Fates had made themselves known in her dreams. It was the night of Regent Etemaad's death. She'd had a nightmare, and the Fate of Purpose had come to her, kissing her cheek and stroking her hair as the dream Lela cried.

"They grant me the gift of their presence. I do not know a better way to explain. They are simply there. Sometimes all three, other times one or two. Even when I don't see them, I feel their presence next to me. In truth, those times rarely feel like dreams at all."

Eyes suddenly wet, Chiku wiped away tears. Then she was standing and moving toward Lela.

She accepted the older woman's tight embrace the same way she had Mosi's caress to her cheek. The Council may not trust Lela in the same way they trusted themselves or Banou, but she never doubted they cared for her—even Yusef.

"You are touched by the Fates." Chiku kissed a cheek before pulling back, eyes full of tears. "Not dreams but visits."

"Visits?"

"Well, I suppose you experience both. Are there times you dream without the presence of the Fates?"

"Yes. I dream of many things. I also have nightmares. But no, the Fates are not always with me."

"Yes, dreams as well as visits. I'm sure we now know the result of your contemplations." Chiku kissed Lela's other cheek, grasped her hand, and then walked toward the table, Lela forced to follow.

Foregoing her own stubbornness and hurt, Lela sat in Reth's abandoned chair. Yusef and Banou also sat, a Council with no regent.

"What I've concluded was that my dreams are too dissimilar from Regent Etemaad's for them to have been the reason why Agala's eyes couldn't control us the way they did everyone else. Also, if it was simply a matter of us both being dreamers that ability wouldn't account for how easily Regent Etemaad battled the illusions."

Eyebrow arched, Banou nodded again. "Quite true. What else then? What are we missing?"

"Nothing that can be easily solved before our battleships leave for Lumeria. Actually, Banou, my intention was to seek your and my father's advice on a list I compiled this morning." A hastily formed list, true, before Ammon's delectable kisses had tempted her back to bed and away from work.

"A list of what?" Banou asked, her elbows going to the table and a hand to her chin.

"Names of band members proficient in the art of Jesenia."

"What is Jes—" Reth began to ask at the same time Banou swore, interrupting his question with her uncharacteristic language choice.

"I was unaware you were trained in Jesenia. Hasani is a true Luminary."

"What is Jesenia?"

"Please explain, Banou. No doubt you are better versed and have a deeper knowledge of Jesenia than I."

"Very well. To answer Reth's question, Jesenia is an ancient mental art form of the Verity Band. For its practitioners, Jesenia aids them in seeing past the veneer of truth to the real truth behind an illusion." Banou swore again, smacking the palm of a hand on the table. "I cannot believe my own blindness. Right now, I feel every bit my one hundred anulls." The hand that had slammed onto the table with force and anger, rose to Banou's chin again, stroking. "Jesenia is difficult to perfect, which is why it is no longer taught at Sagacity. Even when I was in school, few Verity passed the course. Etemaad was an exception. But it took him dekulls to perfect the art . . . for the practice to become an unconscious skill he took for granted."

"Regent Etemaad told me to 'watch and listen.' I misunderstood his directive. I took his order too literally. He must've assumed I knew he meant for me to use what I had learned of Jesenia because he never explicitly said for me to employ the strategy during the mission. I'm still a novice. When I first saw the eye of Agala, it felt as if someone was trying to bore their finger into my forehead. My natural reaction was to push against the mental force. I admit, I did visualize the Fates but only because, when Ab'ba trained me, I used them as my center. Other practitioners have a different point of focus."

"True. Mine is an old-fashioned painting of the Gulf of Serenity that hangs on the living room wall of my childhood home. Etemaad's focal point was the Imp Sunflower, his mother's favorite bloom. How many practitioners are on your list?"

"Ten, not including the two of us and my father."

"Lela, tell us everything you saw or heard as it relates to the threat. I need to know any thoughts you've had then or have now. Anything, Lela, no matter how inconsequential it may seem. Tell us what you know, what you've analyzed, and what you've concluded. Regent Etemaad thought highly of your intellect; put it to good use now."

As she'd done many times, Lela refrained from scowling at Yusef. The Paladin was unbelievable. She had nothing to prove to him or to the others. Yet she despised her traitorous heart that beat for the Council's earned approval, their allegiance born of her merits and not loyalty to the regent they loved and respected.

"Take care," Reth said to Yusef. "I think we've all forgotten how it felt to serve on this Council as a freshman member, how intimidating the experience, how unsure we were, and how isolating it could be, at times." Reth leaned forward in Regent Etemaad's chair, his forearms on the table, his posture rigid, and his headshake a slow side-to-side movement. "You're correct, we haven't treated you as an equal member of this Council. When we look at you, we see our youth and all we lacked when we were your age. We see our impatience, stubbornness, naïveté, irresponsibility, and many other traits that wouldn't have made us an ideal chief magistrate. Apparently, projection is a characteristic inherited with age."

The older man had a knack for leaving Lela speechless with his open self-reflection. She had no ready response to his honesty that wouldn't embarrass her. Lela refused to cry. Anger was an easier emotion to hide behind, but Reth's forthrightness didn't deserve that response either.

Inclining her head, Lela acknowledged his sentiments, accepting he spoke for the Council the same way Yusef had when he'd extended Lela an apology. Both actions reinforced her outsider status on the Council.

All things come in time.

"I've only studied Jesenia for five anulls, so I'm far from an expert. Obviously, one need not be proficient in the mental art to sense the wrongness emanating from Agala's eyes."

"My Paladins don't have five anulls."

"Not only that," Banou said, "Paladins aren't used to the mental exercises required for Jesenia. They've never been schooled to think in such ways."

Lela stepped in, explaining what Banou had not. "Where Paladins are trained to interpret their surroundings as circles, rectangles, triangles, and pentagons, for example, Verity are trained to see the same surroundings as spheres, cones, pyramids, and prisms."

"You mean we Paladins fail to view the fullness of the universe, approaching the world through a two-dimensional lens."

"Paladins can and do see in both 2D and 3D. But to focus on 3D during battle is a distractor that could prove fatal."

"What you're saying is, against the Lumerians and their hypnotic weapon of war, my Paladins have a significant weakness we've never encountered or known to plan for."

"That's correct. But Paladins need not fight this war by themselves. Indeed, if we are to win, Paladins cannot go into battle alone."

Everyone except for Banou and Mosi gaped at Lela. She took comfort in the females' nodded approval, so she proceeded despite Yusef's clenched jaw.

"However the Lumerians use the eyes, I believe the hypnosis has a short range and limited time span. None of the temples dedicated to Agala, on the warring planets, had been destroyed or desecrated. That fact never made sense. But it does if the temples emit a short-distance hypnotic wave that delivers a specific message."

Banou's nod became more vigorous. "Yes, yes, that makes much sense. The short range and impact time would explain why the Amakans, Unbalk, and Yegoth were able to wage war against the Lumerians despite the presence of Agala's eyes on their planet. With the Lumerians' level of technology, it would be a simple enough task for them to build the hypnotic suggestion and deliver it on a subauditory level."

"I don't understand." Reth leaned further onto the table, eyes questioning.

"That's because," Mosi said, "subauditory isn't quite the correct term, although Banou's larger conceptualization is likely correct. If I'm following Lela's train of thought, she thinks the Lumerians have managed to overlay hypnotic messages at the sub-auditory level with sounds at the auditory level."

"Are you saying Agala's eyes are irrelevant?" Reth's brows furrowed. Lela thought he'd fall into the table, so close to the edge of the chair did he perch. "But Lela saw—"

"Spider eyes, I know. But that's how her mind made sense of the double messages being sent to her brain. Because she thought the eyes to be the source of the mental discomfort, that's how the external intrusion manifested in her mind as it sought to make sense of the seemingly unexplainable. Is that what you were going to say?" Mosi asked Lela.

"In part, yes, but I do believe the eyes are significant. I think the way they are formed, circular with alternating bright colors in a specific square and rectangular pattern, it draws the eye, tempting the brain to follow the pattern." Lela pointed to the walls around them, recalling the arrows of light that led to the large Agala's eye in Drassul's ballroom. "The designs around the eyes, I believe, are just as important as the eye itself. I think once someone focuses on the eye, messages are sent to the viewer's brain, combining with other sounds in the area."

"Even if that sound is rustling wind or gunfire?" Yusef asked.

"I believe so."

"A stowaway, of sorts," Chiku added.

"Yes. It's only a theory," Lela cautioned. "Untested and not nearly concrete enough to form a foolproof battle strategy around."

"So why the list of Jesenia experts?" Yusef asked in a tone that challenged Lela's previous contention. "You said Paladins tend to see battles from a two-dimensional perspective, which would prove to be a liability against the Lumerians."

"Yes."

"You think Verity trained in Jesenia can offset the Paladins' limited perspective?"

"That's correct."

Banou tapped her fingers on the table. "There aren't nearly enough Verity proficient in Jesenia to make a difference. But you know that already." Banou smiled at Lela then at Mosi. "That's where the Affiq scholars enter. The Affiq Band has its own methods of training its members to see the full spectrum of the universe. They can be trained in Jesenia, at least enough where they can face an Agala's eye and not succumb easily."

"But you and Lela said it takes anulls to perfect the mental art."

The finger tapping continued, speed increasing as Banou seemed to piece together the final parts of Lela's thoughts. She hadn't viewed her ideas as a battle plan, at least not in the way Yusef probably meant.

"Quite true. As I said, we would only need them to know enough Jesenia to stave off the effects of the hypnotic wave for a short while."

Yusef paused, eyes lowering as he thought, processing all that had been said and implied. When his eyes raised, they settled on Lela. Then a smile formed, not Ammon's this time, but all Yusef's. "You want my Paladins to destroy the temples of Agala."

"I want us to be prepared in the event the governments of Wither, Shin, and Meleris want our help."

"Wither's new leader has already contacted us," Yusef said.

That was news to Lela.

"We agreed to aid them but High Colonel Broiss was reticent for us to deploy our Strikers."

"He's afraid foreign war machines will frighten his people," Reth said. "Paladin Strikers could make us appear more like an invading force than peacekeepers. Furthermore, I believe they've developed their own robot army. Perhaps they can use them to destroy the temples. But yes, Lela is correct. Ground forces may be required."

Lela fingered the ver'ty, the only visual indication of her right to be there among the Council. She could have another chief magistrate robe designed. Indeed, the robe was to be worn whenever a chief magistrate acted in a professional capacity, like attending today's War Council meeting. Fingers slipped from Banou's induction gift. "We can't trust the locals to destroy the temples. They've already proven they cannot, even though they despise Lumerians and reject Empyreanism. We also don't know what else the Lumerians can do with their hypnosis. I'm afraid if we don't purge those planets of Agala's eyes and whatever Lumerians may now be stationed on the three planets, our Paladins will be at a grave disadvantage."

The Council absorbed her words, deliberation the best friend of action. There was much they didn't know, much Lela hadn't paid attention to or remembered. There were no guarantees in war, but the unknowns were uncomfortably high.

"While they may object to the use of Strikers, they may be more amenable to drones. We should explore that option. Unfortunately," Yusef said, "I can't ignore the possibility we may need to rely on civilians trained in Jesenia. I'll discuss these options with my regional commanders, gather their feedback, and share their recommendations."

"Excellent," Banou said. "Hasani and I can review Lela's list, making edits, if necessary, and add any Verity we believe would make good candidates for Jesenia training. Mosi, I'll need you to provide us with Affiq candidates. Lela, while you've ruled out being a dreamer as an explanation as to your and Etemaad's resistance to the hypnosis, I think it's worth exploring with the Devdas dreamers."

"Which means you need me to craft a list of candidates as well."

"Yes, Chiku, preferably today."

"The Paladin Band have few dreamers, but they are yours, if you need them."

"As are the Euridice dreamers. Lela," Reth said, "please create a folder in our shared Council drive and upload your list of Jesenia practitioners."

Accessing her personal drive on the zot tablet embedded in the table in front of her, Lela did as Reth asked. She then watched as the Council opened their individual zot tablets and started typing, adding names to her file.

"It's a start," Yusef said. "But I still don't like it."

Reth stood. "None of us do, my friend. There's still much to discuss but it's time for lunch and we need a break."

Lela remained seated, although everyone else had moved to the sideboard where their lunch had been laid out. She watched them, males and females old enough to be her parents. In Banou's case, her grandmother. Lela could work with them, as long as they treated her as an equal. She could most certainly learn from them. But could she lead them?

17. Pax-Lumeria

Shin
Unbalk Homeworld
Silver Aspen Forest

"I'm scared, Milmy."

Tears warmed Thonet's neck where Nettle's face hid, but nothing else about this night produced heat within her. Holding her two-year-old son closer to her chest, she glanced down at her daughter, wishing she had a spare hand to hold her too.

Thonet rubbed Nettle's little back, his thin bark cold to the touch. The forest was shadowy and forbidding—two descriptors she had never used to describe her beloved forest before tonight.

"There's no need to be afraid, sprout. The soldiers will protect us. They'll get us to safety."

Okacia stared up at Thonet, her red eyes moist, but her steps steady. Her daughter moved closer to her, leaves crunching under her feet, blending in with the sounds of footsteps in front of and behind them.

Quickly and quietly, the caravan walked through the forest, guided by a small platoon of Spirit Strongbark warriors carrying vortex phaser shooters—long guns with a strap for shoulder carry. The platoon had divided into two groups, placing the caravan between them.

Until this day, Thonet hadn't regretted living in the Blinkew Township. Quiet and peaceful, she hadn't cared it was miles from the closest major hub.

"We can stop for a rest, if you want," a Spirit Strongbark soldier said from somewhere behind Thonet, her voice pitched as loud as any of them dared to speak. "But if everyone can push on a while longer, I would rather not stop until we're deeper into the forest."

No one complained or asked to stop, although they'd been walking for hours.

Heavy footfalls sounded right behind Thonet then beside her. She whipped her head to her left, a hand leaving her son to reach for her daughter. But an Unbalk soldier was already hoisting her six-year-old into his arms, his vortex phaser swinging from a gun strap on his back.

"I got her."

Swallowing her fear, she remembered her manners. "Thank you."

"I promised Blister Elm Cycad I would watch after his family."

At the mention of her husband's name and rank, she granted the soldier a smile.

"We thought the Lumis, after the murder of Alder Larchfern, would invade the populated areas first. We miscalculated, so now we're running from township to township, trying to secure those on the outskirts."

Thonet knew, which was why Cycad's unit had been sent to Thousand-Leaf Scrubland, the most densely populated region in Northern Wintercress, and why she was home alone with their saplings when the first invading party landed.

"How bad is it? How many townships have fallen?"

"You don't want to know. Sorry about all of the walking, but it's safer than risking being blown out of the sky or run off the road."

"I understand. What's your name?"

He lowered his head, red mushroom top dull against the fog rolling in. "I'm loxon, Blister Moss Fourth Platoon."

"I'm Thonet. I appreciate your service, loxon. That's Okacia you're holding, and this sleepy sprout is Nettle."

For another two hours, they wound their way through the forest, guided by the half-moon and their Silentwood gods. From the crown of each tree to its roots, a tree spirit dwelled within, a reassuring presence on a long, unexpected trek.

"I'm tired," one of the sprouts in the group said. The statement proved the beginning of similar complaints from saplings of all ages, including Okacia who loxon had to leave to her own bark feet when they'd heard sounds behind them.

Thonet detected no sounds other than them. But an Unbalk's bare feet, when in a forest, felt sound more than their ears heard it. They wouldn't be able to stop for a much-needed rest, not if the vibrations she felt on the forest floor meant what she feared.

Thonet bent to her knees, careful not to displace Nettle. "Get on my back," she told her daughter. "Quickly, Okacia, up, up. Yes, you have it now, my big sapling. Hold on and don't let go."

She didn't need the Blister Elm's order of, "Double-time," to know they had to pick up the pace.

Thonet walked faster.

The vibrations increased, growing in strength and frequency.

Neighbors from the township, some she'd known for years, others barely at all, started running, working hard to keep up with the swift pace set by the Blister Elms at the front of the caravan.

"Hold on tight. No matter what happens," she said, lengthening her stride and increasing her speed, "do not cry out."

Thonet ran. She couldn't see the threat, the danger, but she heard it in the whining of the forest floor and the whistling of the trees. Their beloved forest spoke to her, to them all, and it told them to *run*.

"Okacia, sapling. Are you listening?"

"Y-yes."

"Good." Jumping over thick, aboveground roots, Thonet kept her balance, her feet steady, her eyes on the backs of those who ran in front of her and ears primed for those behind. "If something happens to me, I need you to take your brother and hide. Hide until your feet no longer feel the vibrations from the intruders to our forest. When it's safe, and *only* when it's safe, come out and travel this path to Thousand-Leaf Scrubland. You know how to get there. I've taken you before."

In a transporter, during the day, and with an adult.

Thonet wanted to pray to her tree gods, but she had no time. She needed to make her crying sapling understand. She had to press upon her the importance of saving herself and her brother, of not looking back, of not clinging to her lifeless body, if the worst happened.

Yes, prayer would fuel her spirit and cramping legs. But she had no time to dwell on either.

"Go, go, go," Ioxon yelled.

Gunfire erupted behind her.

Saplings screamed. Feet thudded.

Yellow laser fire streaked across the forest, lighting up the night sky.

Trees burst into flames.

Bodies crashed to the ground.

Thonet didn't stop running . . . wouldn't stop running.

Friends and neighbors fell, arms and legs sliced off, chests and heads blown through. Spirit Strongbark warriors fought, returning fire for fire.

Thonet followed the sound of the Blister Elms up ahead, their vortex phaser shooters a constant cry of resistance leading them through Silver Aspen Forest and to where a large platoon of soldiers awaited them at Thousand-Leaf Scrubland.

I'm coming, Cycad. I'll get our saplings to safety.

She ran through pain and breathlessness, fear and love all the motivation she needed to keep going.

Thick, gray fog settled in the heated space between Unbalk and Lumerians. Thonet saw nothing but the lethal, yellow flashes of laser gunfire moving ever closer to her heaving body.

Don't stop. Keep going. For your sprouts, you need to keep going. You need to . . .

Pop.

Blinding hot pain exploded in her head, dropping Thonet to her knees midstride.

"Noooo, Milmy," was the last sound she heard.

Wither Alpha
Yegoth Homeworld
Slobor Industrial Zone

"Tell me you have good news."

Ful tensed, gray fingers stopping over the keyboard on his hybrid mix analog and digital console. "Well, ahh, I'm not sure."

"Not sure?" Sergeant Valkeld stormed into Ful's lab, his tech assistants scurrying out of the soldier's way. Sergeant Valkeld stopped next to him, pointing to the glass security wall in front of them. "We have no more time. Sure or not, we have to deploy them. We've given you two years."

"Not enough time. Not for what I was hired to do." Ful continued what he'd been doing before the sergeant had barged into his lab again. "They can shoot, fly, follow directions."

"Good, good. Get them in the field."

"But they can't think. They can't anticipate. They can't retreat or alter a course. They have no brain."

"Do you hear that, Dr. Ful?" Sergeant Valkeld asked, pointing to the ceiling.

How could he not? The first wave of Lumerian ships had been silent but when more arrived, claiming Wither's skies as their own, they'd blasted the same message repeatedly: Agala sees all, knows all, is all. Submit to the will of Agala and embrace Empyreanism.

"All I have is a beta-tested war machine army. The Brealorx body armor is the better option. Even you've trained wearing one."

"The Brealorx requires a Yegoth soldier. If you don't remember, Dr. Ful, High Colonel Zirlat funded your research because Wither Alpha is the smallest, least populated planet in the Vargan Solar System. Our Yegoth resources are minimal. We can't afford to lose a single soldier, even one wearing a Brealorx, and we've lost hundreds since the invasion began." With his chin, Sergeant Valkeld gestured to the robots on the other side of the wall. "Ready or not, brain or not, we need those robots out of this warehouse, on the ground and in the air. If nothing else, we can use them as distractors until help arrives."

Ful hit more keys, dreading the possible repercussions of releasing hundreds of beta-tested robots. If his programming failed, they would have more than Lumerians to contend with.

Sergeant Valkeld slapped Ful's back, gentler than he thought the man capable of being. "The Lumerians think we're weak and stupid. They think we don't know they were behind the assassinations. They're wrong. But we're few, and we need help."

"The Asiyans, you mean?"

"High Colonel Broiss contacted the Council of Magistrates. He wanted to speak with Chief Magistrate Lela, thinking she would understand our predicament better than the others."

Ful hit a sequence of keys, bringing the robots online. Metallic storage units, large enough to hold a half dozen Krulx, named in honor of the first Yegoth soldier killed in the Lumerian-Amakan War, opened. Clear doors lifted upward. Ful didn't have to see storage units in other parts of the Industrial Zone to know the same occurred in hundreds of units, his code-protected comm system linked to them all.

"High Colonel Broiss was told that Chief Magistrate Lela was still en route to Asiya but that their Council would make themselves available to speak with him."

"Did they?"

Sergeant Valkeld inclined his head, and Ful blew out a premature breath, remembering, belatedly, how far away the Bazlorian Solar System was from Wither Alpha.

"They agreed to send reinforcements but—"

"They won't reach us in time. They can't save us."

Krulx spilled from the storage units, forming row after row of battle-ready robots, a military formation Ful had programmed. Fifteen feet tall, the armored machines were inspired by Yegoth, who were muscular, strong, and grew to at least seven feet tall.

"Multiload electron shooter," Ful said, hitting keys and going through his list of weapons, making sure all were fully functional before sending the machines into combat. "Cuq eraser, check. Rapid-fire meson gun, check."

"Your Krulx are our best chance at survival, Dr. Ful. If we fall, it won't be because the Yegoth haven't defended ourselves and our planets with all that we have." Sergeant Valkeld bumped his fists together in front of his chest and inclined his head, a high honor granted to a civilian whose specialized work in a military installation gave him clearance above that of a fourth-generation solider who had come out of retirement to defend his homeworld. "It's been an honor. Thank you. You've given us all a fighting chance."

Humbled, Ful duplicated Sergeant Valkeld's gesture, touching his fists together and nodding his head. "My team and I will stay here, lending what support we can. I've upgraded the Brealorx armor since the last time you wore one."

"Brealorx 2.0."

Ful shrugged. "That's a good enough name as any, I suppose. Take care with the new single-load meson gun. It's—"

"Beta tested only. Understood." Sergeant Valkeld pointed to the ceiling again. "All of Wither Alpha is a test site, Dr. Ful. The Vyth Air and the Aark Grounders will provide all the test data you require for Brealorx 3.0 and beyond." The same finger lowered, shifting away from the ceiling and to the glass security wall. "The Krulx will clear the way for the air and ground forces."

"Be safe. Be ruthless. And kill as many of those fulking Lumerians as you can."

"That's the plan, Dr. Ful. That's the plan."

Ful didn't watch the sergeant leave his lab. He wanted to remember the man as he'd looked when he spoke of defending their people from Lumerians—inner strength and hope.

Ful typed, configuring his Krulx to interface with the Brealorx armor, hoping the code would ensure the war machines could distinguish between Yegoth and Lumerians. If the interface didn't work . . . *No, it must work.*

Satisfied he'd done all he could in the time left to him, Ful pressed a key on his console. The ceiling above the Krulx opened like a blooming flower. He typed in code sequences until he'd opened the ceilings to every warehouse where the war machines were stored. Praying to his own god, not the fake god of the Lumerians, Ful typed in one more code.

Up the Krulx flew, their programmed mission simple—Kill the alien invaders.

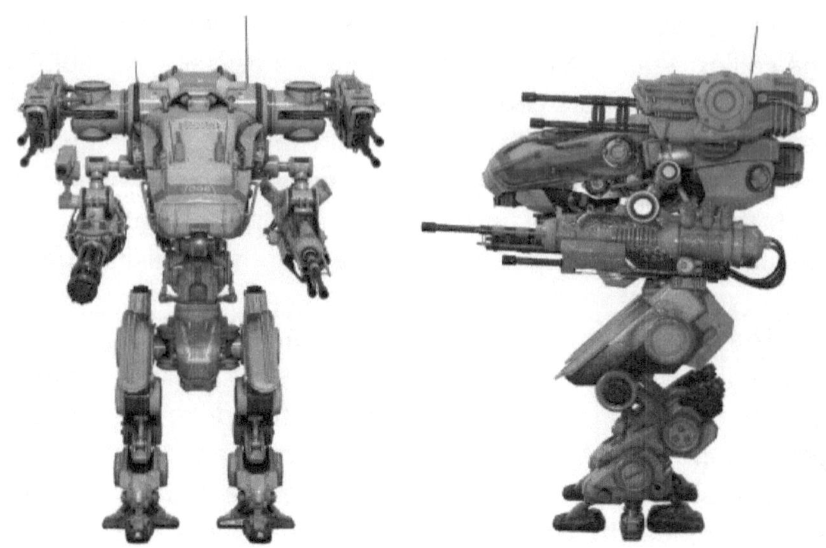

Ful closed the ceiling and sank to his knees. For the first time in days, the skies above Wither did not belong to Prime Minister Drassul. The Yegoth would either rise as one or fall as many.

He drew himself to his feet. Sucking in a deep breath, he readied himself to monitor the Krulx from the safety of his lab. He wasn't a Vyth or Aark, but he could—the ceiling exploded.

He ran, seeking cover as debris rained down, smashing onto irreplaceable equipment needed to manage the Krulx war machines. Worse, much, much worse was the bloodstained rubble. "No. No. No. No." Ful's lunch churned in his stomach at the sight of his crushed tech assistants. *They didn't have a chance. But I still do.* The door through which Sergeant Valkeld had exited was covered by heavy pieces of the ceiling, so Ful crawled toward the only other exit in the room—the glass security wall.

All I must do is reach the door that leads from my lab to the warehouse proper. Once on the other side, I can take the stairs to the lower level. From there, it will be a short walk to the old tunnel that connects the warehouses and the Industrial Zone's buildings.

Taking it slow, Ful maneuvered around the ruined lab. The door in the glass wall was his target, the only path to freedom and life. His hand slipped on a sticky liquid, but Ful refused to look down. *Don't want to know. Keep going. Just keep going.*

His hands touched other things—metal, glass, concrete . . . a shoe with an ankle attached. But Ful made it across the room and to the door in the glass wall. Yanking it open, he rushed through, and that fulking message blared above him—Agala sees all, knows all, is all. Submit to the will of Agala and embrace Empyreanism.

Ful didn't wait to see what would come next. He raced to the stairs, praying his program would hold true, and that the Yegoth would see another sunrise and sunset under a free and independent Wither Alpha.

Vargan Solar System

"Keep firing. Don't let up," Captain Hexosa 27 yelled into her communicator. She could only see Squadron Leader Delta Chirdor 9's fighter jet to her left. Where were the others? Had they all been destroyed? "Fire, fire, fire."

Chirdor 9, one of the best Amakan pilots, followed Hexosa 27's lead, giving the Lumerian troopship everything they had. They couldn't let these flying barracks land on Meleris.

"Speed and agility are our only advantages, Chirdor 9, let's use them to send this burning heap of Agala shilt back to Lumeria."

Hexosa 27 came about, one head focused on the pursuit, the other two scanning the area for more threats. Seeing none, she continued to fire, making sure to stay a moving target.

Hexosa 27 and Chirdor 9 rotated positions, twisting and twirling to avoid being hit by return gunfire.

"We need to destroy the second shuttle bay before anything launches from it." Chirdor 9's deep voices crackled over the line, but Hexosa 27 heard him loud and clear.

They'd studied every type of Lumerian space fleet. Like Amakans, they were divided into three classes: small craft, spaceships, and capital ships. The troopship fell into the spaceship class—military vessels with no stealth capability or cloaking but enviable endurance.

"On it." Captain Hexosa 27 pivoted, flying her fighter around the ship to the opposite side where the second shuttle bay was located. She took a grazing hit to her left wing, but her shields held. They were down to sixty percent. She couldn't take a direct hit from the cannons, but a grazing shot wouldn't send her fighter into flames.

Avoiding the long-range weapons, Hexosa 27 flew as close to the troopship as she dared, laying down fire across the hull as she went, and setting off multiple explosions. The door to the shuttle bay flew off, sending shrapnel in every direction. The two shuttles waiting in the bay lifted off the bay floor, ready to take flight.

Hexosa 27 fired, letting loose repeated rounds of photon blasts. Up in flames the two shuttles went, setting off even more explosions within the shuttle bay.

"Mission accomplished," Hexosa 27 proclaimed.

"Good. Let's head home. This ship is dead in space."

Hexosa 27 flew away from the burning troopship and toward Chirdor 9's fighter. Together, they fired at the dead ship. They may not be able to stop a full-blown Lumerian invasion, but they could guarantee none of the Lumis inside the troopship survived to attack Meleris another day.

She didn't breathe a sigh of relief until they'd punctured a hole the size of their fighters into the ship. Lumerian soldiers flew from the forced hull breach, dying when their bodies met space.

Space.

Hexosa 27's heads glanced around. They were no longer in Meleris space. How had they flown so far without her having noticed?

"We need to leave."

Hexosa 27 heard the panic in Chirdor 9's voices. *He must've realized how far we'd traveled from home in pursuit of the troopship.*

They were on the edge of Lumerian space. Dark and quiet, Hexosa 27 heard and saw nothing. She backed her fighter away, followed by Chirdor 9's. Turning her fighter, she saw something shift in the darkness in front of her. It pulled at the blackness of space, a swirling vortex gathering all it needed to form a creature of nightmares and death.

"Vedem," Chirdor 9 yelled at the same time the monster formed before them.

Hexosa 27 fired at the behemoth, so did Chirdor 9.

"Engage FTL." Silence. "Chirdor 9, did you hear . . . ?" Her question died in her throats. The squadron leader's fighter dangled from the monster's maw, the beast's teeth ripping the ship into morbid chunks of space rubble.

Hexosa 27 slammed her fist down, hitting the red button that would increase her speed and get her away from there. Her fighter lurched forward, sending her heads back against the pilot's chair.

Within seconds, she could no longer see the Vedem or the remains of Chirdor 9 and his fighter. Hexosa 27 flew toward home, hands shaking, heart galloping, and ship set to autopilot.

"Valor One to base."

"Base to Valor One. Status."

"Troopship destroyed, base."

"Good work. Return home, Valor One." There was a short pause on the other end then, "Twelve Valors gone from our radar. We'll mourn them, miss them. Come home, Captain Hexosa 27. The tide of war has shifted."

More than he knows. Vedem. Death. Zisceus, please save your children.

Lumeria
Lumerian Homeworld
Veer River Complex

"Report," Prime Minister Drassul said the moment Lady Junoid entered his office. Nodding to the chair in front of his desk, he reached for the data crystal she handed him as she claimed her customary chair.

"It's all there."

"Wither Alpha, Meleris, and Shin?"

"Yes. I uploaded the most recent reports from our Field Siegers. They've encountered strong resistance on Wither and Meleris, but nothing, without a few reinforcements, they can't control."

"Good, good." Drassul palmed the data crystal. He would review the information later, using it to make tactical plans. But he preferred Junoid's oral summary before diving into the minutiae of his Field Siegers' rambling reports. "Work with the Master Thresher. Tell him exactly what you need and where. He'll take care of the reinforcements you require. What else?"

Crossing her legs, Lady Junoid thumbed her fingers against the arm of the chair, her white dress the color of war and might. The meaning fit her well, as did the tunic. Her happiness radiated in the way she held herself—head high and shoulders straight—and in the way she smiled at him—broad and toothy, every bit the confident advisor he respected.

"Our test run was also successful."

"Ahh, the Amakans took the bait then. You thought they would."

"We now know how they'll respond when we send in our troopships. Sleek, agile fighters with deadly firepower, that's what they sent to intercept the test troopship. Their pilots are well trained, but their fighters can't compare to the might of one troopship. We decimated all of their fighters except for two before they destroyed our ship."

"Good odds."

"Great odds." Uncrossing her legs but still thumbing the arm of the chair, she frowned. "One of your pets got loose and ate an Amakan fighter ship."

"You're piqued, why?"

"Have you news of Asiya?"

Where his political advisor still frowned at him, displeased a Vedem had interfered with her well-ordered plans, Drassul placed the data crystal on his desk, reclined in his chair and smiled at Lady Junoid. The woman had an unfortunate tendency of allowing one unplanned incident to mar her outlook of the larger picture.

"I do not."

"That doesn't concern you?"

"You worry enough for the both of us, my lady. Agala is good. He has protected his faithful servants. He will continue to do so. Asiyans are of no consequence."

Her frown remained, deepening the age lines across her forehead. "She didn't contact you after the attack. As far as I've been able to ascertain, Chief Magistrate Lela returned to her spaceship and left our solar system, all within hours of her regent's death."

"She's young and inexperienced. She also almost died. The fire Malcareon tried to beat her to death. The fool must have some strange fetish because he removed one of his moonrulic gloves. I can only guess he received pleasure from the feel of his skin touching hers when he struck her."

"But the chief magistrate didn't die. Yes, she's tiny. The fire Malcareon should've handled her easily but he didn't. You were there. What did you see?"

"Not much in the dark. The fire Malcareon's glowing hand. Laser fire."

I heard Theimos 105 beg for his life. A wonderful sound. I've never heard anything more glorious than his pleading mouths. He had to have seen Agala that day, knew he'd been wrong about my God. In the end, they all see Agala's eyes, his wisdom but his unforgiving heart to the disbelievers, pagans, like Theimos 105.

"When the Paladins blasted the doors open, letting in the light from the hall, I saw more."

"Such as?"

"The Grul and Malcareons used what was left of the hypnotic messages pumped into the temple to slip past the Paladins. That Grul and the earth Malcareon helped the fire Malcareon out of the room. He'd been stabbed. Badly." Drassul laughed, recalling the man's pained screams in the dark room that contained the dead bodies of his opposers. "How hard can it possibly be to kill a person when you have every advantage?"

"Yet you sit there with that huge grin on your face, as if you haven't a care in the world. The chief magistrate had a weapon, when she shouldn't have. She fought to kill, despite not being a Paladin. She didn't succumb to the fire Malcareon's brutal attack, meaning Asiyans are much stronger than they appear. All of those points should concern you."

Drassul stood, opened his arms, and looked around his office. "Yet they're not here. She fought. She survived. She ran home, taking her naïve regent and useless Paladins with her. Enjoy your accomplishments. We are on the verge of spreading Agala's words throughout this solar system, claiming every planet as an extension of Lumeria. In time, the Amakans, Yegoth, and Unbalk will thank us for elevating them from religious barbarism. They will praise Agala's name and accept Empyreanism into their hearts."

Lady Junoid also stood, brow furrowed, age lines a weathered map of unease. "We need to be cautious. Stay vigilant. The Asiyans' silence worries me."

"You read the report Chief Magistrate Lela sent. She's a fighter but she's first Verity. There was no deception in her report. She may not have contacted me directly, but she did what any good diplomat would, she submitted a detailed report of the attack to a fellow planetary leader. She's respectful, considerate, and no match for our combined intelligence. Take the Asiyans' silence for what it is, Lady Junoid."

"And what is that?"

Stretching arms over his head, enjoying the pop of bones, he wouldn't allow his advisor's paranoia to ruin his day. But he wasn't a fool, and only a dimwitted man would choose arrogance over prudence.

Drassul flopped back into his chair. "Let the Asiyans come, if they dare. The Vedems are hungry."

18. Fated Path

"This is quite unnecessary, my dear. Surely, with the upcoming war, you have more important matters to attend to than keeping a weeping female company."

Like so many older women in Lela's life, Dariya patted her hand with motherly affection. The thought had Lela looking to the female seated on the other side of Dariya—Nenet. When Lela had arrived, her mother had already been there for two herns, offering what support she could to Etemaad's widow.

"I should have come sooner. I would have but—"

"You're a chief magistrate first. The planet needs you more than I do."

Lela could've allowed that partial truth to stand. Indeed, she need not correct Dariya since her assumption wasn't incorrect but merely incomplete. But Lela had skirted the edges of the truth too many times of late. The thought of treating Etemaad's widow with the same strategic maneuvering she'd used with the air Malcareon had her eyes dropping and hands fisting in her dress.

"I was afraid to face you." Slowly, Lela lifted her eyes, catching her mother's knowing gaze first then Dariya's liquid amber. "To see your tears. To witness your pain. To be in this wing . . . this living room without Etemaad here beside you, knowing . . . knowing . . . He should've never left the Hall of Concord. He only went on the peace mission because of me."

She couldn't say she would give anything to trade her life for his, although it was the truth. To do so wouldn't alter the past but it would hurt Nenet to know how deeply Lela's guilt ran. More, Lela's unfortunate truth would only add to Dariya's pain. As it was, she had revealed too much.

Dariya pulled Lela to her and wrapped her arms around her neck. "There is much you do not know. Much Etemaad chose not to share. But he was where he wanted and needed to be, Lela."

"I don't understand."

Withdrawing from their embrace, Dariya kissed both of Lela's cheeks. "Etemaad loved you. Ah, I can see the pain of that truth is a weight on your young shoulders."

Dariya opened her mouth to say more—no doubt to offer Lela kind words and support. But she could no more politely accept Dariya's empathy than she could silently send Ammon off to war. Yet, as Dariya continued to speak, Lela knew she had no choice but to do both. So, a condolence visit had turned into an unbearable hern of mothering from a female who had never borne a child and who no longer had a mate.

Through it all, Nenet said little until Dariya's energy had waned and her melancholy filled the room—smoke whose fire source couldn't be easily doused.

"Come, my friend, allow me to take you to bed." Nenet helped Dariya to her feet. "After your nap, I will insist you leave this wing and have dinner with Hasani and me."

"You'll insist?"

"Only if you prove troublesome."

"Troublesome? Well, yes, you've known me too long for me to fake an affront. Lela, dear, will you also join us for dinner?"

She hadn't planned on dining with her parents. With Ammon's departure looming before them, she hoped to spend most of her free time with him—talking, lovemaking, but not planning for a future not guaranteed them.

"Lela is worse than you. She eats only if reminded and never enough for my liking. Say goodbye to our daughter, so she can return to work. Who knows what trouble Yusef will get up to if left to his own devices?"

Dariya's smile warmed places where Lela still felt cold. It wasn't a bright, sunny day kind of smile but a smile conjured from the depths of a soul in need of relief from pain—even if the reprieve proved fleeting.

"Yusef will come to understand as Etemaad did. But he won't accept the truth until you do, Lela. Until that time, the war you'll wage against the Lumerians won't be the only war you'll fight."

"I don't—"

"Understand, yes, I know." Dariya embraced Lela again, clinging to her for comforting merns. "I will see my beloved Etemaad again in the Realm of Thuraya. We are bound souls—destined to find each other after my soul has rejoined Mother Cosmos."

Lela tightened her arms around Dariya's thin waist. "Not yet. Please, Dariya, it isn't yet your time. Not. Yet."

"No, my dear, not yet. Nenet, Banou, and I still have much to teach you before we allow the Fates to call us home."

The Fates hadn't called Etemaad home. He'd been forced from the mortal plane by a power-hungry religious zealot who needed to be stopped.

"I can hear your vengeful plotting . . . feel it in the tensing of your body. Yes, we will have our revenge, Lela." Dariya stepped back. "When your thirst for vengeance has been quenched and your sight restored, return and we will speak of what Etemaad saw, knew, and hoped . . . for you and for all of Asiya." Dariya squeezed her hand—a strong woman despite her loss. "You need not be perfect, Lela. No one expects it of you, and you should not expect it of yourself. By the time you reach your mother's and my age, the list of your mistakes will be as long as you are tall."

"That's not exactly comforting."

"The truth rarely is. Now," she said and turned to Nenet, "I think I'll allow you to escort me to my bedroom and tuck me in like a good little Verity."

"You haven't been good since the day we finished Sagacity."

"Yes, well, yet another truth. We won't bore Lela with tales of our youth. Does she look afraid we'll do just that?"

"A little, yes."

"Good. Then my work here is done." Dariya glanced over her shoulder at Lela. "The regent's signet ring is yours. This entire wing is also now yours."

"I can't. I won't."

"Yes, I know. Your position is understandable, even acceptable. For now. But with the coming war, Asiyans *will* need a regent."

"Even a reluctant one?"

Dariya's headshake didn't answer Lela's question. Neither did her weak smile or her retreating words. "Have dinner with us tonight. The road to war will be far too short and food will become less appetizing with every life given and soul taken."

Lela wandered onto the balcony, standing by the railing instead of sitting on the bench. Tolurs sang from the trees below, while the gray clouds above matched her mood. An enclosed walkway led from the balcony to the center of the courtyard below, branching off in three directions, granting the user access to any part of the Hall from a single-entry point. Only the regent's wing of the Hall of Concord had such a private walkway. To enter from any end required a voice command.

She'd traveled the regent's walkway before, beginning on the balcony with Etemaad's voice command of "Unlock for Regent Etemaad of the House of Sanna." The doors would slide open and they would enter, sometimes with a purpose no greater than "walking meditation."

Etemaad had once told her, "This walkway is a visual reminder that a regent must be connected to all of Asiya. That even when I choose to walk one path, the others are still there—options not yet taken. But there are always opportunity costs to every decision, Lela. Some are greater than others, true, but there are always costs to our decisions."

The balcony doors behind her opened then closed.

"Her eyes are closed, but she isn't yet asleep. Pretending for my sake. You and Dariya are alike in that vein. Come here, daughter."

Knowing she shouldn't but unable to stop the tide of need, Lela turned to her mother, sinking into her embrace in a way she hadn't Dariya's. Even Ammon's arms couldn't compare to what she found within her mother's. But Lela wouldn't weep again.

"It's all right, my sweet girl. You are home now. No one will lay hands on you ever again. Your father and I will not allow it."

Lela hiccupped a laugh that was part sob. She buried her head against her mother's neck—the scent of her body oil fruity and familiar.

"I'm too old for you to fight my battles."

Nenet's soft hands cupped Lela's cheeks and lifted. "I can see remnants of what you did not want Hasani and me to see when you called us from the peace cruiser. Whose idea was the audio-only communication?"

"The Council's. Yusef's."

"Yusef's. I see." Nenet sucked in a deep breath then released it on a slow nod. "You must've been quite the sight, if the recommendation came from Yusef. He can be thoughtful. Not always sensitive and rarely tactful but he's never insincere. He's fought in many wars, on the side of innocents like the Amakans. He's seen much and has likely done worse."

"Why are you telling me this?"

Nenet lowered her hands from Lela's face. "There is a reason why so few Paladins have ascended to the position of regent."

"I do not think Yusef seeks the regency."

"Perhaps not but that is due more to his lack of imagination than will. To lead effectively and well, daughter, one must be willing to see and accept the complexity of the universe, including within oneself. Perhaps even more within yourself. Yusef is neither that insightful nor that brave."

"But you think I am?"

"Don't sound so doubtful." Nenet grasped Lela's hand and led her to the doors of the enclosed walkway. "To answer your question, no, you are not yet there. But also, yes. All that our planet requires in a great leader dwell within you. It takes time. Most things of value typically do. Time but also patience."

"But everyone wants me to wear Etemaad's robe and ring now."

"In the beginning, both will ill fit, but they won't always. Speak and allow us entry onto the walkway."

Lela tried to back away from the doors, but Nenet held fast to her hand. "I can't. It's not programmed to my—"

"Speak, daughter, and let's discover the universe's plan for my only child."

I know my future—blood and death. The road to war might be short, as Dariya said, but I fear this war will last—testing and stretching us in ways I don't want to imagine.

Lela laughed to herself, strangely amused that no matter Nenet's support of Lela as regent, she still expected her to submit to a mother's order.

As always . . . well, mostly always, Lela complied.

"Please open for Chief Magistrate Lela of the House of Asheema."

Although Lela hadn't expected the doors to open, she also hadn't anticipated the sense of conflicted disappointment when they did not part under her request.

"If you want to take a stroll, A'bra, we cannot begin it here. We should—"

"Try again."

"I don't see how—"

"With the proper title this time." Nenet released Lela's hand and stepped back, as if either action would affect the outcome of a second command to doors programmed for a person who would never ask for entry again. "Humor me and try once more." With a hand to Lela's lower back, Nenet pushed her toward the closed glass doors.

"I think it is you who now sounds doubtful."

"Never. I have faith."

Perhaps, but it felt like a pointless test. What would the doors opening under her command, or even staying closed, prove? No higher power controlled the doors. And, if Lela sought to discern a sign of her fitness to rule billions of Asiyans, she would not find it on either side of the walkway doors.

She touched the glass, creating smudges that would disappear with the removal of her hand. Futilely, Lela searched the doors for Etemaad's handprint. She found none, not only because Etemaad would've had little reason to touch the doors, but because the glass had been treated with mor'up, a security protocol taken to prevent the stealing and duplication of handprints.

Letting her hand fall to her side, she uttered the title she had rejected for welks. "Open for Regent Lela of the House of Asheema."

To her surprise and dismay, the doors parted—a soundless recognition of a truth she still refused to accept.

Behind her, Nenet chuckled—from relief or with joy, Lela did not know.

"It means nothing."

"It means everything."

"No, A'bra, this only means that someone, likely Yusef or Reth, maybe even Banou, had Elan override Etemaad's voice code with my own. Not that I've ever submitted to having myself recorded."

Lela thought back to the oral report she'd given the Council from her living room aboard *Ibor Peace 01*. She supposed any of the chief magistrates could've recorded her then, thinking ahead when Lela couldn't see past her current pain.

"This is Dariya's home, not mine. I won't take it from her."

Nenet walked around Lela and onto the walkway, colored crystal glass as far as the eye could see. She turned. "Without Etemaad to share the dwelling, this wing is no longer a home for

Dariya. When Hasani and I leave for Aureen, Dariya will travel with us. She claims she hasn't been to the Verity region in too many anulls. West Asiya is lovely this time of year, so now is a perfect time for Dariya to reacquaint herself with the city of her birth. So," Nenet said, shifting to the side and raising her left arm in the southern direction of the walkway, "which path will you take, daughter?"

Lela recalled the last conversation she'd had with Gayora, and how she'd used double meanings but to little effect on the seasoned High Star. Lela would have to speak with her security team, especially since she too intended on returning to Aureen. Not to her parents' home, where she'd resided before becoming Etemaad's disciple and moving to Khatra and into the Hall of Concord, but to the Towers of Truth, the seat of power for the Verity Band's chief magistrate. It's where she belonged, where Banou had lived before stepping down from the post of chief magistrate.

She laughed, stepping further onto the walkway, eyeing first her mother then three doors. Each door led to a different walkway and a different part of the Hall of Concord.

"Double meanings," Lela muttered to herself. To Nenet, she said, "I do wish to be regent. But not now. I don't think I'm yet the leader our people deserve. I'm afraid I'll fail them, Etemaad, and myself."

Nenet lowered her left hand then lifted her right to Lela, who grasped it the way she used to when she was a girl and afraid of being separated from her mother while visiting a crowded marketplace.

"In this case, Lela, fear will serve you and the people of our great planet well."

Nenet looped their arms and walked, leading Lela from one end of the walkway to the other, passing each door without stopping. When they reached the end of the enclosure, Nenet turned them in the opposite direction. Before Lela knew it, they were back on the balcony, the glass security doors closed.

"If you aren't ready to decide on a path, then do not. But understand this, Lela, if you choose not to become the official regent of Asiya, you must give our people something of equal value in return for their patience and faith."

Lela knew her mother was correct, but . . . More gray clouds had moved in, bringing with them the scent of rain and the chill of late afternoon. "I have nothing of equal value to offer the citizens of Asiya."

"There you are wrong. You can lead us to victory against the Lumerians. When Drassul's mercenaries killed Etemaad but failed to murder you as well, the road to war began with your survival."

Lela hated the thought of being a war leader more than she did the idea of staking claim to all that had once been Etemaad's. Neither appealed but both would prove true. Lela could see the inevitability of both—the doors through which she would eventually walk.

"Bring Ammon with you to dinner."

The sudden topic switch jarred Lela. Avoiding her mother's eyes, she walked away and sat on the bench near the doors that led from the balcony into the living room.

Nenet didn't follow but she looked at Lela with a mother's improbable knowing.

In the end, Nenet asked Lela a single question. "Is Ammon your soul's mate?"

Chin dropped to her chest and hands fisted in the skirt of her black mourning dress. She sucked in a breath and held it until she had no choice but to let it out in wispy breaths.

There it was, the question Lela feared Ammon would one day pose and she would, out of duty and respect, have to answer.

Lela loved Ammon. She wanted him as part of her present but also her future. They'd given themselves to each other—profound grief a convenient excuse to shed propriety. Yet . . .

"I don't know."

Lela had never lied, not even to spare herself pain, embarrassment, or punishment. But when she had opened her mouth to speak the truth, an unforgivable lie rolled off her tongue instead.

Lela, Chief Magistrate of the Verity Band, heir to the regency had lied, and she felt . . . *unworthy of everyone's trust and faith.*

What was worse were her mother's downturned lips. Perhaps for Lela's shameful lie but likely for the distasteful truth she couldn't bring herself to admit or to accept.

A welk later, when Lela rested in Ammon's arms, his warmth surrounding her, the scent of him on her skin and his taste on her tongue, her shame warred with her hope for a happily ever after with him.

He kissed her forehead. "I'll return to you."

Lela believed he would, but no one fought a war and returned untouched by its ugliness. She should speak from her heart. Share her fears. Instead, she kissed him until they were breathless, their arousal reawakened and their joining, like his departure from her life, inevitable.

"I can't bear to watch any more. Turn it off."

Chiku didn't wait for Yusef, who had turned on the communication system and displayed the holographic images in the center of the conference table, to comply. She struck her zot with pounding fingers until the scrolling images winked out.

No one spoke. No one had since the message from Dr. Ful of Wither Alpha had played.

"My name is Dr. Druirt Ful, a weapons engineer on Wither Alpha. By the time this message reaches you, it will likely be too late for me. But I must try. The Lumerians want the man behind the design of the Krulx robots, and that's me. They'll find me, but I won't make it easy on them. I know High Colonel Broiss already asked for your help. Well, I'm also asking and with an urgency that can't be understated. We're dying. Being slaughtered. That fulking Drassul doesn't simply want converts, he wants everything. Our souls and our planet. He thinks he is unstoppable. Maybe he is. I don't know anymore. Chief Magistrates, Asiyans, I beseech you, return to the Vargan Solar System, not under a banner of peace but with battleships of war and retribution.

My lab was destroyed, so I no longer have a way to make more Krulx, not that it matters. Two years of my life spent building them and the Lumerian ships shot them from the sky with ease—flying and armed weapons but ultimately inconsequential fodder for a dead cause. And maybe a dead people. If you need any more motivation, beyond the fact that the Lumerians killed your leader as they did mine, I've attached images to this message. Death and despair. It's what our lives have become under Lumerian occupation. Please, Chief Magistrates, send help."

Lela sat in her chair, eyes cast down to her zot, while recalling similar images displayed by Theimos 105 during the befouled peace negotiations meeting.

Lifting a neck that felt the weight of three planets' worth of innocent lives, Lela asked, "Any word from the leaders of Meleris, Wither, and Shin?"

"No." Yusef, who had been uncharacteristically quiet, added, "Communications with the Vargan Solar System have gone dark."

"Meaning?" Lela feared she knew the answer but, considering the result of the awful miscommunication between herself and Etemaad, there was no luxury found in assumptions.

"It means my Paladins will enter the solar system with no intel other than Dr. Ful's message. It means, most likely, the leaders of those planets are either dead or in Drassul's custody. It means," Yusef said and looked to Etemaad's vacant chair, "we need a regent willing and able to lead the war against Lumeria." Dark eyes shifted to Lela. "Either become that leader or renounce your position as Etemaad's blood-chosen heir, so someone else can be appointed to the post."

"Yusef—"

"No, Reth. I'm already exhausted, and we haven't sent our first squadrons into Vargan space. We don't have time to train our troops in Jesenia, no more than we have time for Lela to gain experience and confidence."

"What do you suggest then?" Mosi asked, her tone lethal enough to slice through the hull of a warship. "You become regent and your son and disciple, Gurion, fill your vacated seat?"

"That's not—"

"Who do you think, after spending two dekulls grooming Lela for the Council, the Verity Band can nominate who is capable, or even willing, to replace her? Lela hasn't even had time to select her own disciple."

"Mosi, I—"

"It isn't Lela's fault she isn't yet prepared to take Etemaad's seat. But if we compel her to renounce his dying wish, the planetwide outrage that decision will incur will be our doing, or rather our undoing."

"You're speaking of a civil war."

"A divided people will fall first from within. Our planet was there before, Yusef. I assure you, none of us want to be responsible for returning Asiya to the days of internal fighting and barbarism."

"Where does that leave us then?" Yusef asked, not of Mosi but to Lela.

Paladin, Affiq, Devdas, Euridice, they all looked at Lela . . . *to* Lela.

Four bands, four chief magistrates but only one regent. There were two paths before Lela—forward or fear.

No, only one fated path.

Sending a silent prayer to the Fates, Lela pushed from the table and stood. Not giving herself time to second-guess her decision, she walked to the head of the Table of Wisdom and Guidance, pulled out the chair, Etemaad's chair . . . *her* chair, and sat.

Lacing her fingers on the table in front of her, Lela nodded to her Council. "We have a would-be empire to topple, a regent to avenge, and innocents to save. Let's begin."

TO BE CONTINUED

About N. D. Jones

N. D. Jones, Ed.D. is a USA Today bestselling author who lives in Maryland with her husband and two children. In her desire to see more novels with positive, sexy, and three-dimensional African American characters as soul mates, friends, and lovers, she took on that challenge herself. Along with the fantasy romance series Forever Yours, and a contemporary romance trilogy, The Styles of Love, she has authored three paranormal romance series: Winged Warriors, Death and Destiny, and Dragon Shifter Romance.

Other Books by N. D. Jones

Winged Warriors Trilogy (Paranormal Romance)
Fire, Fury, Faith (Book 1)
Heat, Hunt, Hope (Book 2)
Lies, Lust, Love (Book 3)

Death and Destiny Trilogy (Paranormal Romance)
Of Fear and Faith (Book 1)
Of Beasts and Bonds (Book 2)
Of Deception and Divinity (Book 3)
Death and Destiny: The Complete Series

Forever Yours Series (Fantasy Romance)
Bound Souls (Book 1)
Fated Path (Book 2)

Dragon Shifter Romance (Standalone Novels)
Stones of Dracontias: The Bloodstone Dragon
Dragon Lore and Love: Isis and Osiris

The Styles of Love Trilogy (Contemporary Romance)
The Perks of Higher Ed (Book 1)
The Wish of Xmas Present (Book 2)
The Gift of Second Chances (Book 3)
Rhythm and Blue Skies: Malcolm and Sky's Complete Story
The Styles of Love Trilogy: The Complete Series

Sins of the Sister (Dark Fantasy Short Story)

Fairy Tale Fatale Series (Urban Fantasy)
Crimson Hunter: A Red Riding Hood Reimagining

Feline Nation Duology (Urban Fantasy)
A Queen's Pride (Book 1)
Mafdet's Claws (Book 2)